Tempting SYDNEY

ANGELA CORBETT

BOOK ONE *Tempting*
SYDNEY
A TEMPTING NOVEL

Dedication

To A.B. for all of her dating stories

One

"It's an epidemic, Sydney. A freaking epidemic." Brynn's face was scrunched into a frown as she slid into the chair next to mine. She put her salad and Diet Coke down on the table. We were at Soup and Spoon, our favorite lunch spot a block from Easton University campus. I'd been at the table awhile, my face buried in a book, trying to study for my law school prep class. So much information was packed into the short summer class that I felt like all I did was study.

I set the book to the side and took in Brynn's tight crimson v-necked tee that showcased her fantastic cleavage, bootcut jeans that hugged her ass, and thick espresso colored hair that fell in curls all the way to her waist. My hair was long, but I didn't have the commitment required to take care of a mane like hers. She was stop-and stare-gorgeous, though I'd never convince her of that.

"What's the epidemic?" I asked, unwrapping my ginormous chocolate toffee cookie. I'd been saving it as a reward for finishing going through my notes. It's the little things.

"Small dicks." She shook her head in frustration. "Cocktail weenies are bigger than what I've had to deal with lately. I'm going to start making guys tell me their size before I go out with them. I'm sick of wasting my time on tiny weenies."

This should have been shocking, but not much surprised me anymore when it came to Brynn Harper. I laughed, thoroughly amused, as I broke off a piece of cookie. "I guess your date last night didn't go well?"

She threw her arms up in disgust. "No. It didn't. You just don't understand because you haven't been investigating. Just wait, you'll be disappointed."

I considered that as the toffee and chocolate melted together in my mouth. While I wasn't a virgin, sex had never been a big priority for me. I was very goal-oriented. Currently my goals included graduating from my excellent law school at the top of my class, and then moving on to a fantastic law firm, and becoming one of the best attorneys in the country. Pregnancy would hamper those goals. Since no form of birth control was one hundred percent effective, I'd

decided to stay away from sex until I at least had my law degree…and maybe forever. It hadn't been too difficult. My experience with sex in the past hadn't been memorable. If history was any indication, I really wasn't missing much.

I raised a brow. "I didn't realize an investigation was underway."

Brynn heaved an exasperated sigh as she dribbled her lettuce with light dressing. "You've known me since we were freshmen in college, Syd. I've been investigating dick sizes for years."

"I thought you were just hooking up. Not taking notes."

She waved me off like I was being ridiculous. "Of course I was hooking up! But it's been impossible not to notice the current state of weenies. The situation is horrifying!" Her eyes were so wide that her long, thick lashes practically hit her perfectly arched eyebrows. "It's all those hormones in milk—I know it. I bet dicks have been getting smaller and smaller for at least thirty years. Someone should study that." She paused, her brows knit together. "I wonder if I could make it a topic for my Master's thesis?"

I broke off another piece of my cookie. "You might want to wait until you actually start grad school before you propose that as your research concentration. It would be bad to get kicked out of the program before you even start."

She rolled her eyes. "You worry too much, Syd,"

she said, stabbing a forkful of lettuce. "You need to learn to relax."

I nodded. "I will. Once I have my law degree and my dream job."

"'Gather ye rosebuds while ye may'," she said, quoting one of my favorite poems by Robbert Herrick. "You're not really doing that, you know."

I tilted my head to the side, thinking. "We just have two different versions of seizing, Brynn." I pointed to my text book. "Mine involves studying books, not men."

She lifted her hand, opening and closing it as she mouthed the words blah, blah, blah. "My version is *way* more fun. You're going to regret not doing stupid things while you were young and had an excuse." She lifted her eyes, scanning the room and then abruptly stopped, her gaze totally focused somewhere behind me and to the right. "Speaking of *doing* things, the guy behind you is throw-me-down-and-screw-me-now hot."

Brynn had hot guy radar. *That* should be the study of her thesis. We'd done the hot guy assessment routine so many times that it was habit. I waited for her to glance away—which seemed to take a lot longer than usual—counted to ten, and turned slowly, scanning the room in the direction she'd been ogling. My lips parted in a surprised "O" at the man—and he was definitely all man—sitting two tables away. Brynn had reason to stare.

His short, dark brown hair had a little curl to it and

was styled like he'd just gotten out of bed. Judging by the shadow across his square jawline, he'd also forgotten to shave. His eyes were what really captivated me, though. I'd only seen such a vibrant shade of blue once before. I'd taken a high school graduation trip to Cancun, Mexico, and thought the colors of the ocean were the most stunning hues I'd ever seen. This guy's eyes were the exact same bright blue. If I'd seen him in a photograph, I'd have sworn they were Photoshopped. His arms strained the seams of the white tee shirt he was wearing, and I had no doubt that everything under his clothes was probably as captivating and sculpted as his face. A matte black, beaded bracelet wrapped around his wrist. Most men wouldn't be able to pull it off, but on this guy, it looked masculine, and just upped his sexy factor even more.

I'd mastered the two second check-out years ago, but this guy had caught me completely off guard. I'd been looking—some might even say leering—for far more than two seconds. Just as I got my wits back, the guy looked up, straight at me. He met my gaze—and held it.

And held it some more.

A flutter started in my stomach. His expression was full of unabashed self-assurance. Clear eyes were trained on me with a brazen focus that made the flutter descend much, much lower. Sparks felt like they were jumping across the room, and my breath caught in my throat. Just when I thought I might pass out, one corner of his lips lifted slightly and he cocked a brow expectantly. I knew how to flirt. And if I was reading him right, he'd just issued a dare to come over—one I wasn't sure I was capable of accepting. I hadn't said a word to him, but it was obvious this guy had almost as much confidence as he had testosterone.

He gave me about five seconds to decide what I was going to do, then tilted his head down, lifting a shoulder in a half shrug that seemed to indicate I'd had my chance and lost it. He stood, grabbing his tray filled with trash left over from his lunch. His jeans hung low on his hips, held up by a wide black belt with a square, distressed silver buckle and I couldn't help but watch him as he walked away. It was a *really* nice view.

"*What* the hell was that?" Brynn asked in a half whisper. Her voice brought me out of my trance. "I think you just had eye-sex with him!"

"Sorry," I muttered, glancing back at her for a brief second so she knew I wasn't totally ignoring her. I watched the guy empty his tray into the trash, and stack it with the others above the bin. Every fiber of my being was willing him to turn back around and look at me again.

Every.

Single.

One.

My fibers failed me. He walked out the door without a second glance. I blew out a disappointed breath. "Sorry, I got distracted."

"No shit!" Brynn practically yelled. "I could feel your chemistry with Blue Eyes from here!"

I waved her off, trying to act like it wasn't a big deal, when really, I was a bit jolted by it. I'd never felt something like that before, especially for a guy I hadn't even talked to. He could sound like a chipmunk for all I knew. And chipmunks were *not* a turn-on for me.

"Well, I bet *he* has more than a cocktail weenie," Brynn said, her eyes bright with teasing. "Why don't you find out?"

The guy passed by the front window and out of my line of sight. I shifted my eyes away from the windows and back to Brynn. "Because that would get in the way of my goals."

She laughed. "You realize you've barely looked at me for the last five minutes?"

I took a drink of my dark chocolate iced coffee. It was my third one today. "I can appreciate nice things without having to try them. He was hot, Brynn. That's all."

She grinned conspiratorially. "Trying them makes it *so* much more entertaining." She leaned back in her chair, contemplative. "I haven't seen him around town or campus before. I wonder if he's a student? Or if he just works around here?"

I'd seen the veins visible through his huge arms, and when he'd stood up, I'd noticed his thighs were pretty darn substantial, too. "I don't know. Maybe he's a trainer at a gym or something?"

She put a finger to her lips. "Maybe..." she

paused, thinking about it. "Nah…I bet he does something mountain-manny. Like chopping wood."

I rolled my eyes. She'd been spending way too much time watching stripper movies.

"What?" she said, noticing my dismissal. "I'm just saying he probably has a nice, big ax." She slowly licked her lips and I could practically see the images forming in her head. "And I bet he knows *exactly* how to use it."

That thought made my mind immediately wander to what he'd look like shirtless chopping wood—which would be great if I was home alone in my room, with the secret box only Brynn knew the location to in case of my death so my mom didn't find it and have a stroke over the dirty things her daughter liked—but it wasn't so great in the middle of a restaurant. I quickly changed the subject. "What's the plan for this weekend?" Brynn always had our weekends planned by Wednesday at the latest.

"Party at Collin's."

I sighed. I hated Collin's parties. "I don't know why you still hang out with him. He's like the President of douchebags." Really, he was the President of his frat until we graduated a couple of months ago, and that's pretty much the same thing as being the President of douchery.

She lifted a shoulder in a half-shrug as she pushed her food away. She'd hardly eaten any of it—typical. "He has free food and beer. Plus, he's a great singer when he gets drunk enough."

I nodded in concession. He really was a good singer, and if I was being honest, he wasn't a bad guy. I just despised frat boys in general...which was a problem since Brynn spent so much time with so many of them. Brynn's phone vibrated and she glanced at the screen. "I have a meeting to go to, but I'll see you at the house later?"

"Sure."

The phone vibrated again. She grinned as she read the text and quickly replied, her fingers flying over the screen.

I eyed her skeptically. "You're not going to a meeting. You're going to hook up with someone."

She flashed a sly smile as she slid her phone into her back pocket and stood. "Well, it *could* be considered a research meeting. I do have a Master's thesis idea I need to gather information for. I'll have to start carrying a notebook, and make a chart."

I shook my head, a little jealous of her spontaneity, and wishing I was a bit more fun as opposed to focused. "Let's hope you find more than a cocktail weenie, then."

She gave me an evil smile and lifted her hand with her index and middle finger crossed as she walked away. I took a sip of coffee, thinking about the current state of my non-social life, and then pushed it to the back of my mind so I could review my notes one more time.

Two

White smoke billowed out from under the hood of my car. I glanced at the temperature gauge; it had passed the danger zone about five notches ago. Great. Overheated…again. I pulled over to the side of the road as it sputtered to a stop. Ugh. I loved She-Ra, my cobalt blue classic Camaro, but it wasn't the most reliable car in the world. At least I could identify everything under the hood, unlike the newer, boring cars my friends drove. Then again, their cars started—and ran continually. Point to them. But mine was sexier. Point to me.

I put my hazard lights on and got out of the car. As I lifted the hood, a sweet, familiar smell hit me. Anti-freeze was sprayed across the entire engine

compartment like a neon green version of stars. I could probably find the Big Dipper in the dripping dots. I blew out a long sigh followed by a string of curses. Usually, I could just wait for the car to cool down and add some distilled water or anti-freeze to the radiator. Judging by this particular liquid explosion, I was going to need more help than what I could get from my emergency car kit in the trunk. I grabbed my phone and hit the button for Red's Garage. Red was number three on my speed dial, behind my parents and Brynn. Red and I had become good friends since I moved to Winchester, Colorado, for college. I was in constant need of a tow truck and mechanic.

"Howdy, Syd. What's wrong?"

I wondered how many emergency calls it took to make it into your mechanic's phone contacts. I'd been there a while. "Don't you ever think I'm just calling to chat?"

"Yeah. About what's wrong with your car. You should've bought a Ford. Then you wouldn't have these problems."

I sighed. "I'm sure I'd have this problem with any car as old as you...or my dad. I'm on Fifth West and Second South. Something's wrong with my radiator and it's spewing anti-freeze like the girl in *The Exorcist*. Can you come help me?"

I heard something crash in the background on Red's end. "Yeah." He paused. "I'll send the flatbed tow truck just in case."

"Thanks!"

I wasn't far from town, so by the time I finished texting Brynn to tell her I'd probably be late for the party at Collin's tonight, a bright red truck with a long flatbed had pulled in front of me. Flatbed towing is better for She-Ra, so I always insisted on it, but Red would have done it anyway. He loved She-Ra almost as much as I did. I'd been sitting on her trunk—only because my jeans didn't have any buttons on the back that could scratch the car—but stood when the truck came to a stop. I shoved my phone in my back pocket and waited for Red to get out and save my paint job from the anti-freeze assassin. Red was a handy guy to have around.

The light from the setting sun glared off the truck door as it opened. The person was in shadow, but his outline showed a large, tall, imposing frame. Wide shoulders, narrow waist, full head of hair. I thinned my eyes. Since Red was just a little above hobbit size and balding, I figured this must be one of his employees, and not one I recognized by silhouette. I lifted my hand to block the light and try to get a better view. It didn't help. He kept walking toward me and was five feet away before I realized who it was.

Confident, gorgeous blue eyes held mine. It was *the* guy. And he was standing in front of me…about to work on my engine. I had a momentary hot flash and took a deep, steadying breath to try to calm down.

"Hey," I said, shoving my hands in my front

pockets. There was no telling what my hands would do if I gave them freedom—but I was sure it would be mighty embarrassing, and perhaps illegal.

His eyes raked over me, dark and with purpose. I felt like I was being undressed with each shift of his gaze. "Hey," he said back, his voice deep and smooth. Shit. Even his voice seeped testosterone. Why couldn't he have sounded like a chipmunk?

After what felt like a thorough inventory of my assets, his gaze slowly made its way up my body to meet my eyes. I felt like I'd been measured—and was suddenly completely self-conscious about my clothing choice: low-rise jeans, a rose pink sequined tank that complimented my cleavage, fair skin, and blonde hair, and a beige moto jacket. I'd been pretty happy with the ensemble when I'd left the house, but wasn't sure how I felt about it now. I wished I was one of those confident girls who could grab a guy's attention with a smile and keep it for as long as I wanted. But I wasn't Brynn, and there was no point in pretending I was. Mindless flirting with guys I couldn't care less about was one thing—that sort of flirting I could do. But this guy was hot. Like, break-the-rules-and-to-hell-with-my-goals hot. This guy was in a whole different ballpark, and I was completely out of my league.

He'd practically had eye-sex with me at the Soup and Spoon, but I didn't want to make it obvious that I remembered who he was. Though, really, who wouldn't remember him? He could star in an ad for muscles. So, I went with something utterly stupid instead. "You're not Red."

One eyebrow went up like he was contemplating my lack of IQ. "Nope."

I nodded, feeling like an idiot for beginning the conversation that way. At least I hadn't started with an ode to his eyes and bicep circumference—because that had been on the tip of my tongue. I decided to try again. "I think I saw you the other day at lunch. Do you go to college at Easton?" There, that was good. An acknowledgment that I recognized him, but not an affirmation that I'd thought about him in seriously inappropriate ways that required me dipping into my secret naughty box on several occasions since I'd ogled him earlier this week.

He eyed me again. "Nope."

"Then you live in Winchester?"

"Yep."

And he wasn't talkative. So we'd established that.

He stood back and looked at the curvy lines of my car, almost the same way he'd looked at me. I took that as a good sign, since my car was pretty damn hot. "She's gorgeous."

"Thanks."

"A '69?"

I was impressed he identified the year with a glance. Though cars were his job, so I shouldn't be. Maybe my impression of his probable chest

measurement was seeping into my impressions of him in general. "Yeah. And she exploded."

I explained what had happened, and he followed me to the front of the car. He put his tools down on the gravel next to the road and started checking the radiator.

"Any idea what's wrong?"

He didn't answer for a minute. "A few."

He was a man of little words.

We were quiet for what seemed like eons. I felt awkward just standing there, watching him inspect my car in silence. I'm not good with awkward—I tend to just make things more awkward. But I couldn't stand the no-speech zone any longer. "Have you lived in Winchester long?"

Again, he waited more than a minute to answer. "A few weeks."

"I'm surprised I haven't seen you before." I would have remembered. Those eyes. Those arms. It was suddenly much warmer than it had been a few minutes ago.

"Because you're an expert on all the men in town?" My cheeks flamed and I was about to respond when he said, "I just started working at Red's, so it's not really that surprising."

Okay. So we weren't friends, and there was a good chance he thought I was an absolute idiot. Or maybe he just wasn't interested in talking. In any case, I already felt dumb enough, and I had no further interest in talking to a man who didn't want to talk to me, regardless of his criminally low levels of body fat, or tight jeans and shirt that fit him like a second skin. He worked in silence, and I watched in silence. It was even more awkward than before. He seemed totally fine with that.

I felt deflated. Why wasn't he talking to me? Or even attempting to flirt? We'd flirted during our eye-sex encounter, so what was his problem now? He'd barely said a word, which made him so difficult to read that I couldn't tell what his issue was. But his issue was giving me issues, and I didn't like it. I toed some gravel on the ground, wishing I could speed up time and get this service call over with.

"Why isn't your boyfriend helping you with this?"

I started at his voice, surprised he was instigating a conversation. I was even more surprised he was instigating a conversation that was fishing for information about the state of my relationship status. Since it seemed he'd already put me in the epic loser category, I decided not to give the Superman body double any other ammunition. Instead, I lifted a shoulder, non-committal—which was how I felt about my dating life—and pretended I was actually in a relationship, "The guys I date don't usually do cars."

He placed his hands on the front of She-Ra and looked at me sideways, one corner of his lips lifting. "What *do* they do?"

I shrugged.

"So…not you?"

I felt my cheeks redden.

He smiled wider, turning his attention back to the mess under my hood. "With a car like this, you should really have someone who appreciates it and wants to help you take care of it. It's a lot of work."

That whole statement seemed like it had a lot of double-meaning attached to it. I wasn't sure what to make of it, but I wasn't the type of woman who wanted a man to take care of me, and I didn't want him to assume I was. "I can do the work myself. I don't need anyone else."

He braced his arms against the edge of the car, his muscles even more defined with the added strain of his weight. He held my gaze. "You definitely needed me tonight." My eyes widened and he grinned. It took me a second to realize he was talking about my car, and not about all of the other ways he thought I needed him.

I folded my arms over my chest. "I call for help when I can't take care of something on my own."

He laughed softly.

"What's so funny?"

"Just wondering what else you get 'help' with."

He took a towel from his tool box and wiped the antifreeze off of She-Ra. I watched his large, strong hands move over the engine compartment, cleaning it with precision. If his car maintenance skills were any indication, he was a perfectionist, through and through. I couldn't help but wonder what other things he approached with such determined focus, and what else he could do with those hands.

"Did your friend at the Soup and Spoon find some research material?"

My jaw dropped. So, *now* he was acknowledging our previous wordless exchange…and informing me that he'd been eavesdropping. "How did you know about that?"

"Your friend wasn't exactly whispering. Did she find what she was looking for?"

I was kind of annoyed he was asking. What? Did he want to be part of her research team? Geez. I scowled at the thought. "Brynn usually gets what she wants."

He licked his lips, his eyes focused on mine. "Do you?"

I had no response, and was too stunned by the scorching heat radiating off of him to answer. The way he looked at me made me think I should stop for a pregnancy test on the way home because he might have inseminated me with his eyes.

His lips lifted slightly, amused that he'd made me uncomfortable. "The tube for your radiator overflow popped off and the overflow container is leaking, too," he said, throwing the towel back in his tool box. "It's a hazard; you should get it fixed, or your radiator will leak—and overheat— constantly." He latched the clips on the front of the box and picked it up. "You'll be

fine to get it home, just don't take it on the freeway or for long distances until you bring it into the shop and we install the overflow."

Still overcome with all the lip licking and eye-sexing, I barely comprehended his explanation of my car issues. His brow lifted like he was waiting for a response—which was a problem since my throat felt like cotton. I attempted a swallow. "Great," I managed to get out. "Thanks for your help."

"I work in the afternoons," he paused as he passed by me, his arm brushing mine. Heat raced through my veins at the slight touch. He leaned down next to my ear, and in a low tone said, "in case you want me under your hood."

He said the last part with blatant innuendo. I felt my cheeks go hot as he picked up his tool box.

"See you around, sixty-nine."

"Blue Eyes called you sixty-nine?" Brynn asked, her mouth gaping. "That. Is. Awesome!"

I took a sip of my soda. "It's the year of my car. That's why he said it."

"Uh huh, sure it is," she said, rolling her eyes. "If you really believe that, you're way more gullible than I thought."

I shifted my eyes away from her, taking in the

room. Standard college party. The air smelled like alcohol and too much perfume. The girls were wearing next-to-nothing, and the guys were hoping they'd get to take the next to nothing pieces off. I wasn't interested in the guys, but Brynn liked going to these parties, and I liked spending time with her. Plus, I didn't want her going alone, without someone to have her back. "You're making a bigger deal out of the situation than you should," I reasoned, also trying to convince myself.

"He made sexual references all through the conversation with you. That's a big deal." Her voice went high and sing-songy. "He liiikkkes you."

"He doesn't like me. He barely talked to me, and made me feel like an awkward teenager again."

"But when he *did* talk to you, he totally flirted." Brynn watched me with a knowing expression. "I saw the way you looked at him at lunch. And the way he looked at you. It was like he was hungry, and you were absolutely willing to be eaten."

I gasped. "I am *not* willing to be eaten," I said, affronted. "In fact, I've been very good about not being eaten in the past! Law degree first, remember?"

"That's what you've always said, but this time is different." She studied me for a moment, tapping a finger against her lips. "You're interested in him. *Really* interested. I think he might just be the man who breaks your no-sex streak."

I made a pssh noise, though my heart was

pounding at even the thought. "You saw him. A nun would be interested! But I'm only interested in looking. That's all."

My mind was racing with thoughts about Blue Eyes—I still didn't even know his name—and our interaction. I'd replayed it over in my head at least thirty times in the past three hours. I had it memorized. I'd probably dream about it. I'd even considered pretending to be sick so I could go home and analyze it some more—with aid from my naughty box. I couldn't keep talking about it, though, or it would make me even more crazy. "How was your 'research session' the other day?" I asked, changing the subject.

Brynn made a disgusted noise like she was completely over it. "Not great. My research is underway, though. I've started taking notes and compiling a list of my past observations."

I burst out laughing. I didn't realize she was taking this so seriously. "Do you tell the guys about your research before, or after, they drop their pants?"

Her brows shot up. "Are you crazy? I don't tell them at all! If word got out, I might start getting sizes that aren't normal, and that would skew my results. I need an unbiased study."

I didn't point out that she was probably the most biased person in the world when it came to penis size, and that her research project had started *because* of her bias. "But if people knew you were looking for bigger sizes, it would help you reach your ultimate goal:

getting laid by guys you actually want to have sex with."

She tilted her glass back, taking a drink. The yeasty smell of cheap beer perfumed the air. "True. But now I'm focused. I really want to get some data on this."

"I'm sure you do." I took another sip of my drink—Coke. "Have you found anyone here worth studying?"

"No," she scanned the room, "I already have info on most of these guys."

My mouth fell open. We were at a party with a bunch of current and former frat guys. There were at least fifty of them here. "I didn't realize you had that much time."

She looked at me like I was nuts. "I haven't slept with *all* of them. Just some. And the others, well, you hear things."

My eyes got even wider. "I guess I'm not hanging out with the same people you are. Because you're the only person I know who openly discusses the size of their partners."

"That's because you hang out with books instead of girls."

I shrugged. I was fine with that.

"I know some guys who'd like to be studied," a voice behind me said.

I shifted and turned to see Collin. He used one hand to brace himself on the back of the couch, then jumped between me and Brynn. There wasn't a lot of room between us to begin with, but that didn't deter

him. "Hey!" I yelled, trying to steady my Coke. "You almost spilled my drink all over my shirt." I glared at him. He was wearing dark wash jeans with a black tee that had a deep green dragon design on it. It looked like something that would be sold at a sci-fi / fantasy convention.

"I would have helped you clean it up," he said, brows waggling.

I rolled my eyes. Collin was a massive flirt, often annoying, and occasionally, a nice guy. He and Brynn had hooked up before, and were still friends. I put up with him—and all of her dates and booty calls—because she was my bestie. "I would have taken my chances with the stain."

He shrugged and moved on. "Can I get you ladies anything? Food, drinks, condoms?"

I gave Brynn a look that said, *this is unbelievable*. She grinned, amused. "You could tell me when you're going to start singing. Because that's what I really came for."

His lips spread revealing a bright smile. "I aim to please," he said, jumping up and standing on the cheap, fabricated wood coffee table in front of us. He lifted his hand, miming a microphone, and started singing a teen pop song about love gone wrong at the top of his lungs. It was off-key, horrible, and he was making a total spectacle of himself. I was glad I'd stayed for it. Just as he got to the chorus for the second time, I heard a loud crack and the coffee table legs gave out. The table crashed to the ground, taking Collin with it. The room fell silent at the abrupt end to his performance. I stood up to see if he was okay or needed help, but my assistance wasn't required. Collin popped up off the ground and in the middle of the coffee table wreckage, he picked right back up where he'd left off in the song.

Everyone clapped and laughed. My initial thought was that I was glad he was okay. My second thought was that if he kept treating his house like this, he wasn't going to get his rent deposit back. Looking around at everyone else in the room having a great time, I was pretty sure I was the only one who'd had that thought.

Three

After the party, I'd spent some time thinking about my extremely practical reaction to Collin's coffee table destruction. Instead of laughing and having a good time like everyone else, I'd immediately gone into "adult" mode in my head, ticking off the reasons Collin had been irresponsible, and the issues that would arise from his error in judgment.

Part of my problem was that unlike most people, I analyzed every action, and its potential consequences, before I made a move. There was a reason for that. For a long time, things in my life had been completely unpredictable—and scary. The uncertainty made me feel like every day I was treading water, unsure whether that would be the day my legs finally gave out. It had affected me to the point that I tried to control my environment as much as possible. I liked things safe, organized, practical—and apparently, pretty damn boring. That made me pretty damn boring myself. I was sick of being practical, and I wanted to have a little fun. Not "get knocked up" fun, but I'd convinced myself some flirting wouldn't be a bad idea.

So, in the spirit of trying to be more social and act twenty-three instead of fifty, I decided to get She-Ra's overflow fixed. While that might not seem like anything out of the ordinary, it was. I'd purposefully waited until four o'clock in the afternoon, when I knew Blue Eyes would be there to work on my car. I was going to get She-Ra fixed, and possibly even flirt. And if that went well, maybe I'd do something completely irrational like not fill up my gas tank until it got below a quarter of a tank instead of a half. Baby steps.

"Hey, Syd!" Red said as I opened the glass front door of his shop waiting area. He was standing behind the counter; an office with a door was behind that. Red's mechanic shop was on one of the busiest streets in town. The outside of the building had wood siding, painted white with bright red trim. Four gas pumps sat in front of the garage. A sign declaring it Red's Gas and Auto Repairs hung above the large garage shop doors. He had a waiting area with popcorn, drinks, and candy for people who didn't have to wait long for a repair to

be done—you know, the people with cars that weren't as old as their parents.

"Hey." I leaned against the counter, kicking one leg out and resting an elbow on the laminate countertop. I was trying to pose in a flattering way in case Blue Eyes made an appearance. I'd already done a scan of the outside of the shop. He wasn't there. Maybe he'd lied about his hours. I frowned as I thought about that. Red would surely tell him when I came in. Then he'd know I was there during the afternoon and make assumptions about why. They'd be correct assumptions, but that didn't matter as much as the fact that they'd be embarrassing assumptions that would confirm I'd come to the shop at the exact time he'd told me to. I sighed inwardly. Nothing I could do about it now. If I ever saw Blue Eyes again, and if he asked, I'd just say this was my only free time. I almost laughed at that. I was already rationalizing things, thinking of worst-case scenarios, and coming up with ways to manage them. I needed to stop; I needed to learn to relax. And, I reminded myself, I was here to try to change that exact problem. "I came in to get my overflow fixed."

Red nodded, pulling out his keyboard from under the desk. He pushed his glasses up higher on his nose as he typed. "I heard about that."

"Yeah. The new guy figured it out pretty fast." Red nodded. "He's been here for a few weeks. I was lucky to get him. He has a lot of experience."

"I bet he does," I mumbled, thinking his experience probably encompassed a hell of a lot more than cars. An image of Blue Eyes from the other night, leaning over She-Ra, popped into my head. The muscles in his back bunching with each twist of his wrench—the same muscles that would be flexed if he was leaning over me instead. I dragged in a ragged breath before Red coughed, trying to get my attention.

I blinked, and noticed Red looking at me over the top of his wire rimmed glasses, like he was analyzing me or something. I was fine with analyzing myself, but I didn't like when other people did it. I quickly changed the subject. "So," I said, absently picking up a card from a stack on the counter and tapping it against the laminate, "can you fit She-Ra in today?"

Red hit a button and his printer started up. He grabbed the invoice and started to walk to the door between the waiting room and the garage. "Park her in the first bay."

I put the card back down and noticed what was printed on it for the first time. An ad for a local haunted house. It was only August. I shook my head, thinking that haunted houses seemed to be starting earlier every year. I picked it back up and slid it in my purse. Haunted houses weren't practical and boring, and they were definitely out of my comfort zone. I might have to drag Brynn to it with me.

Red guided me as I pulled She-Ra into the garage and parked. I felt a little more deflated as I looked

around and saw three employees, none of them with bright blue eyes or an attitude. The jerk. His work hour declaration had been a trick.

I got out and opened the hood, showing Red the hose and damage.

"It's an easy fix. Shouldn't take long."

"She could probably fix it herself," a deep baritone voice that was *so* not chipmunk-like said from behind me. My stomach jumped and my legs felt like soup. Where in the world had he been hiding? I'd looked for him! I turned slowly, taking in his messy hair that peeked out from under his black ball cap, jeans, and tight black tee shirt with Red's name and logo plastered in white and red on the front of his chest. I licked my lips, and wondered if it was normal to suddenly be jealous of a logo. My reaction wasn't lost on him—one corner of his lips lifted as he continued, "When I rescued her on the side of the road, she told me she's pretty good with," he paused, his eyes glinting, "cars." That particular discussion had also involved innuendo, but I saw no reason to clue Red into that.

Red looked from Blue Eyes to me, a knowing expression passing over his face. "She is," Red said, "and what she doesn't know, she picks up on pretty fast. Her dad was a good teacher."

I smiled, thinking of him. "He didn't let me leave the driveway with the car until I knew how everything under the hood worked, and could fix the basics on my own."

Blue Eyes tilted his head to one side. "Smart dad."

"I agree," Red said. "Why don't you take care of this, Jax. I've got some stuff to do in the office."

Jax? His name was *Jax?* Red *had* to be joking? My eyes darted around outside, searching for a Harley. I didn't see one, but I really hoped he had it parked out back—and that he was channeling a *Sons of Anarchy* season two version of Jax Teller.

Red stopped before going through the door connecting the waiting area to the garage. "You can stay out here and watch Jax if you want to learn how to fix it, Syd. It would be good to know in case it happens again."

"Thanks." The word came out slowly, like it was stuck in my throat. My voice felt as hesitant as my feet. I wasn't sure what the best plan of flirt action was here. I'd shown up when Jax had told me he'd be working, so he already knew there was some level of interest on my part. If I stayed, would that make me seem even more desperate? Ugh. The analyzing had to end. I inwardly shook myself out of it. I needed to stop planning every possible situation, and just act. Now.

Jax pulled a piece of candy from his pocket, unwrapping it as he watched me, like he was waiting for my next move and totally amused by the internal struggle I seemed to be having. He put the candy in his mouth, rolling it against the inside of his cheek, then cocked a brow. "Hey, sixty-nine. Want a piece?"

I shook my head, candy the very last thing on my mind.

"Want a piece of candy, then?"

I froze, totally unprepared for the brazen flirting. My heart was sprinting in my chest, and with my blood currently occupied in so many other places, the best I could come up with in response was, "Funny."

A smile tugged at his lips. I brushed it off and squared my shoulders, pushing up my sleeves. "So, what's first?"

He eyed me, his lips widening into a grin as he walked over to a large, silver tool chest and moved it next to the car. I was standing close enough to smell the strawberry candy in his mouth, and he kept moving it around like he was massaging it with his tongue. It was distracting. "It's pretty simple. I just take off the old container, attach the new one, and put on the new hose."

"Your name is Jax?" I asked, watching him unbolt the container. "You didn't tell me that before." "You didn't ask."

"What's your last name?"

He rolled the candy around some more. "West. Jackson West."

Jackson West? It sounded like he should be in a John Wayne movie. "So, do you ride a Harley, Jax?"

He looked up at me, sucking the candy between his teeth. "Yeah. I also have an insane mother, and kill people. That's why I'm here. I pissed off the gun runners and had to find an unassuming place to stay until the heat dies down."

"Sarcasm. Nice. You get points for watching the show at least."

"Is that all it takes to get points with you?" he asked, throwing the old overflow in the trash.

"You also get points for carrying on an actual conversation—which means you now have two more points than the last time we talked."

He looked up, his dark hair falling over his forehead as he bolted the new container to the side of the car. "Is that all?"

I took a breath, wondering if I could really do this. Flirt with a guy who felt a hundred miles out of my league. I went for it. "You also got points for—other things."

"Other things?" he asked, eyes wide with interest. "Like what?"

I shrugged, letting my gaze trail over his arms and chest before coming back to rest on his face again. The corner of his mouth hitched. "Point taken," he said, attaching the new hose. "I thought you had a boyfriend?"

I leaned against the car. "No, you assumed I had one, and I didn't correct you."

He cocked a brow, intrigued. "Girlfriend?"

I could see the wheels turning in his head at the thought. "No," I said, narrowing my eyes. "I'm just too busy for boys."

He looked up at me from under the hood, his eyes holding a distinct glint, like my statement had been

some sort of challenge. My stomach fluttered immediately in response.

Jax stood, wiping his hands off. "She's all done."

It really was simple. The whole process took less than ten minutes. I could have done it myself if I'd had all the tools—and knew what I was doing. "Thanks for fixing She-Ra for me," I said, flashing him my sweetest smile. "And for teaching me how to fix it so I can take care of the problem next time."

"She-Ra?" he asked, incredulous. "Shouldn't you have at least named it after She-Ra's horse?"

I gave him a disgusted look. "It's a Camaro, not a Mustang."

He put the hood down, gently dropping it in place. "Horsepower applies to all engines, not just the ones built by Ford. You don't know much about cars if you don't know that."

I glared, annoyed. "I know plenty about cars. And She-Ra's unicorn's name would have sounded silly."

He leaned against the side of the car, crossing his arms over his chest. "I don't know. I think Swift Wind and She-Ra are mutually ridiculous."

I was pretty stunned he was so well informed about He-Man trivia. That gave him another point, but I wasn't going to tell him that. "She-Ra is super strong and super fast. Just like my car. It's the perfect name. Don't mock me."

His lips lifted slightly. "I'll do my best. Not to, I mean."

I eyed him. "For some reason, I don't believe you."

He grinned. "Probably for the best." He stepped away from the car. "You're ready to go."

"Thanks."

He walked past me to the bay door and opened it while I went inside and paid Red. He gave me his frequent customer discount—even though I was pretty sure no one else got the same deal. I waved goodbye to him and met Jax outside the shop. He pushed off from the side of She-Ra, and opened my door for me. "You shouldn't have any other problems with it."

"'Shouldn't' being the operative word. I'm sure I'll be back in here next week—if not sooner."

His azure gaze flashed with interest. "I'll look forward to it."

Four

Brynn came through the house like a storm, dropping her bag on the floor, keys in the wood tray next to the door, and kicking off her shoes in the middle of the dark, hand-scraped distressed hardwood living room floor as she made her way to the kitchen—it was her usual entrance. She came back with her custom water mix of lemons and limes. She drank it all day, every day. She said it was good for detoxing. She made me drink it sometimes, too…against my will.

Two hours ago, I'd finished a batch of cookie dough, and sat down in the living room to relax for a minute. I'd switched on the TV and landed on *House Hunters*. I was now on my fourth episode. I couldn't stop watching. So far, I'd argued with a woman who wanted the paint color changed before she'd agree to put an offer on a house, a man who refused to go in a house because his spirit guide told him not to enter, and a couple whose deal breaker was ghosts. I could start a drinking game for every time someone used the word 'character.' The show was like crack. As soon as a new episode started, I was immediately invested and couldn't look away. I was alternating between snacking on Reese's Pieces, and nuts—because that's how I justify copious amounts of candy, by adding a little protein—when Brynn got home.

She plopped down next to me on the grey, suede couch, leaned against the teal throw pillows, and crossed one leg underneath her. "I've seen this one," she said, nodding toward the TV. "The couple picks the house with the most space for a sex room."

I'd seen the preview and watched with a combination of interest and shock. They were on national TV, totally comfortable with everyone in the world knowing about their sexual preferences. I could barely admit those things to myself. "I can't believe they're so open about it."

Brynn shrugged. "They have good communication skills." She took another drink. "I like watching the relationship interactions between people on the show. Their personality traits, and the way they deal with conflicts and compromises are really interesting case studies."

I agreed. Though Brynn's potential career in psychology made it even more interesting to her. I

popped a couple of pieces of candy in my mouth. Brynn frowned at the sugar—she wouldn't even have it in the house if she had her way—and she took a small handful of nuts instead. "My textbooks just cost me as much as our rent," she said. "My professors can suck it. I'm not looking forward to starting school next week. What have you been up to lately?"

I muted the TV. "I finished my law school prep class a few days ago, so I was just working hard on that. Oh, and I got the radiator hose on my car fixed." Her brows went up as she swallowed a chug of sour citric water. She didn't even wince. That had to be some sort of super power. "How did that go?"

"Good," I said, replaying the highlights in my head—for the fiftieth time.

"And?" she prompted, rotating her free hand in circles to encourage me to go on—now. "Was Blue Eyes there?"

I nodded. "He showed me how to fix it in case it happens again."

Brynn snorted. "Why would you want to know that when you can just take it back to him and watch his ass as he bends over and fixes it for you?"

Yes…I'd had a similar thought. The view was well worth the money. Now that I knew how to fix the hose and overflow, I could easily dismantle it—or something else on the car—and go back for more maintenance. "I spend almost as much time at Red's getting my car fixed as I do at school or home. I'm sure I'll be in there for something else soon."

She nodded. "That's true. And you can look at his ass again when you go back."

I shifted my leg underneath me as I laughed. "And everything else. His name is Jax."

She choked on a nut—something she'd probably done before, only this one was actually edible. She took a drink to wash it down. "You've got to be kidding," she said, her voice still a little raw.

I shook my head. "Nope. And when I made a reference to *Sons of Anarchy*, he totally got it. So he gets points for that."

"Hell, with that ass and face, he didn't need more points, but good for you. You need to get on that. And by 'get on,' I mean get on him and ride him like a horse before someone else does."

I worried my bottom lip. I had no doubt Jax had a lot of experience in the riding arena. It made me nervous, and a little excited, too. "Maybe," I said, relenting a bit. I'd already told her about my plan to try to have a little more fun. She was highly supportive. "We'll see where it goes."

"What are you talking about?" she asked, her face lined with disbelief. "Stop wasting time and just do it!"

I lifted my leg, resting it on the white coffee table stacked with magazines, and decorated with teal and black candles. My parents had insisted on buying all of our furniture and decor. I'd argued at first, but no child

has a chance against the resolve of their mother. My parents had insisted they wanted to do it, and I'd let them because I knew my mom's reasons went deeper than just a parent wanting to spoil her child. "I'm not like you, Brynn," I sighed. "I can't just hop into bed with a guy. I think it's risky, and I need an emotional connection. I have to feel something more than attraction—I need to really *know* him. I have to feel like there's the potential for something more than a meaningless hook-up—even if I'm *so* not ready for a relationship yet."

Brynn stood and grabbed her now empty cup. She could throw back water like a frat boy throws back bad beer. "Sometimes there's not more, Syd. Sometimes it's just fun, and that's all it is. Do yourself a favor and have some. Blue Eyes looks like he'd be a blast."

"You know his name is Jax."

She grinned as she walked away. "He'll always be Blue Eyes to me."

I laughed, and glanced at my watch. Brynn and I volunteered at CARE—a lodging facility for families from out of town with loved ones in hospitals. We went in a few times a month. CARE tried to handle everything for the families so they could concentrate on helping their loved ones get better. Tonight was our night to serve dinner. I grabbed the candy and nuts off the coffee table and walked into the kitchen to put them away. "Are you almost ready?" I yelled to Brynn. "We need to leave soon."

"Yep, I just need to change," she yelled back from her room down the hall. "Be there in a minute."

I opened the fridge and grabbed the cookie dough I'd made earlier.

I really enjoyed volunteering at CARE. It was a cause close to my heart. Being with the families was such a humbling experience, and the people were truly grateful. Hearing their stories inspired me to want to make the world a better place, and help as many people as possible. I wasn't sure how I'd do that yet, but it was one of my many goals. I knew that after I got my law degree, I wanted to keep working with CARE in some capacity.

CARE housed everyone from parents of patients to extended family members. After we'd finished serving dinner, a bunch of the kids helped me roll the peanut butter cookie dough into balls. When the cookies were done, I had several eager assistants help unwrap Hershey's kisses and press them into the warm cookies.

After we'd cleaned everything up, Brynn and I sat down and chatted with some of the residents, and read books to a few of the kids.

"Read it again!" Macy cried when I'd finished *Rapunzel* for the second time. She was four years old,

with strawberry blonde colored curls, and she was adorable. Her brother was in the hospital being treated for spinal injuries he'd suffered after a car accident.

"Again? Don't you want a different story?"

She shook her long, bright locks. It was pretty obvious why she liked this story so much. "This one!"

I tugged her hair. "I bet your hair is long enough to climb up. Wanna try?"

She giggled, shaking her head. "You're so silly, Syd." She picked up the oversized book and turned it page-by-page back to the beginning, careful not to drop the cookie she was holding in her left hand. I wasn't sure how many she'd eaten, but it was probably more than her mom had authorized. I knew the peanut butter kiss cookies were her favorite, so I tried to make them a lot. I started the story over again, reading until her mom came to take her to bed.

"She's had some cookies," I warned. Her mom, Patti, laughed and nodded as she walked away. I stood, rubbing my eyes. The end of my law school prep class had kicked my butt, hard. It had been a long week, and I was looking forward to my bed. "You're good with her," Charlie said. Charlie had been with CARE for a long time. He'd come here originally for help while his wife was going through chemo. Charlie had been so moved by the love and support of the people at CARE during his stay that he'd started working with the organization, and had been their executive director for the past five years. I admired him, and his strength. Working at a place like CARE was an emotional rollercoaster. One day you'd get to celebrate a triumph, and the next, mourn a tragedy.

I stretched my arms above me, letting my muscles loosen. "She's easy to entertain."

"Well, we appreciate all you do to help out." I looked around at the toys, couches, and TV. The home-away-from home for everyone CARE helped. "It means a lot to me."

He patted me on the back. "I know."

"The construction seems to be going well." CARE was adding on to the house so they could accommodate more temporary residents.

Charlie nodded, looking toward the back of the house where the construction was taking place. "It should be done in the next couple of months."

"I'm glad you'll be able to help more people with the addition."

"Me, too."

Brynn came up to me, her purse hanging from her shoulder. "The cookies are gone and the kids probably won't sleep tonight. Our job is done."

Charlie laughed. "We'll see you girls soon."

"Have a good night," I said.

"You, too."

Brynn and I walked out to the car and I went home to fall into bed, and hopefully some dreams starring a sexy mechanic.

Five

F ew things were more annoying than car problems. With a car like She-Ra, I was used to the unexpected. But a car problem that required me to change my tire at seven in the morning in heels before my first class on my first day of law school was even more annoying than my usual car issues. My hands were covered in mud and dirt by the time I was done, but my jeans, button-up lilac colored shirt, and black blazer were fine. I said a silent thanks to my dad for teaching me how to change a tire in less than ten minutes, and rushed out the door to my class. I was frazzled, but made it through the first day without getting an ulcer—at least, as far as I could tell. Part of that was because of my friend, Cade. He'd been in my law school prep class over the summer, and we'd helped each other on a few assignments. When I got to school this morning, I was happy to see we had some classes together. We'd made plans to get together and study later in the week.

When school was done for the day, I checked my hair, makeup, and did a quick assessment of my ass in my jeans. Finding all of the above acceptable, I was ready to take She-Ra and my spare to Red's to get the tire fixed. If I happened to see a hot, blue eyed mechanic while I was there, I was totally prepared. Okay, not really. Every time I saw him, my stomach contorted into shapes reserved for circus performers, but I was as prepared as possible.

"Hey, Red," I said, pushing the door open. He stopped writing and looked up. "I caught a nail last night and need the flat fixed."

"How did that happen?"

"Went through a construction zone." At least, that's where I suspected the nail came from. I hadn't been too careful about where I'd parked at CARE, and with all the building going on, a flat tire was bound to happen at one point or another.

He nodded. "We have some other cars in front of you, but if you want to wait, we'll get to it in about thirty minutes."

"Sounds good." I glanced through the office door window, out into the shop bay.

"Looking for someone?" Red raised an eyebrow, his lips lifting in a knowing grin.

I could feel my cheeks flaming. "What? No!" I

said, trying to throw him off the scent. I didn't need Red—or anyone else for that matter—knowing about my obsession with Jax. I was barely comfortable knowing about it myself. "I was just looking around."

Red chuckled. "Uh huh."

"Really!" I said, in my most affronted voice. "I was!"

"Whatever you say, Syd."

I narrowed my eyes, annoyed that I'd been caught, and dropped my purse next to one of the lobby chairs. Red disappeared into his office and soon I heard the muffled sounds of his voice coming through the door. He must be returning phone calls. I stole more glances at the shop bay as I grabbed a bottled water and some chocolate from the vending machine. I wasn't hungry, but I needed an excuse to get up and investigate the employees currently working. Plus, I needed to calm my nerves. Chocolate was very soothing. I saw two other guys in the bay, neither of them Jax. I frowned, letdown, and sunk into one of the chairs. I was surprised at my level of disappointment, actually. As I thought about my reaction, my analysis led me to the unnerving realization that I'd become absolutely infatuated with Jackson West. There was no other explanation for it. I checked my watch. It was only eleven in the morning. That must be the reason for Jax's absence. He'd said he worked in the afternoons.

Thirty minutes later, She-Ra was in the bay, getting her tire patched. I'd been disappointed all over again when Devon, one of Red's other employees, had come to get my keys. No Jax today. I wondered when I'd see him again. I could always make up a car problem so I'd have an excuse to stop—stabbing various things under the hood with a screwdriver should do the trick. But there were only so many times I could use that method without Jax—and Red—seeing through it, and me looking like stalker.

I glanced at my bag full of textbooks and assignments. I thought about starting them, but I knew the tire wouldn't take long, and I didn't want to get interrupted in the middle of my work. I pulled a paranormal romance novel from my bag instead. Romance novels were my guilty pleasure. I feared no real man would ever be able to live up to them. I'd left off at a particularly rapturous scene, and was eager to get back into the story. I started reading, going through pages, and chocolate, like the world was about to run out of words and sugar. Completely enthralled with the story, and oblivious to everything else, I jumped out of my skin when I heard, "You're a fast reader. With all the thrusting going on there, I'd think you'd want to savor it a bit and not rush through."

I jumped, dropping the last of my chocolate on the ground. Luckily, my water had a cap, or there'd have been an even bigger mess to clean up. I glared up at Jax, annoyed about my lost chocolate, though it was hard to stay mad when he looked even more delicious than the candy. His jeans sat low on his waist, his red

work shirt straining over his chest and arms. I wanted to lick him. I marked my place in the book and folded it shut. "I took a speed reading class." I refused to be embarrassed by the fact he'd just seen me reading something much more than R-rated. "How long were you standing there, anyway?" I asked casually.

"Long enough for him to change from werewolf to human, rip off her clothes, and impale her with his massive member."

I pursed my lips as my cheeks heated. He'd been there awhile. At least ten pages by my count. "It's not nice to spy on people, you know."

"It's not my fault you weren't paying attention."

My eyes narrowed to slits "And it's not my fault you're kind of an ass."

He grinned. "So was the werewolf. I'm taking notes."

I rolled my eyes and changed the subject as I picked up the remains of the chocolate from the floor and threw it in the trash. "I didn't know you were here today." And he hadn't been when I got there. I checked!

"Again, not my fault you're oblivious. Your car's done. The hole was from a nail. It was small and easy to patch. I changed it out and put the spare back in the trunk. I also did a tire rotation for you since your records show you haven't had it done for more than five thousand miles."

I lifted my brows in surprise that he'd had the

forethought to check that. "Thanks. I thought Devon was working on my car?"

"He was. Then I got here."

I pushed my brows together. That was weird. Usually the same mechanic who started a project was the one to finish it. Plus, it wasn't even noon yet. "Don't you usually work later in the day?"

"I'm here early today."

I couldn't help but wonder why. My mind immediately wandered to Red's knowing look when I'd scanned the shop like I'd been tactically trained to find washboard abs by the FBI, and then Red's phone calls. A part of me—a pretty big part—wanted the reason Jax had come in early to be me. A thrill went through me at the thought.

Jax walked to the counter and printed off an invoice. I paid for the flat fix and grabbed my stuff. I wasn't expecting him to follow me outside, but he did. The warm breeze danced through my hair as I threw my purse on the passenger seat. "Well," I said, trying not to sound too awkward, "thanks again."

"Leaving already?"

"You have to work, and I have things to do."

"Werewolves?"

I pressed my lips together, owning the embarrassment. "If I can find one."

He grinned. "And if I didn't have to work?"

My brows gathered, unsure what exactly he was asking. "If you didn't have to work, what?"

"Would you still have things to do?"

This time it was my turn to grin. "Wouldn't you like to know?" The fact was, if he was offering himself up as one of the things on my to-do list, I'd take it—with a condom and no hesitation. The act first, think later Syd was taking charge.

He watched me for several seconds, like he was trying to figure me out. "Well, I can promise you one thing, you wouldn't want to rush through it if you were with me."

I widened my eyes. "Pretty ballsy to compare yourself to a paranormal being who can bench press six hundred pounds and change his dick size at will."

His lips slid into a slow, sexy line, his eyes raking over me like I'd just been undressed. "Sweetheart, there is *no* comparison."

He'd rendered me speechless. Absolutely no words. I'd been interested in the muscle-bodied, blue eyed God before, but now, I could barely contain my curiosity. He hadn't really opened up to me at all, and our conversations mostly consisted of innuendo. He was guarded, arrogant, and sexy as hell. All things that made me want to get inside his head even more. He was drawing me in, and I just kept getting more and more invested. Jax was my *House Hunters*! I couldn't turn away. I swallowed. Hard. "Your ego is off the charts."

The afternoon sun highlighted his bronzed skin, and the lighter cocoa tones of his hair as he fixed his gaze on me. "I'm not the type of person who lies to myself. I know what I have to offer. And I can promise you it's better than anything you've ever read." I widened my eyes at that. Clearly, he didn't know about my romance novel expertise. He grinned like he knew what I was thinking. "As a bonus, with me, you wouldn't have to worry about claws, or the chance of being ripped apart mid-orgasm. I'm a far better choice than fiction."

It took me a few seconds to respond. "Noted," I managed to get out, still a little shocked by his opinion of himself—and trying to decide if his statements were an actual invitation. Yeah, we'd flirted, and we had chemistry, but was he as attracted to me as I was to him? I almost snorted at the thought. It seemed impossible. We had nothing in common but our love for cars and banter.

Jax pulled She-Ra's keys from his pocket and dropped them into my hand. "How'd you get this car?"

We'd gone from werewolf sex to car questions in less than ten seconds. I felt like I had verbal whiplash and it took me a minute to get my bearings after the subject change. My mind was still stuck on what he'd look like naked—with or without claws. I shook it off and answered his question, "I stole it. How do you think I got it?"

His lips tilted in a half grin. "It's a pretty unique car. Red mentioned your dad made you learn about it. Was it his?"

I usually hated when people stereotyped muscle

cars as not for girls. I also hated when people assumed my dad / grandpa / boyfriend / sugar daddy bought my car, but Jax seemed genuinely interested, not condescending. "Yeah. My dad bought it when he was in high school and drove it on the weekends when I was growing up. I loved going out with him and riding in the car. He told me that if I kept my grades up, he'd give me the car when I turned sixteen. He made me spend a year learning about the car and how it worked before he let me drive it. And even though he wanted to give it to me as a sixteenth birthday gift, I didn't let him. I got a job and paid him back. He agreed to that, but insisted on paying for the maintenance and insurance. He said it was the least I could do for being born with boobs and not making his insurance premium skyrocket."

Jax grinned, his eyes sliding down to my lilac shirt, the top three buttons undone and hinting at the lacy purple bra I had beneath it. He'd clearly noticed the cleavage tease. "I'm also really fond of your boobs— for other reasons."

"I'm sure you're fond of boobs in general."

"Yours are special."

My stomach fluttered and I looked down, trying to hide my smile as I answered, "Uh huh."

"You look more dressed up than usual today." His eyes went over me again, taking in the tailored jeans, silk button-up shirt, and black heels. "Did you have a job interview or something?"

"No. It was my first day of law school. I'm going to go home and study, then try to relax before things get even more hectic tomorrow."

His expression changed from a guy checking me out, to a guy slightly more intrigued with my brain than my bra size. It's a rare thing to see. "I didn't know you wanted to be a lawyer."

"It runs in the family. I love the law, though, and I think it's great that I'll get paid to argue."

He laughed. "I imagine that's something you excel at."

Now it was my turn to grin. "I had years of practice debating my dad. He's an attorney, too."

He cocked his hip out and leaned against the car. "So you have a good relationship with your dad?"

I nodded. "My mom was the cautious one. My dad let me have fun. It was a good parenting combination. Maybe not for them—I'm sure they argued like crazy over what I should be allowed to do—but, it was good for me to have them both, and see both sides."

"Do you have siblings?"

"Nope," I answered. "What about you? What's your family like?"

Jax's face shuttered. "Complicated. I don't see them often."

His immediate shutdown of all things emotional made me wonder about the backstory behind his feelings and his family relationships. "Siblings?"

"Yeah. I'm the oldest."

"Ah, so you were the test child," I said. I'd had

friends who were test children. They were all pretty bitter about the advantages their younger siblings got from their pain.

"Still am."

I shifted my bag on my back, adjusting the weight from all of my books. "I always felt like I missed out on something by not having siblings. Growing up, I thought a brother or sister would be a lot like having a built-in friend." Jax crossed his arms over his chest as he listened to me. "Now that I'm older, though, I realize that just because you have a sibling, it doesn't mean you're always going to be close. People change as they grow, and sometimes that means drifting apart."

He looked off into the distance like he was thinking, and then nodded. "Families can be complicated." He opened the car door for me and I got in, fastened my seat belt, and started the car. "Let me know if you have any problems with the tire—" he paused and leaned down into the window, his face inches from mine. His contemplative look had been replaced by a mischievous one—"or if you need someone better than a werewolf."

"He actually said to let him know if you need someone better than a werewolf?" Brynn asked, eyes wide.

I replayed the conversation in my head, licking my lips as I did. I nodded, and Brynn laughed. "You want him. Bad."

"No!" I shook my head fervently. "I totally don't. Really." Even I knew I didn't sound believable.

She snorted a laugh. "You stare off into space every time you mention him, and you always lick your lips when you're thinking about him. I haven't seen you this obsessed with a guy since the Henry Cavill look-a-like lived on our dorm floor freshman year."

I gave a dreamy sigh, remembering doppelganger Cavill's perfect...everything. "Damn, he was hot."

Brynn picked up her purse and took one last look in the mirror. She swiped a finger over her lip line, checking to make sure none of her Wicked Crimson lipstick had escaped to unauthorized places. She liked to draw attention to her mouth.

"Who are you going out with tonight?" I asked.

After getting my tire fixed, I'd spent all afternoon buried in text books, case studies, and homework. Brynn had apparently used the time differently. Her classes for her Masters in Psychology had started today, too. It seemed she'd already found more research candidates. "A guy in one of my classes. He looks like a pirate. I hope he's up for role playing."

I gave a disbelieving laugh. "How do you get guys to agree to all of this?" My sexual experience landed far more on the vanilla side of things than Brynn's—not by choice, however. In fact, every guy I'd suggested

something more creative with had almost gone flaccid at the thought. Maybe it was because they were too young and inexperienced. It wasn't my fault I'd been reading romance novels since I was a teenager and had plenty of interesting sexual knowledge to draw from. The guys I'd dated definitely hadn't read romance novels, and weren't up for the challenge. My mind went straight to Jax, and what he would be up for. I mean, hell—he was apparently better than a werewolf. The train of thought immediately made me hot—everywhere.

I took a few deep breaths, trying to keep calm until Brynn left at least. I had a vibrator upstairs fully-powered and ready to give me some relief, but I'd rather wait until she was gone to retreat to my room.

"I'm excellent at persuasion," she said, grabbing her keys. "And in the heat of the moment, it's not difficult to get a guy to do pretty much anything." Huh. That hadn't been my experience. "I'll let you know if I have another entry for my research file when I get home."

I rolled my eyes as she walked out the door. I took a drink of my ice water—which did nothing to help alleviate the ache between my thighs, or the seam in my jeans that was pressing into *just* the right spot.

Jax.

Naked.

My body heated as I thought about what sex with Jax would be like. Him, naked and on top of me, his strong arms flexing as he held himself above me. Naked and behind me was even better. Or maybe me on top of him, riding him fast and hard. My face flushed and my breath became ragged. Relieved I was finally alone, I took a deep breath and started straight for my bedroom when the doorbell rang.

I muttered a string of curses under my breath and briefly considered pretending I wasn't home. Then the doorbell rang again. I wanted to be upstairs behind the privacy of my bedroom door. Not worrying about people on my porch. But I didn't think I'd be able to concentrate if I thought someone was still outside, casing the joint. This time, a solid, thudding knock hit and I jumped. I scowled, marching to the door. So help me, if this was a salesperson or someone asking me to find Jesus, I would take off my sock and throw it at them. I had priorities, and they had nothing to do with chatting about my preferred religion, or cable company.

I swung open the door, totally annoyed at the interruption, and came face-to-face with a wide, sculpted chest. My eyes quickly traveled up to his perfect face and panty-dropper eyes. Jax was holding a box of pizza, six pack of beer, and wearing his standard jeans and a tight black tee shirt.

I wanted to rip them all off.

Right there.

I probably wouldn't even take the time to close the door.

My current agitated state didn't help matters. I'd been on my way upstairs to take care of the images of Jax in my head. Now I had the real-life man standing in front of me looking like he seriously needed to be relieved of clothes and thoroughly kissed. I reminded myself to stop being so horny and focus on the goal. Jax's lips tipped up, his expression a little sly, like he was holding a secret behind it that only he knew. My brows came together and I smiled, a combination of confusion and amusement. "Umm…hi."

"Hey, Syd." His perfect mouth curved up and I couldn't stop thinking about what I wanted it to be doing—to me.

I shook myself out of his lip spell. "What are you doing here?"

He glanced down at the cargo in his arms and arched a brow before meeting my eyes again. "What do you think?"

"Well, it looks like you're about to have dinner."

"I am. With you."

His sudden appearance had jolted me enough that some of my blood had started flowing to my brain again so I could focus. I folded my arms across my chest. "I don't remember you asking me to dinner."

"I just did."

Oooookay. That was assertive. "How did you find my house?"

He smirked and leaned against the door frame.

"Your address is on the invoices I print out for you at Red's. I noticed."

I wasn't sure whether to be freaked out or impressed. "That's kind of…stalker-y."

He leaned into me. "Sweetheart, if I wanted to stalk you, I wouldn't show up with pizza and a movie."

I didn't want to think of what he'd do if he was really stalking me. Well, I did want to, but I wasn't upstairs alone in my room, and I didn't know if I could refrain from attacking him like a puma, so I thought it best not to think about that at all. I opened the door wider, cocking my hip to the side. "Well, since you brought pizza and I haven't had dinner, I guess you can come in."

He raised one brow. "That's the kind of invitation I like to hear."

I rolled my eyes.

He put the food on the coffee table and I went to the kitchen for plates, glasses, and napkins. When I came back, he was putting a movie in the DVD player. He already had a slice of pizza in his hand and was half way through it. The pizza looked like it had every possible topping the restaurant offered. I knew I'd drop pieces of it all over the place and make a mess, so I grabbed a knife and fork from the kitchen.

I sat down on the couch, took a piece of pizza from the box and put it on my plate. I also grabbed a napkin for my lap. Jax sat down beside me. My heart skipped a beat as our knees touched, and my mouth

went dry. He grabbed the remote off the coffee table and turned the TV and DVD player on, queuing up the movie.

"What are we watching?"

He glanced over at me, his eyes sparkling with mischief. "Something with werewolves."

I tried to push down my rising blush, but didn't succeed. He gave me a cocky grin. I looked down at my food like cutting my pizza was the most important task in the world. I was still blushing, but it would have been worse if I was staring right at him.

"Uh, Syd?

"What?" I asked, my focus held on my plate.

"Are you seriously eating pizza with utensils?"

I pushed my brows together, not understanding why that seemed weird, but glad I had something to take my mind off of werewolf Jax, and my embarrassment. "Yeah, I'll make a mess if I don't." I turned my head, and pointed at him with my knife. "Unlike you, I'm not a caveman." He shook his head, still chuckling. "Were you always like this? Or did something happen in your childhood to make you this uptight?"

I wrinkled my nose. I'd never really thought about it like that before. I didn't like the description. "I'm not uptight. I'm just organized, clean, and well-mannered."

He grinned. "If that's what you want to call it, sweetheart."

I thought more about his questions as we both ate. And the more I thought about it, the more irritated I got. He was making it sound like I had a stick up my ass. I felt the need to defend myself. "I've always been a perfectionist. I want to be my best, and I don't like creating additional work for myself. If I do it right the first time, I don't have to worry about that." I paused to chew. Then swallowed and took a drink of my beer, Blue Moon, my favorite. I wondered how he knew that. I watched an olive drop onto his plate; he picked it up, and popped it in his mouth with his fingers. "Just like that," I said, pointing. "If I didn't have utensils, I'd be picking up lost pizza pieces over and over again. Why make the extra work for myself when I can be efficient—and much more civilized—with a knife and fork?"

He shook his head. "I suppose you think some epic disaster will happen if you lose a pepper?"

"No. It just doesn't look very nice when a grown woman eats like a toddler."

"I don't have a problem with it. In fact," he said, smiling slowly and licking his lips, "I'd like to see you use your hands."

The look-and-lick did nothing to help my girl parts. They were overjoyed someone as swoon-worthy as Jackson West was paying any attention to me. My ovaries hadn't gotten the message that the hot man currently rubbing his leg against mine in an effort to make my blood pressure explode would absolutely not be getting naked with me tonight.

I gave a small smile, shaking my head at the

innuendo—and how freaking sexy he was. "You're a guy. You have a different set of rules that allow you to occasionally act like a Neanderthal. You should thank your dad and his Y chromosome."

Jax grabbed another slice of pizza and leaned back, kicking a leg up on the coffee table. His plate rested on his stomach like his abs were a slab of granite. Hard and thick. He looked over at me as he ate, watching me for far longer than I was comfortable with, almost like he was studying me. "Tell me more about the pretty, perfect Sydney Parker."

I wiped at my mouth with my napkin and took a drink, but inside, I was doing tiny jumping jacks of joy that Jax had called me pretty. I'd already committed the statement to memory, and deconstructed it five times. "What do you want to know?"

"Where did you grow up?"

I shrugged. "All over the place. We moved around a lot. My dad was military."

"So I should be worried about guns when I meet him?"

I arched a brow. "You're pretty confident if you think you'll be meeting my parents someday."

His mouth slid into a shit-eating grin.

He was so…aggravating and attractive at the same time. It annoyed me on a visceral level. "Yeah. Guns, grenades, and probably even ninja knives."

He whistled, his eyebrows coming together in mock concern. "Good to know."

"I told you earlier that I'm an only child," I said, taking another drink of my beer. "My parents are protective…especially when it comes to men."

"Thanks for the warning." He grabbed another slice of pizza. I was damn jealous of his ability to eat so much junk food and still look like his body was carved by the gods. "How many men—or boys—would you say they've protected you from?"

A smile tugged at my lips. "Is that your way of asking for my dating history?"

He shrugged. "I'm just trying to learn more about you."

I watched him closely. It felt like he was trying to gauge his level of competition, but I didn't think Jax was the type of guy who wanted a relationship, so I couldn't understand why he'd care. "I've had boyfriends, but no one serious. School has always been my focus."

He thought about that for a minute as he ate, then said, "Interesting. So, you were an only child who moved around a lot. I bet that was hard. Must have been tough to make friends—and have relationships."

He was right about that. Every time I really started to connect with someone, it seemed like my dad would get transferred. "I don't think I had any true friends until I came to college. Then I met Brynn, and we've been attached at the hip ever since."

"You seem pretty different from each other."

I tilted my head as I thought about it, trying to see

our friendship from another perspective. Jax had only watched Brynn and I together once—at the Soup and Spoon. From the outside, I could see his point. We had different goals, and different personalities. But when it came down to core beliefs, we were actually really similar. "In some ways, but not in others. We share the same opinions about a lot of things."

"She dates—if you can call it that—way more than you, though, right?"

I couldn't argue. "She has an active social life. I think we just define college success differently. She measures it by friends, guys, and parties. I measure it by my GPA." I took another bite of pizza. The rich, red sauce was my favorite. "What about you?" I asked. "Have you met a lot of people since you moved to Winchester?"

He shrugged and took a long drink of his beer. "I've met a lot of people, but no. I don't have a lot of friends." He took another drink, and I thought that might be the end of the conversation, but he surprised me. "I'm not really close to many people. I don't like to burden others with my problems. It's easier for me to deal with things on my own."

I slid a glance to him, wondering what in his life had caused him to decide solitude was the best way to deal with his issues. "That's a pretty lonely way to live."

"Maybe," he paused, his gaze dipping to me, "but you've been…a surprise."

I blinked, shocked. I wasn't expecting that confession, and I wasn't really sure how to take it, either. "Thanks…I think."

He smiled faintly, and changed the subject. "So, tell me more. What other finger foods do you eat with utensils?"

I laughed, setting my plate on the coffee table. "Chocolate."

His eyes went wide and he stared at me, dumbfounded. "Chocolate?"

I nodded.

"Why?"

"It melts on my fingers if I hold it."

He grinned and shook his head, watching me for a long time. He sat up and leaned forward, his left elbow resting on his knee as he held my gaze. "Someone needs to make you come completely undone, Sydney Parker." His tongue moved slowly over his lips. "That someone is going to be me."

I inhaled a rattled breath, ensorcelled by his eyes and his words. "We'll see about that," I said, hoping my voice didn't sound as shaky as it felt. He affected me in a way no one had before, and I didn't want him to know how much. I was barely capable of admitting it to myself.

"No. We won't," he said, his tone authoritative. "I've already decided it."

He hit play on the DVD remote, and leaned back, his arm now brushing against mine in addition to his leg. I spent the next two hours watching a movie about a werewolf, completely turned on, next to the man who had taken my breath away.

Six

J ax's 'undone' comment stuck with me for days.
Yes, days—despite my efforts to remedy that.
Through five days, one test, two quizzes, my
volunteer hours at CARE, at least ten movies, and an
attempt to read a book that I'd abandoned once a
werewolf showed up. I couldn't stop thinking about it,
or him, or about what I might want from him. And that
scared me. Because the thought of a potential
relationship—with anyone—made my stomach knot,
and seriously screwed with my five-year plan. But
wanting a relationship with someone like Jackson West
was terrifying, and would impact my whole life plan
like a natural disaster.

However, the fact was that She-Ra needed gas. It

was far below my half tank comfort zone; it was even below a quarter tank. I couldn't let it go much more or I'd be stuck on the side of the road calling Red to bring me gas, and Jax would probably be the one to rescue me. I could go somewhere besides Red's shop to get it, but he always gave me a deal, and I liked supporting him instead of one of the big chains. But at Red's, I might run into Jax. My current state of indecision about what exactly I wanted would be made worse if I stopped for gas and Jax's abs were there.

After he'd started the movie last week, Jax had sat next to me, our bodies pulling toward each other like magnets. He occasionally moved, his hand brushing against mine, his leg pressing into my own, creating an energetic friction that seemed to flow straight to my core. The movie was two hours long. I spent the entire time thinking about Jax, and what I really wanted to be doing to him instead of watching a movie. I was pretty sure he knew it, too. I caught him smirking a few times. When he'd finally gotten up to leave, the air in the house had been charged with so much sexual tension that I considered dragging him up to my bedroom, or back to the couch. Hell, even the living room floor would do. I just wanted him. More than anything. I'd managed to contain myself, however, and let him leave. And then I wore out the batteries on my vibrator.

The feeling had scared me, though. I'd never wanted sex, or a man, as much as I wanted Jax. When I thought of what I wanted more: hot sex with Jax, or

graduating in the top one percent of my law school, sex with Jax surpassed my goals. That had never happened. Not once in my life. No man had ever taken precedence over my school and career plans. I wasn't sure how to handle the information, but I knew it was something I needed to work through before I ran into him again or I might do something really out of character.

Seeing Jax at Red's wasn't really a problem so much as a threat of serious temptation. The number of my fantasies Jax had starred in since I'd known him—and especially during the *week of the werewolf*—could make him a card carrying member of the Screen Actors Guild.

I'd checked my watch, though—ten o'clock—and decided to chance the gas tank refill since it was still morning. I popped the pump into the tank and flipped the lever, switching it on. I kept discreetly scanning Red's shop windows, but hadn't seen Jax yet. So far, so good. I could live in denial for another day.

I finished filling up and took the pump out of the car, but there was gas left over in the pump. A few beads of gas caught on the edge of the tank and dribbled down the paint. "Shit." I whispered. I rushed to put the pump back on its holder, and grabbed a paper towel next to the window squeegee. I crouched down to wipe the gas off.

"You should use a cleaner for that." I glanced up and immediately forgot to breathe. Jax towered above me. Backlit by the morning sun and dressed all in black, he was practically glowing—like a freaking dark angel, coincidentally a costume he'd also worn in my mind. He looked like he'd just come from the gym. His sleeveless black shirt hugged his chest, and his biceps were corded with muscle. A blue and black tattoo of the number seventeen mixed in with a tribal design framed his upper arm. His matching black workout pants sat low on his hips, and his dark chocolate hair was clumped together in wet pieces. He was only a few feet from me, but I was confident that I'd be able to smell his pheromones from at least twenty paces.

Images of his SAG card earning roles started flashing through my mind. Between that and lack of air, I almost passed out. I remembered to inflate my lungs at the last second. He grinned, totally aware of my reaction to him. I narrowed my eyes, annoyed. I was acting like a giddy teenager with a crush. This was stupid. I was an adult. I needed to act like it. Yeah, he was attractive. So what? I spent time with a lot of attractive people and managed to function. This should be no different.

But it was.

And that was the problem.

"Move the car out of the pump lane, and I'll grab something to clean it with," he said, moving toward the garage.

"Okay." I pulled She-Ra to one of the parking spots in front of Red's. Jax came back out holding a paper towel and bottle of cleaner. He poured some cleaner on one of the towels before handing the bottle

to me and rubbing the area the gas had dripped on. "This will take care of it, and you won't have to worry about your paint."

"Thanks," I said, watching him. A chilly gust of wind kicked up out of nowhere. I shivered, and wrapped my arms around myself, eager to get back inside the car.

Jax noticed. "Are you cold?" He stood, tossing the paper towels in the trash. Reaching over, he put his palms on the sides of my arms and pushed gently, methodically, as he rubbed his hands up and down from my shoulders to my elbows. I shivered again— for a completely different reason—feeling like sparks were arcing at his touch. He was so warm, probably from his workout, and the contact was heating me up in more ways than one. The caress sent a thrill of excitement straight through me. I inhaled a rattled breath, trying to pass it off as another shiver. One corner of Jax's lips lifted in a knowing expression. I didn't think my fake shiver had worked.

"I'm fine. September just gets chilly sometimes in the mountains." I loved this time of year, but wasn't thrilled about the looming threat of winter.

"This is my favorite season," Jax said. "I love watching things change, and the temperature is perfect…most times."

"Mine, too," I agreed. "I love driving through the mountains to see the fall colors on the trees. And I love when it's still sixty or seventy degrees outside."

He bent down and wiped the car one more time

with a dry paper towel. When he finished, he straightened back up, turning to me. "Plus," he said, slowly licking his lips, "sex in a pile of leaves is always fun."

I tried not to register my surprise, but it was definitely present. I added 'sex in leaves' to the fantasy list in my head, as well as a reminder to inhale—and another to exhale. He didn't need to know all of that, though. I attempted a blank face as I responded, "That seems unsanitary."

He eyed me. "Do you ever have fun, or is everything by the rules for you?"

"There's nothing wrong with rules," I said, defensive. "They keep things organized and in line."

He leaned toward me, curling his finger for me to move closer. I held my ground—mostly because I couldn't decide if I wanted to acquiesce to his demand, or if I wanted to run from it. Running was a much safer choice. "I could keep you in line," he said, moving his lips to my ear. "I definitely think you could use a spanking."

I hadn't been threatened with a spanking since I was a toddler. The proposition shocked me so much, I didn't realize I was still holding the bottle of cleaner and squeezed it. Hard. Liquid exploded out the top like the cleaner bottle was going through an embarrassing bit of puberty. It hit Jax directly on the lower stomach, and immediately started dripping down onto his pants. "Oh my gosh! I'm so sorry!" I was mortified as I

grabbed more paper towels and started trying to mop up the mess, though I was careful to avoid his crotch area…an area that seemed to be growing larger despite the cold cleaner and crisp air.

Jax laughed and grabbed my hand, stilling it. He held my eyes. "Come on."

"Where are we going?"

"To my apartment. I need to change."

I wasn't sure why I needed to go along. I was pretty sure he was well versed in all skills related to clothing removal—his, and women's. But I was the reason for the clothes situation, and felt like I should probably tag along since I'd caused the mess and he'd asked me to.

We walked across the street and down the block. I'd wondered why I'd never seen his car. Now it made sense. I usually only saw him when he was at Red's, and he didn't need to drive when he lived this close to work. His apartment was part of a new duplex. The outside was a combination of grey brick and stucco. There were only three steps to get to his front door. I waited behind him while he opened it and motioned me inside. His apartment was modern and clean. Two toned walls in neutral beige and brown, with matching light brown carpet. Grey and blue slate tile in the kitchen complimented the stainless steel appliances. A flat screen TV hung above the fireplace. The couch was black leather. I thought of how much easier leather was to clean, then immediately thought of the naked girls who had probably been on it and frowned. I made a mental note not to sit on any of his furniture.

"Come on back." He motioned for me to follow him.

I watched him walk down the hall. I took several beats to decide whether or not to follow him, but my curiosity finally got the best of me. I stopped before I came to the room he'd walked in. The door was wide open and he was standing next to his huge black sleigh bed with matching nightstands and dresser, stripping off his workout shirt as he toed off his shoes onto the carpeted floor. My eyes were huge, and I quickly looked away. Not that I wanted to, but because it seemed like the right thing to do...and I wasn't sure if I could keep the desire off my face if I maintained him in my line of sight.

He started to laugh. "I didn't realize you were shy."

Now I'd been challenged. I wasn't good at backing down. It was a problem. My eyes shot up past his ripped stomach, and held his gaze. His lips formed a half smile in acceptance of my challenge, and then he moved his hands down to his waist. He held my eyes as he untied the string on his pants, then slowly slid his index fingers under the waistband and pushed. As I heard the fabric drop to the floor, I did my best not to gulp—or look down. But I was tempted. Very, *very* tempted.

"Are you afraid to look, Syd?"

I pressed my lips into a thin line. I wasn't shy, and I wasn't a chicken. Plus, I felt like he'd just issued me another dare. Dares are my weakness. Tell me I can't do something, and I'll do it every time just to spite the person who said I couldn't.

I crossed my arms over my chest, and held his gaze for a split second longer just to let him know that I wasn't going to give in. Then I let my eyes trail slowly down his body. I got stuck on his abs for a few seconds, but eventually hit his waist. I breathed a sigh of relief when I realized he wasn't birthday-suit ready. He was wearing black athletic shorts that hung to his knees. A band of grey—boxers or briefs?—peeked out under his shorts. I wasn't sure whether to be relieved at his lack of nudity, or disappointed…I was a little of both.

Still, he was half-naked—shorts and socks were all that remained. And he was sooooo freaking hot! He had the body of someone who spent all their free time running Spartan Races. Every part of him was toned, sculpted, and huge—Every. Single. Part. I had to mentally slap myself to force my eyes away from the lower half of his body. On a scale of one to five, I was at drool-threat level six. The important thing was to not let him know that, though. Better-than-a-werewolf had a big enough ego as it was. "Boxers, huh?" I said, taking a guess at his underwear preference.

He raised a brow. "How do you know I'm wearing anything at all?"

I raised mine back. "You go commando often?"

He slid his index fingers between the cloth of his shorts and his tight, toned skin. He started to tug down. "Wanna find out?"

The devil on my left shoulder was screaming: Yes, please! Luckily, the angel on my right shoulder was exceedingly boring with far more sense. The angel reasoned that if seeing Jax fully clothed made me want to hump him like a bunny and to hell with graduating at the top of my class, then seeing Jax naked would be trouble. Lots and *lots* of trouble. I agreed. "I'm good, thanks." I pointed to his waist. "Plus, you're not hiding it very well."

He looked down, noticing how much of his underclothes he was already showing me, and flashed an unapologetic grin. He watched me for several moments before leaning against his bed. "How many men have you been with, Syd?"

I felt like I'd just been hit with verbal whiplash—again. It seemed to happen frequently with Jax. "Excuse me?" I said, completely affronted.

He reached down to pick up his socks on the floor and throw them into the square laundry basket next to the wall. I was so pissed, I didn't even really notice how the muscles in his arms, shoulders, back and abs moved with tightly honed, perfect fluidity. Really. I didn't. "Come on," he said, straightening back up. "I'll tell you my number; you tell me yours."

"Absolutely not."

"Why? Embarrassed?"

"No! But the only way that would be your business is if we were in relationship. We're not. So screw you."

"We could be."

I blinked in shock. "No." A relationship? We hadn't even been on a date, what was he talking about? Though the thought sent a flutter through my stomach that met the flutter already percolating a bit lower thanks to Jax's lack of clothes. "We couldn't do that," I said, flushed and off-kilter. I was not prepared for this decision yet.

"Why?"

"Because I'm not ready for a relationship right now. And from what I can tell, neither are you."

He eyed me. "I guess it depends on what your definition of 'relationship' is."

"Mutual love, respect, and quality time. Passion, friendship, intimacy, common interests. Caring about each other, being there for one another. I thought those were all pretty common relationship themes."

"Every relationship is different. Some people just want to have fun."

"I'm guessing that's you."

"If you go into it with expectations already set, no one gets hurt."

I snorted. "Right. I'm sure you have a lot of experience with this. Maybe you can shut your emotions off and screw anything that moves, but I can't."

His eyes hardened ever so slightly. "I didn't say that was *my* definition. I said it was *a* definition. You wouldn't even answer my question about how many men you've been with. You're uncomfortable with the thought of opening up and relying on someone else. It seems like you're the one who can't handle a relationship—by *any* definition."

My brows came together in an angry line. "I really don't think you know me well enough to make that call."

He shrugged. "I know your type."

I was about to tell him off again, but he dropped his shorts and my witty comeback was lost. My mouth fell open and I stared.

He smirked. "Never seen a mostly naked man before, huh? Guess that doesn't say much for your previous boyfriends."

The jab brought me back to my senses enough to stop staring at the huge bulge confronting me. He wasn't completely naked, but he was close. The only thing delineating him from being a living version of the Statue of David was his gray boxer briefs. I refused to acknowledge that thought further. "Don't be dumb. Of course I have."

"On TV?" he asked, his tone infuriating.

"Screw you."

He walked toward me, pushing into my personal space, getting closer and closer. "Be careful, sweetheart. One of these times, I might take you up on that offer."

My mouth fell open. It was at that very moment my phone rang…which was strange. Not many people actually used the phone to talk any more. I was used to texts instead. I took a step away from Jax's danger zone, and turned my back toward the very tangible temptation that stood a few strides from me. I looked at the phone. Brynn's name was on the display. "Hey, is something wrong?"

"No, I just need you to come to a bar with me tonight."

"That's the emergency that warranted a phone call? A demand to meet you at a bar? I thought something was wrong with you! You could have just texted me!" *I was in the middle of something!,* I wanted to scream. *Something super important!* The image of Jax in nothing but a tiny piece of cotton covering a massive piece of man was making me breathless.

"No! I need to give your name to the guys so they can get us into the VIP section. I had to make sure you were coming with me first."

I sighed. "Where?"

"Edge. It's the new, all glass building on Third."

"Well, I seriously doubt anything Edgy is going to be happening if the building is all glass."

I could feel her rolling her eyes. "You need a better imagination."

I rubbed the bridge of my nose with my thumb and forefinger. "What time?"

"Nine. And don't be late! I'll meet you there."

"Yeah, yeah. See you then."

I turned back around and caught my breath. Jax was in the exact same position as when I'd moved, and he was still watching me. Judging by his intent stare, I got the impression he'd been watching me through the whole conversation. I couldn't tell if he was interested in the discussion, or annoyed. "You have a date?"

I snorted. "Or something."

He waited, and the awkward moment got even more awkward, prompting me to keep talking and give way more information than I should have. "I just get dragged to parties, bars, and anywhere else Brynn wants to go because she loves being social."

He watched me. "You don't love it, though. So why do you go?" He always seemed so interested in my answers that it sometimes made me feel like everything I said was being dissected. Now was no different.

"Because I don't want her to go alone. She needs someone to watch her back."

He folded his arms across his chest, drawing my eye to his massive pecs, which was good so I had something else massive to focus on that wasn't in the same vicinity of his crotch. "And who watches yours?"

I lifted one shoulder. "Mine doesn't need watching." I pulled my keys from my pocket. "Looks like you've got everything under control here." I gestured to him and his lack of attire. "Thanks for the show. I'll see you next time I need an oil change."

I immediately winced at my choice of words.

He grinned and held my eyes like he was trying to decide his next move. I knew mine, though, and it was out the door, far away from this volatile situation that wasn't at all helped by my hormones. "Sorry for squirting you." I winced again, then recovered with, "thanks for showing me your place." I waved as I speed-walked out of the room and back down the hall.

I got to the front door before I heard, "Syd."

I turned.

He was leaning out of his bedroom, hands braced on the top of the doorway, abs just as tempting as they'd been a few minutes before. "Be careful tonight."

I nodded. "Thanks. You, too..." I shut the door behind me, then practically hyperventilated on his porch before I made it back down the street to Red's parking lot, and She-Ra.

Seven

I hated bars. And clubs. With a passion. The music is loud enough to recalibrate your heartbeat, and you can hardly hear yourself think, let alone try to carry on a conversation with another person. Everyone judges you completely on appearance, and they're all there for a meaningless hookup. I wasn't interested. But Brynn was. And she was well on her way.

"Karl thinks you're hot," she said. Her mouth was pressed directly against my ear. It was the only way to hear her. The VIP section was slightly quieter than the regular dance floor, but really, the only luxury it afforded was a guaranteed place to sit, and faster drink service; also, the experience of being behind a rope that proved you were more important than ninety-eight

percent of the people there. It seemed silly and stupid to me.

I turned and put my lips practically in her ear. "Karl's been feeling up every girl who walks by. And the girls don't seem happy about it. Karl's a douche. Why are we here again?"

Brynn looked over at the tall, tan guy with the face of a movie-star sitting across from her. His lips formed a slow, cocky smile as he ran a hand through his shaggy, shiny locks. Brynn's eyes immediately went starry. "Because Derrick is freaking hot!"

He was attractive, I'd give him that, but his eyes were also glued to anything with boobs, and he didn't seem to care who he ended up with tonight, as long as it was a woman, and he got to screw her—in more ways than one.

Brynn had met Derrick and Karl through mutual friends at dinner the night before. They'd invited her— and any of her hot friends—to go out with them tonight. They'd looked at me like I was a nun when we walked up. I guess I did look pretty out of place; my pleather skirt went all the way down to mid-thigh and wasn't showing off my vulva, and my lacy indigo shirt had fabric covering my chest *and* my back. Judging by their reaction when we walked up, I didn't pass the "hot friend" requirement, but it seemed they were putting up with me to keep Brynn around. Which was fine. I wasn't interested in either one of them.

Derrick caught Brynn's eye and grinned, motioning for her to come over to him. Her smile widened like she'd just won the lottery. And in this world, I guess she kind of had. She grabbed my hand, dragging me with her. "Hey," she said coyly, twirling one of her dark curls.

"Hey, yourself, beautiful." He patted the bench seat next to him, "Why don't you come sit with me?"

She looked at the seat, then at me. "There's not enough room for my friend."

He glanced in my direction, giving me a quick once-over, and finding me lacking. "Sure there is, babe," he grabbed her wrist and pulled her down onto his lap. He scooted over, making room for me to sit between him, Brynn, and Karl. Great.

Derrick lifted his hand at the server, signaling to bring us more drinks. I hoped the server knew I was drinking water. Brynn loved getting drunk. I didn't. So, we made a good designated driver team.

Brynn and Derrick flirted while Karl and I ignored each other. That lasted about five minutes before I felt a large, rough hand on my knee. Pretty sure it wasn't mine, I looked down, and followed the hand up the arm of the jerk who had the nerve to grope me. Karl's lips tipped up in an arrogant smile. He leaned into my ear. "You should sit on my lap. I have a present for you."

I gave him a too-sweet smile as I pushed his hand off my leg. "Keep dreaming, asshole," I yelled over the pounding bass.

His smile shifted slightly, no longer as smug, and definitely more annoyed. "You're a bitch."

"And you're a douchebag who probably has a tiny dick. We all have our problems to overcome." I turned away and looked at Brynn. Her eyes softened like she was asking if I was okay. I waved my hand in front of me like it was no big deal. She believed me, and went back to kissing Derrick again until our drinks came. Brynn got something so bright orange it looked neon. I shook my head, thinking that couldn't be healthy. I took a sip of my water and frowned. It was carbonated, and had a hint of lemon. I liked lemon in my water, but I wasn't a fan of water with fizz. It just tasted…wrong. Like soda without the sugar. I decided to ask for a non-fizzy water as soon as the server came back, but for now, this would have to do. It was hot as hades in the club and I needed to stay hydrated.

After what felt like a few minutes, I looked down at my drink and it was half gone. I shook my head, confused. How had that happened? I didn't even like the bubbles. Bubbles? What was wrong with me? My head felt fuzzy and I was having a hard time thinking. Then I felt myself being pulled on top of someone's lap. I looked up into a fuzzy face I barely recognized. "Karl?" I asked.

"Come on, baby," he said, his hand going around my waist and resting on the curve of my ass.

I shook my head repeatedly and my skull felt like it was being hit with Thor's hammer. "No," I said, trying to push him away and stand. I was unsuccessful at both attempts. "No, I want to stay with Brynn." I looked for her, and she was now across from me in a tiny bean bag with Derrick. I frowned. She shouldn't be there. We needed to stick together. We always stayed together. I stood again and stumbled, trying to make it to the bean bag next to her. Derrick was leaning into her, kissing her like he was trying to put out a fire with his saliva, while his hand moved under her wispy, see-through shirt.

Suddenly, an arm was around my waist again, pulling me in the other direction—away from Brynn. "Your friend's going to hang out with my buddy for a while, so you and I can spend some time together. I'm going to show you how big my dick really is." His voice sounded harsh.

My brow furrowed. I didn't want to see his dick. I wasn't at all interested in it. I needed to tell him that, and tell him to go to hell, too. But I couldn't form the words. Something wasn't right. My head felt cloudy, and the pounding against my skull was increasing. Brynn was drunk off her ass, and I was…something. And whatever it was, the effects were becoming worse with every passing moment. I'd had my drink close to me and hadn't noticed anything slipped into it, but I'd also been babysitting Brynn, so maybe someone drugged me when I wasn't looking.

Karl held my upper arm and started dragging me down a hall, away from the dance floor—and all of the people.

That's when I heard the noise. Like a furious

animal roaring. And before I knew it, I was being pushed out of the way, and Karl was being pushed into—and almost through—a wall. I stood across the hallway, bracing myself against a table so I wouldn't fall. My legs felt like jelly as I watched Karl get pounded. Some guy was using him as a punching bag. I wanted to cheer! He was getting the shit beat out of him! He deserved it. I wished I could do it myself, but I could barely stand.

Without warning, the whole world started to tilt. It felt like it happened in slow motion, and I wondered why the earth had abruptly fallen off its axis. I felt myself start to fall and suddenly, I was weightless. Like a feather floating in the breeze. I laughed and waved my arms. I was flying! Cold wind hit my cheeks and I looked up into the sky, but a face passed over my point of view. It was a gorgeous face with a strong jaw, sexy, messy dark chocolate curls, and bright Caribbean colored irises. I smiled widely. "Blue Eyes!" I said, wrapping my arms around his neck. I realized he was holding me. Tightly. "You're here!"

His lips were pulled into a thin line, his features a study in barely contained violence as he looked around. They changed when his gaze came to rest on me, though. "You're going to be okay, Syd. Let's get you home."

"But...Brynn! I need Brynn!" I flopped my head to the side of his arm, trying to look around. "Brynn!" I yelled. "Brynn! Come with me!"

"Sshhhh. I'll get her, Syd. Let me get you out of here first."

When we got to his truck—he had a truck!—he gently put me inside, shielding my head, and belted me into the front seat. He left, telling me not to move. I didn't. I fell asleep instead. I woke up when he got back, cradling Brynn in his arms. She looked as sick as I did, but her clothes all seemed intact.

I'd been saved by Blue Eyes. Brynn too. Full-on, knight-in-shining-armor, this-only-happens-in movies, saving. I tilted my head and tried to focus on his gorgeous face. "You saved us," I murmured.

There was a long pause, or maybe I'd already fallen asleep and dreamed his next words, "This time," he whispered "And I won't let this happen to you again."

I tried to sit up, but my head was pounding so hard I thought drums were playing in my brain. I immediately lay back down, tightly closing my sensitive eyelids against the bright morning light, and covering my ears while I rubbed my head with my fingertips and groaned.

I felt hands brush over my hair, replacing my own. Pads of fingers pressed into pressure points on my head and I moaned as I slitted my eyes open, trying to figure out who the angel head healer was.

Even through my sliver of vision, I could see his sculpted features and messy brown hair. He was

wearing a tight fitted white shirt, his muscles bulging beneath it. He pressed gently, but firmly along the front of my skull, rhythmically making his way around to the back, pushing deeply into the base of my neck. His touch was perfection, and absolutely what I needed after such a horrible night. As he moved around to my jawline, pressing under it, he cupped my cheek. I opened my eyes a little wider. "Jax," I breathed.

"Hey, sweetheart," his voice was as tender as his touch. "Glad you're awake."

I moved to get up, but he shook his head, and kept massaging. I was in heaven. "What happened last night?" I asked. I had bits of memory including some dickhead named Karl, but I was having a hard time piecing it all together.

"From what I could tell?" he said, still focused on his task, "Your drink was spiked with something. I'm guessing a date rape drug."

My mouth dropped. "Seriously?" The whole reason I went to stupid parties and events with Brynn was to make sure shit like that didn't happen. Ever. We were always careful to stay together. "I don't know how it happened. I had my drink with me all night."

A muscle worked at his jaw. "It happened because you were hanging out with assholes."

I couldn't argue with that. They were definitely douchebags of the highest order. "I was careful, though. I don't know when they could have put something in my drink."

"You can't watch your drink every second, Syd. I'm sure he slipped it in when you were busy monitoring Brynn to make sure she wasn't getting in trouble."

I shifted my eyes to the door, and her room down the hall. "Is she okay?"

He pressed his fingers against my temples and I sighed. "She's hung over, but that's it. I don't think they drugged her. The probably didn't think there was a need since she was hanging all over the guy, and she was drunk."

I wasn't functioning on even half of my brain-power yet, but that piece of information hit, and stuck. "You saw her? Us?"

He didn't say anything for a minute. He licked his lips before replying, "I did."

A question—and realization started to form in my head. "Why were you at Edge?" I remembered him standing in his bedroom in his boxers, listening to me talk to Brynn about our plans. I hadn't even said the name of the club, but he must have pieced it all together.

"Because you were."

I widened my eyes and immediately regretted it. Jax saw me wince and reached over to the window above my bed, pulling the purple curtains shut. "Thanks," I mumbled. "Why would you go to the club just because I was going?"

He took a deep breath, and scrubbed his hand over his chin. "Call me crazy, but I don't like when

people go into situations they could get hurt in. You said you're Brynn's backup. I'm yours."

My stomach did a flip-flop. "I didn't ask you to be," I whispered.

"You didn't have to."

For some reason, Jax's protectiveness felt a lot like a man reacting to someone he cared about being in danger. Jax might have feelings for me, but I wasn't sure how far those emotions extended. I didn't think he was looking for a relationship, though. As much as I wanted him to care about me, and take care of me, I didn't know if I could handle it. If I let him in, I was afraid I'd get too invested, and be destroyed when he left. "What if that's not what I'm looking for?"

He stared down at me. "Too bad."

A warm feeling coursed through me, followed by a giddy rush of excitement at his protective behavior. I wasn't even annoyed that he'd eavesdropped on my conversation with Brynn and then followed me to the club like a stalker. I couldn't deny the fact that I was grateful for his presence. If it wasn't for him, I would have ended up in a horrible situation. I couldn't thank him for that enough. I put my hand on his arm, his bicep moving under my touch. His gorgeous gaze met mine. "Thank you for being there. I would have been..." I paused, tears pricking my eyes, "I don't know what would have happened without you."

He pursed his lips, the muscle ticking at his jaw again. I felt like there was more he wanted to say, but instead, he cupped my cheek with his palm, his thumb rubbing lightly, back and forth, on my skin. "It should be almost out of your system by now."

He turned away, and handed me a cold bottle of water. "Only take a little, and let me know if you feel sick."

I took the water, gingerly lifting it to my lips. No beverage had ever tasted as wonderful as that sip; I felt like I hadn't had anything to drink in days. I wanted to gulp it down, but knew that wouldn't end well, and vomiting all over Jax probably wouldn't impress him much.

When I'd managed to keep down half of my water, Jax handed me some fruit and yogurt mixed with granola. "Little bites," he said.

I chewed my food slowly, trying to make digestion as easy as possible. I dropped a piece of granola on my shirt, noticing my clothes for the first time. Blue pajama shorts and a matching tank top covered me. Well, thank Thor I wasn't naked. I amended the thought when I realized that I probably wasn't the person who got me in my jammies.

"Did you stay here all night?"

He nodded. "I watched you and Brynn to make sure you'd be okay."

I hadn't noticed the dark circles around his eyes, or his heavy lids until now. I couldn't believe he'd saved us both from our own stupidity, and then stayed up all night to keep checking on us and make sure we

were okay. My heart constricted and I swallowed the lump in my throat. He was a good guy. A really good guy.

I heard Brynn moving around in the other room. "I should go check on her," I said, shifting to get out of bed.

"She's fine. She's already eaten."

I gaped at him. "Seriously? Sheesh. She bounces back like she's a professional drunk."

His lips lifted in a small smile. "I gave her some food, so I'm sure that helped."

"She had enough alcohol to take down a large mammal. She should still be barfing in the bathroom, or at least in bed. Yogurt or no yogurt."

"She got french fries."

My mouth fell open. I was totally offended. He clearly liked—no, *loved*—her way more than me. "She got fries? And I got fruit? You hate me. Admit it."

His smile widened a bit more. "Her problems were caused by too much liquor. The greasy french fries helped sop up the alcohol left in her system. You had other problems, and I doubt grease would have made you feel better at all."

I scrunched up my nose, knowing he was right. I was shocked he'd put so much thought into it, actually. And when had he had time to go out and get us breakfast? I was impressed at his nursing abilities. "You saved us from total jerks, watched over us all night to make sure we were okay, and brought us breakfast? I kind of hate to admit this, but you're amazing."

He grinned. "So I've heard. And in more ways than one."

I smiled back. "Your ego is as healthy as ever." I paused. "Seriously, though. Thank you for being there last night, and for staying with us, and nursing us both. You didn't have to do that, and I really appreciate it. I know Brynn does, too."

He lifted a shoulder in half-shrug like everything he'd done was totally normal. "If you're feeling okay, I should go. I need to get to work."

I looked at the clock and was horrified to see that it was almost noon. "Holy crap! I didn't know it was so late."

"I let you sleep it off."

"Thanks," I said, lowering my lashes as I picked absently at a piece of thread on my quilt.

He stood, grabbing his jacket from the floor. His jeans hung off his hips, and great goddesses, he had a perfect ass. Like two grapefruits. I just wanted to bite it. Holy crap! Where had that come from? I couldn't bite Jax's ass! I couldn't bite Jax at all. That would be totally inappropriate. He was my mechanic, and after last night, I was pretty sure he was my friend. Friends don't bite the asses of friends, even if they have the potential to be more than that.

He slipped his arms through his jacket sleeves. "Let me know if you need anything."

I shook my head. "You've done more than enough, Jax. I'll never be able to repay you."

His eyes lit with mischief "I can think of some ways."

Heat rose in my cheeks. I could think of some, too. They involved biting.

His smile fell a little as he opened the door to my room. "Seriously, though, you don't have anything to repay me for. I did what any decent guy would have done. Choose one of them next time you and Brynn go out, will ya?"

I nodded, thinking that even though I had no business wanting him, the decent guy I'd like to choose was walking out the door.

Eight

Brynn and I had both recovered from our previous weekend adventures. The thought of what could have happened if Jax hadn't shown up was terrifying. At least once a day, I gave a silent thank you that he'd been there. I also spent far too much time analyzing why he'd shown up at the club. Part of me, a really big part, hoped it truly was because he had legitimate feelings for me. It seemed like a crazy thing to hope for since he could have any girl he wanted, but I couldn't help myself. No matter how hard I tried to fight it, I could feel myself falling for him, and I wanted him to want me, too.

Brynn had bounced back from the incident much faster than me…maybe because she'd just been her

usual drunk self instead of being drugged. She'd been horrified when I told her what had happened to me, and vowed to kick Karl and Derrick straight in the nuts as hard as she could if she ever saw them again. She'd sat on the bed next to me, crying as she told me she never wanted me to be in that position again. I told her I didn't want either of us to be in that position again, so something needed to change. She agreed she'd vet the men she spent time with better. I wasn't sure that would solve the problem, but at least it was a start. She seemed pretty shaken up by everything that had happened. For the past week, she hadn't been as social as usual, and had spent a lot of time with me watching *House Hunters* and sexy superhero movies. I wondered how long her priority change would last.

Brynn had a wild streak, brought on by her past. I understood why approval from men was so important to her. I wasn't sure what would eventually knock her out of her need for constant attention from the opposite sex, but I hoped it would happen soon. Nothing broke Brynn. She was who she was, and she didn't apologize for it. She took things in stride, and seemed to think she was above disaster. So far in life, she had been, but that wouldn't last forever. If she continued like this, at some point, there'd be a time when I wasn't there to save her, and the thought made me sick to my stomach. I'd keep doing what I could to make sure she was okay, though, and from now on, I'd bring my own water—bottled, with a lid.

I was sitting at our distressed wood dining table

with my homework. "Distressed" was a nice way of saying "used." We'd picked it up on the side of a street when we were college freshmen, where it was sitting with a big cardboard FREE sign on it. Brynn only agreed to the procurement after several sanitizing sessions. Free is free, though, and nothing is more appealing to college students, even obsessively clean ones. I told my mom we'd bought it at an antique store, or she probably wouldn't have let us keep it during her redecoration of our house.

I popped some Reese's Pieces in my mouth as I studied, and jumped at least a foot when I heard Brynn's voice. She came out of nowhere. Like a freaking ghost.

"Put your books away," Brynn said, sweeping into the living room and slamming my tort reform book shut. "We're going out."

"Where are we going?" I asked, flipping the book back open, trying to find my lost page.

Brynn stomped her foot and grabbed the book, holding it behind her. "Away from all things school-related for at least two hours. It's a Friday night! You've been doing homework for days—which, unfortunately, isn't unusual for you. I demand you get out of the house and enjoy yourself, even if I have to force you to do it." She pointed down the hall. "Get a sweater, coat and gloves. We're going to the haunted mine."

I'd grabbed the card advertising the haunted mine while I was at Red's, and shown it to Brynn a few weeks

earlier. Really, in the midst of school and daydreaming about better-in-bed-than-a-werewolf Jax, I'd forgotten the mine completely.

"We're going alone?" That seemed unwise. Scary situations were always better in a group. That way when you peed your pants, you had a lot of cover—or people who were as equally wet as you.

"Don't be silly," she said, throwing my gloves at me as I pulled an emerald toned sweater over my head. "The whole point of haunted houses is to have a big, strong arm to grab onto and keep you safe from the crazy people scaring you. You've got nice arms, but I seriously question your ability to fight off demons and clowns. So, I found us dates."

I stared at her, surprised she was ready for dating again already after last week's disaster. "Are you sure, Brynn? After what happened last week, I'm a little leery about going out with strangers."

She looked down, playing with the zipper on her coat. "I know. I am, too. But, there's nothing I hate more than fear. I won't let my life be controlled by it."

I considered her words, and knew she was right. If we let one situation dictate the rest of our lives, we'd be sitting home until we were ninety, experts on home decorating style trends, but not on life. "Okay," I relented. "Who are the guys?"

"Some boys I met last year. I know them pretty well, so we'll be safe."

That didn't make me excited. I'd been hanging out with a *man*. I wasn't even sure how old he actually was, but he definitely wasn't still going home on the weekends to have his mom wash his laundry. He was a manly man who got shit done. Boys weren't the least bit interesting to me anymore. "Can't we just go with some other girls or something? I'm not really up for a blind date."

Her lashes shot up to her brows in disbelief. "A group of girls? To a *haunted* mine? Are you out of your freaking mind? We need someone to hold onto who won't be running for the exit!"

I sighed. She was probably right. I still wasn't enthused. Part of me wanted to call Jax and invite him to come be my date. But that seemed a little forward when all we'd really done was flirt, and I wasn't sure where we stood. It was silly, and so not in sync with my feminist attitudes about everything else in the world, but if we ever went on an actual date, I wanted Jax to be the one to ask first. I wanted to *know* that he wanted me. I blamed that particular attitude on the plethora of romance novels I loved, and I was totally fine with it.

Brynn, thinking I was still listening to her and not daydreaming about Jax, had continued talking, "Plus, the guy I'm going with is highly *gifted*." I shook my head, remembering she was there, and tried to focus on what she'd said. It didn't make any more sense the second and third time I replayed it in my mind.

"Gifted?" I asked, stuffing my wallet and phone into my coat pockets.

She shook her head like I was completely dense. "You know…hung."

I stopped to stare at her, totally stunned. I shook myself out of the shock. "Where in the world do you get this information? Are you subscribing to some newsletter I'm not aware of?"

She lifted her index finger to her cheek and looked contemplative. "A newsletter would actually be really helpful."

"Seriously, Brynn. How do you find this stuff out?"

"It's out there," she said, waving her hand in the air, "in the wind."

I rolled my eyes, grabbing my keys from the table next to the door. I decided I needed to spend more time listening to the wind. Maybe it would have some intel on Jax.

Thirty minutes later, we were at the entrance to an old silver mine high above the city. Every October, they opened it up as a haunted house attraction. Tonight—according to the huge black banner hanging over the entrance—all ticket sales went toward a fundraiser benefiting a foundation that raised awareness to stop reckless driving.

I love Halloween, ghosts, and scary stories, but I'm not a big fan of haunted houses. They're all shock factor and fake scares. Give me a real haunted house with an actual ghost any day. But I reminded myself that I was trying to broaden my horizons and get out of my comfort zone. Plus, it was for a good cause.

We started walking toward the entrance, but detoured away as Brynn pulled me in the direction of two guys. She'd told me on the way up the mountain that we were meeting them there. I'd gone along with it because I figured she was probably right—I did need to get out of the house. But I could care less about the date, or the boy she'd set me up with. Brynn, who had far more experience in the man department than me, swooped in next to a tall, blonde surfer type, and grabbed his bicep with gusto. "Damn, Chet! What do you bench, five-hundred pounds?"

That was one of the more ridiculous things I'd ever heard come out of Brynn's mouth—and I'd heard some whoppers. "If so, you should check him for fangs," I said, "because five-hundred pounds is vampire territory."

"I wouldn't mind a vampire." She looked up at Chet, batting her eyes. "Wanna bite me?"

I rolled my eyes and turned to the guy standing next to them. He was wearing a coat, but his shoulders were wide and he seemed sturdy enough to climb if I needed to get away from an evil clown. His light brown eyes were soft. I smiled, trying to be a good sport about the date. "Hey, I'm Sydney."

He smiled back, his cheeks dimpling in an endearing way. I wasn't going to marry the guy, but if I had to go through a scary haunted house, he wasn't a bad person to partner up with. He was attractive, I'd give him that. Brynn had done a good job. "Drew. Nice to meet you. And I'm not a vampire."

I frowned inwardly, and tried to keep the expression off my face. Huh. *Drew.* I hadn't had great experiences with Drews in the past. I had a theory that any guy named Drew was destined to be a raging, egotistical asshole. I hoped this one proved me wrong. I smiled and said, "Good to know. I'm glad I won't have to worry about being turned tonight."

Chet and Drew had already bought our tickets, which was nice of them. Brynn and Chet stopped groping each other long enough to direct us inside the mine entrance. Drew and I followed them into the elevator that took us three hundred feet down into the ground.

The first obstacle we came to was a watery pit covered by a few 2x4s we had to navigate across in the dark. It was like walking a plank, only each plank was about as wide as my shoes, and precariously placed. The smoke rising from the water made it difficult to see anything, let alone the boards. I could already tell this haunted attraction would not be my favorite experience, and I longed for the case study on tort law that I was working on at home, instead.

Unsteady on the skinny boards, I almost fell, but felt a firm hand grab my waist and stabilize me at just the right moment before I would have tumbled. I looked back and saw Drew's dimples. "Thanks!"

"Any time," he said, his hand lingering on my waist. Whether it was for support, or an excuse to touch me, I wasn't sure. I'd take the support, though.

We stepped off the wood walkway and into a

tunnel. We had to crouch down and crawl through it. The tunnel was pitch black, and I was constantly on guard for something to jump out from the sides, or in front of me. The confined space wasn't helping my claustrophobia, either. Without light to guide me, there were more than a couple of times I thought I was going to get stuck. I felt a hand on my ass. I figured it was probably Drew, but couldn't fault him for it since he was trying to feel his way through the darkness, too. I was surprised I hadn't accidentally fondled someone myself.

I finally reached the end of the tunnel and pushed through a heavy black curtain into a room pulsing with a bright strobe light. I had no memory of my birth, but figured it probably felt a lot like this, and was just as disorienting. No wonder babies are so pissed when they're born. I was a little pissed off myself.

I found Brynn and grabbed her arm. "This is ridiculous," I hissed into her ear. "I'd rather be doing homework."

She rolled her eyes, still hanging onto Chet. "You'd always rather be doing homework."

"And his name is Drew! You know how I feel about Drews!"

"Stop overreacting. You're on one date with him, not having his babies. Plus, you're obsessed with a Jax. Jaxes are *way* higher than Drews on the douchebag name meter."

I scowled at the reminder. After he'd followed us

to the club and rescued us, Brynn had become even more convinced that Jax was my soul mate.

Drew came up behind me, standing a head taller than me, and pressing into my back. "Hey, you made it!"

I turned from Brynn, trying not to let my pissy mood show and gave Drew a forced smile. "There were times I questioned if I would, but the tunnel eventually birthed me."

Loud music started blaring and we were all pushed into a room full of mirrors, multi-colored lights flashing in quick patterns meant to be disorienting. The strobe light had been tame compared to this. I kept pushing around the mirrors, trying to find my way through the maze. I finally realized it was useless and they'd provide an exit when they were ready for our group to move on. I decided to stop fighting my predicament, and stood, waiting. I grabbed Drew by the arm so we wouldn't get separated. He smiled wide. "Don't worry, I won't let anything get you."

Great. My knight in shining armor.

After a few minutes, we were herded into another room. This one had macabre scenes that made photos I'd seen of the plague look like cupcakes and rainbows. It wasn't scary—it was absolutely disturbing. Each scene was dark until we passed by it, then the scene would flash and come to life. A girl smashing a guy's head with an ax; a red-eyed monster threatening to attack; a man tied to a rack, arms and legs being pulled apart in four different directions as he screamed in pain. The final scene was a terrified woman sprawled out on what looked to be cobblestone streets. The guy above her was laughing maniacally as he held a knife over her, eyes wild. The screeching music was a horrifying companion to the scene. Just as the guy looked like he was about to do something even worse, like rip off her clothes, the scene went completely black, and the music cut out. I took a deep breath, relieved that part was over, and waited to be herded to the next room of horrors. My eyes tried to adjust to the inky blackness surrounding me, but there was no light at all; I couldn't even make out shapes.

That's when I was pulled a few feet away. A strong arm around my waist.

I was glad Drew was so committed to our buddy system, but his grip was a little tight. We stood there, the sound of heavy breathing the only noise in the room. I felt a large hand cup my cheek tenderly—the gesture somewhat familiar. Hot breath hit my face like a warm, beachy breeze. My chest heaved in response. The combination of total darkness and an unfamiliar area where anything could happen had my heart racing, but not with fear—something else. I could feel him in front of me, strong, stable. I liked the feeling more than I wanted to admit. My contemplation was interrupted by soft, silky full lips pressing against mine. He pushed lightly against me, coaxing my mouth open. Our tongues twisted together and the kiss deepened before he suddenly broke away.

His lips, hands, everything—gone.

A blood curdling scream pierced the air and the lights kicked back on, highlighting the woman now dead and bleeding in the scene. The man smiled, his lips curled in a way that seemed to radiate insanity. The actors in this haunted house were pretty damn impressive.

And I was totally disoriented. I looked around the room; Drew was a few paces away. It didn't *look* like he'd just kissed his blind date. But his name *was* Drew and he *was* probably an epic asshole, so I couldn't be sure if he was the type to kiss and pace. But jeez, that was an amazing kiss!

I licked my lips, tasting a fruity strawberry flavor. It reminded me of something, but I couldn't put my finger on what.

I moved closer to Drew, silently studying his face for any sign that he'd just pulled a ninja kiss. He gave nothing away. A door opened and I followed Brynn and Chet, with Drew bringing up the rear. We went through a few more scenes, but my mind was preoccupied as I tried to figure out what had actually happened in that dark room. We rode the elevator back to the top and I managed to nod and give appropriate—albeit short, responses—where I needed to as we were herded through a maze of hay bales, at the end of the attraction.

We were penned in by a chain link fence, and were trying to figure our way out when the obligatory Jason with his chainsaw, minus the chain, was suddenly in the cage with us. He paused to look each one of us in the eye, tilting his head like the psychopath he was. When he got to me, he stopped and stared longer than he had with everyone else. I was uncomfortable with being the subject of his fixation.

Brynn grabbed onto Chet. I had mixed feelings about grabbing the possible stealth kisser Drew, and managed not to until Jason came rushing for us. I screamed and tried to pull Drew with me to the other side of the fence, but he stood there, frozen in place. Great. The guy who was supposed to be protecting me was a pansy. And I wasn't sticking around to get attacked with him, even if the attack wasn't real.

I ran to the other side of the fence, leaving Drew by himself. Jason had the chainsaw right above Drew's head. At first Drew tried to keep it cool, but as the chainsaw lowered more and more, Drew's fight or flight response kicked in and he eventually ran away, too. Now Brynn, Chet, and Drew were all by the exit and I was alone, on the other side of the enclosure. And really, *really* pissed. I wasn't going to be terrorized by a fictional character wielding a fake weapon while my date, best friend, and her alleged big dick scampered away. Some protector Drew had been. He had one job and didn't do it.

Annoyed, I narrowed my eyes and I started to march past Jason. He stalked toward me, pushing me back toward the fence—the last place I wanted to be

trapped. Fake chainsaw and fake Jason notwithstanding, the actor still played the part well, and it was hard to be ballsy when I was being detained by a nightmare.

He stood back, holding the chainsaw in front of me, blocking my path. Every time I tried to move, he blocked me again. Finally, I'd had enough. "This is ridiculous," I said, pushing past him. He grabbed my arm and I swiveled my head in his direction, looking first at my arm, then at him. I'd had friends work as actors in haunted houses. The number one rule was not to touch the attendees. I shifted my eyes up to meet his. They were indiscernible dots through the mask. "Let me go," I hissed.

The voice that answered was muffled through the mask, but held a familiar, deep tone. The words he spoke were unmistakable, "Not a chance, sweetheart."

Nine

I had one question plaguing me. The same question that had been running through my head all weekend. Had Jackson West kissed me in a dark, haunted mine? And if he had, was it creepy, or romantic? I couldn't decide.

I went over the facts—again. The strawberry flavor left on my lips after the kiss had reminded me distinctly of the strawberry candy Jax had popped in his mouth when he fixed the overflow on She-Ra. But a lot of things smelled and tasted like strawberries—including the actual berries—and a lot of people ate strawberries, too. Based on that, I didn't feel like there was a big enough connection.

Jason's voice had sounded a lot like Jax's, but he

was wearing a mask, and the voice was hard to distinguish. And the "sweetheart" tacked onto the end of the conversation was a word he'd used in place of my name before. Sweetheart was a pretty common term of endearment, however, so between that and the muffled voice, I had enough uncertainty to drive me nuts with curiosity about whether or not it had actually been Jax. My gut didn't have any questions, though. My gut told me Jackson West had full-on kissed me—and it had been fantastic. I wasn't sure how I felt about that revelation. Admitting it even to myself was scary.

I'd gone over and over the night in my head all weekend. Number one, Jax as an actor in a haunted house seemed…odd. I just didn't cast him as the acting type. Football, wrestling, hell, even baseball, I could see, but drama as an extracurricular? It seemed completely out of character. But maybe I didn't know him well enough to make that judgment. And if he was that good at drama, no wonder he thought highly of himself in bed. He probably knew quite a bit about role-playing. I got lost in thoughts of that, and the scenes from my fantasies that he could probably act out like a true thespian, before I shook myself out of it and went on to my next point.

Number two, if Jax had pulled something like that off, he'd have owned up to it by now…at least, I thought he would have. Then again, the last time I saw him was at my house the morning after he'd rearranged Karl's testicles a week ago, so maybe he was waiting until our next meeting to deliver his "I kissed you and you didn't know it" speech.

Of all the possible kiss explanations, Jax as the kiss ninja made the most sense. It would explain the fact that Drew didn't seem at all phased by what had happened during the haunted adventure, and—despite his name—was nothing but a gentleman the rest of the night. We'd stopped for hot chocolate after the mine and Drew even bought my drink. Though if he'd stolen a kiss in the dark and still wasn't owning up to it, hot chocolate was the least he could do.

After calling me sweetheart, "Jason" had terrorized me a bit more before letting me leave with Brynn and the boys. If Jax really had kissed me, he'd broken the rules by touching me—twice: once during the kiss, and again as Jason. A thrill of excitement fluttered through me. Maybe he did like me? I was also a little pissed because why kiss me in the dark, instead of kissing me in a normal lighted area where we could both be privy to the lip lock, and the lead up? You only get one first kiss with a man; it's really not something you want screwed up. If we'd had a magical moment, at least one of us was unaware of the identity of the other magic maker. That seemed grossly unfair, and gave him the upper hand. I didn't like that. I preferred to be in control of situations.

"I just wish I knew if it was him," I said to Brynn. We were doing yoga in the living room, trying to decompress from the weekend. Which meant I was

trying to relax, and Brynn was trying to shake a hangover from her second date with Chet on Saturday night.

"Well, it wasn't Drew," she said. "I asked."

"You asked?" My mouth hung open as I switched into Warrior Two pose. "I can't believe you asked!"

She lifted a shoulder, concentrating on her balance. "Drew was there when I got up this morning, so I took advantage of the situation."

"Yeah, I noticed you didn't come home last night. So, are you and Chet an item now, or what?"

She rolled her eyes as she changed positions. "When am I *ever* an item with anyone, Syd? You know I'm just having fun."

"You had fun with Chet two nights in a row. That's unusual for you."

"Chet's man parts are unusual. They warranted further investigation…you know, for my *research*."

I laughed and shook my head. "You're using research as an excuse for a lot lately. I take it the info you got from 'the wind' was correct, then?"

Her lips stretched into a smile. "It was. And Chet might be my new go-to booty call. I'm sure Drew would like to be yours. He seemed interested, and was pretty deflated when I told him someone else had ninja kissed you on his date."

"Ninja kiss" was even funnier when someone said it out loud, and it wasn't just in my head. "I can't believe you told him that, either. But it is pretty funny.

His date got stolen right under his nose and he had no clue."

She laughed. "Did you even get Drew's number?"

"No. He was a nice guy, and hot—so good job on that—I'm just not really interested."

"Yeah…that's because you're interested in a guy who pretends to be a chainsaw wielding psycho killer, and probably stalks the bowels of the earth searching for his next conquest—like an evil dragon. Congratulations on falling for Smaug. How many girls do you think Blue Eyes kissed in the dark Friday night besides you?"

I frowned. "I hadn't thought about that." I didn't want to think about it now, either. Surely, he had girls interested in him. With his face and biteable ass, he probably got hit on hourly. The question was whether he followed through on any of the invitations. I didn't get the vibe that he did. He was so guarded, and I knew it wouldn't be easy to get him to open up—for anyone. I could tell he had plenty of experience with women, but he wasn't some frat boy just trying to get laid. He was older, and seemed to be past that stage of his life. I got the feeling he didn't do much without first knowing the potential reactions and consequences from every party involved—kind of like me.

"I thought you liked Jax," I said to Brynn. "You suddenly seem to think he's evil."

Brynn shook her head. "No, not evil. I just don't know what his game is. He's hard to read."

Brynn stood and we both finished with Mountain,

and then sank down into Child's pose. My breath was even and calm. The yoga had helped me think. I sat up, brushing hair away from my face.

"You need to confront Jax about his ninja skills," Brynn said, her arms still flat in front of her, face pressed into her mat.

"I know. I'll talk to him about it the next time I see him."

She sat up slowly, and grinned. "Maybe I'll pop your tire so it happens sooner than later."

I narrowed my eyes. She better not, but I wouldn't put it past her. Brynn usually got what she wanted—one way or another.

Brynn was doing her weekly version of dance party at the apartment. It involved a lot of jumping around and singing at the top of her lungs while she cleaned like a maniac. She loved doing it. The domesticity of the action seemed so strange in relation to Brynn's other activities, but I was happy to let her clean if she wanted to. It meant I didn't have to do it. I couldn't study with that commotion going on, though, so I took my books and went to the Soup and Spoon to do some work, and get lunch.

I was reading my textbook and taking notes between bites of my grilled cheese sandwich—which I was holding with a napkin to prevent grease prints—and tomato basil soup.

"A tornado could go through here and you wouldn't even notice."

My head shot up at the sound of Jax's voice. His jeans were tight around his hips and ass, and his dark blue tee shirt was straining to contain him. He looked good enough to suck. I inwardly shook my head, shocked at myself. Good enough to suck? Where had that come from? I couldn't just go around *sucking* people! Or biting and licking them!

"I was watching you while I got my food. You didn't look up once. You get seriously caught up in your study time." He put his tray—holding a sandwich, chips, soup, and soda—down on my round table, and pulled his chair around closer to mine before sitting.

"I *was* seriously caught up in it until you got here. And yes, you can sit at my table."

He raised a brow like he was amused I was giving him permission when he clearly just did whatever he wanted. I watched him back, neither of us saying a word. I expected a lot of things at this point. Like a ninja kisser confession, or at least a reference to the haunted house to get things started. What I didn't expect was Jax to kick his leg out, lean back in his chair, open his sandwich and chips, and start eating without another word. I stared at him, totally dumbfounded. He was completely comfortable with the awkwardness, and not the least bit phased. I was pinging. He needed some of my neuroses, and I needed some of his zen.

I tried to go back to studying, but the visual orgasm sitting next to me made that pretty damn difficult. Not to mention that I couldn't stop thinking about the kiss. Finally, half a sandwich, full bag of chips, and most of his soda later, I blurted, "So, what did you do this weekend?"

He lifted his soda and took a long drink. When he finished, he slowly ran his tongue over his lips. I couldn't look away. His bottom lip was so full, with moisture clinging to it. I wanted to take his lip in my mouth and suck it. Hard. I shook myself out of the thought as Jax's gaze latched onto mine. One corner of his lips tilted up. He'd noticed me having eye-sex with his mouth. Dammit! His lips slid into that slow, sexy grin that promised everything from dark kisses to werewolf sex. "My weekend was—" he paused, searching for a word, "enlightening." His brows went up, almost in challenge. "How was yours?"

I narrowed my eyes. He still wasn't owning up to the kiss! He wasn't even admitting to being at the haunted house…yet. But he would. "Fantastic. I had a date."

He widened his eyes. "Did you? And how did that go?"

"Great. It was a blind date. Brynn set me up. But he was hot, and nice. I'm sure I'll see him again."

Jax lazily scooped some soup onto his spoon and took a bite. "That's all it takes? Hot and nice? Do you have a future mate characteristics list somewhere with 'hot' and 'nice' written at the top?"

It was all I could do to keep from sticking my tongue out at him. So what if I really did have a list? That was none of his business. And hot and nice weren't at the very top, so there. "I'm sure hot is at the top of *your* list," I said. "That and 'willing to put up with my shit'."

He laughed outright. "Good to know what you really think of me."

"I don't know what I really think of you…yet."

He ate some more of his soup before responding, "Why is that? Last week you seemed to think I was a pretty good guy."

I scrunched my brows and watched him. "I still do, most of the time." Thoughts of the ninja kiss he wasn't admitting to ran through my head. "But you're a hard guy to read, and an even harder guy to get to know."

"You want to know me?"

I shrugged. "Maybe."

His lips formed a half smile as he looked down into his bowl and got another spoonful of soup. "You think you could handle it?"

I lifted my brow. "Are you harboring secrets that would be difficult to handle?"

His face shuttered to a blank slate again. That made me think he really did have some serious secrets he didn't want me to know. I was suddenly uncomfortable with the prospect.

"Ask."

I was taken aback. Considering the way his face

had closed up like a prison, I didn't expect him to volunteer any information. "Ask what?" "Whatever it is you want to know."

Well, I wasn't prepared for this. I had a list of questions at home—typed up and everything—that I was dying to ask him, but I was so off-balance from his willingness to chat that I couldn't remember most of them. I did remember the kiss, however. And I wanted to know if it had been him. But I didn't want to ask him outright; I wanted him to admit to it. "I went to a haunted house this past weekend."

"Did you?" he asked, sounding intrigued. "How was it?"

"It had some scary parts," I answered. "Some more scary than others. The costumes and actors were pretty convincing."

He quirked one brow, and looked like he was absolutely enjoying himself, and our conversation. "That's surprising. Maybe I'll have to check this place out. What was your favorite part...would you say?"

I narrowed my eyes. He knew that I knew, but he still wasn't admitting it. Crafty ninja. "Probably the part where my date kissed me," I said.

A muscle ticked at his jaw.

I looked down, hiding my smile. I'd purposely not given him more info. I wanted him to wonder whether I'd really kissed Drew, or if I was just attributing Jax's ninja kiss to someone else. It seemed to be working.

"So," I said, changing the subject. "What's your

favorite holiday?" I took a gamble that it might be Halloween since he'd been acting in a haunted house.

"Halloween."

I took a drink of my chocolate iced coffee. "Do you dress up?"

The annoyed lines on his face smoothed. "Mmmm, yes." His eyes glinted with amusement. "For a lot of reasons."

My brow lifted. "What reasons?"

His lips slid into a slow, sexy grin. "Certain things require costumes."

I caught the insinuation, but chose to press on with my questioning. "Like, say, a theater production of some sort," I offered.

He watched me closely. "I imagine that's one of them."

He wasn't going to give. And I wasn't going to flat-out ask. "What are the other situations that require dressing up, Jackson?"

He dropped his soup spoon in the container, then folded his arms on the table and leaned in toward me. His scent hit me like a fifty pound weight. He smelled like the mountains after a rainstorm, clean and earthy. He had invaded my space an entire lean ago. If I leaned just a little forward, we'd be nose-to-nose. The realization that our lips would be that close and suckable—again—made my breath short. He held my eyes the entire time before saying, "Maybe I'll show you sometime, Sydney."

With that, he moved back, and stood. I realized my mouth was hanging open and picked it up.

He noticed, too, his lips lifting at the corner in a cocky smirk. He gathered all of his trash on the tray and looked like he was going to leave without another word, but stopped, locked eyes with me, and said, "Go out with me."

I couldn't have been more stunned if he'd just told me he was raised by howler monkeys. "What?"

"On a date. Go out with me."

I shook my head. "I don't think that's wise."

"Why? You can't tell me that you don't date, because obviously you do." His lips quirked up slyly. "I'll pick you up on Saturday. Does noon work?"

"I'm volunteering at CARE this weekend. I won't be off until two."

Surprise flashed across his face before he continued, "CARE is downtown, so I'll pick you up there."

I nodded without even realizing I'd done it.

"See you soon." He grabbed his tray and as he brushed by me, he leaned down and whispered, "Sweetheart."

Saturday. That meant I had six days to get my heart back to a normal rhythm.

Ten

The week flew by, mostly because I spent every spare moment analyzing Jackson West. When I told Brynn about Jax's reaction to my questions at the Soup and Spoon, she'd also been convinced that Jax was the ninja. She said I needed to call him on it. Maybe I was just stubborn, but I wanted him to admit it on his own.

I was at CARE, sitting on a bean bag in the corner, reading a Dr. Seuss story to Macy. She giggled every time I used the word "sneetch." "That's a funny word," she said, laughing some more, and pointing at the star-bellied sneetch picture.

"And they have stars on their tummies," I said, pointing to another star-bellied sneetch.

She nodded, and leaned her head against my shoulder as I read the last few pages. "All done." I closed the book, and put it back on the shelf.

Her bottom lip pouted out. "Don't worry, we can read it again next time I come over," I reassured her.

She smiled, and jumped up out of my lap. I noticed Jax leaning against the doorway, watching me steadily, his eyes soft. Charlie was standing next to him. I waved at them both and started to stand, but Macy came rushing over and wrapped my thighs in a bear hug. "Thanks for coming, Syd. I love you."

My heart constricted at her tiny arms squeezing me, and I felt lucky to be involved with an organization that was so good about helping families make a difficult time a little easier. Memories floated back to me of a time when I'd been the one looking for a distraction as I waited to hear the latest news from the hospital. I knew first-hand what it meant to have a home away from home during a family member's health crisis. Nothing buoyed a spirit like feeling the comfort of a familiar place to go, and people who care. "I love you too, sweetie." I leaned down, whispering in her ear, "I left some peanut butter cookies on the counter."

Her eyes lit up and she made a beeline for the kitchen.

I smoothed my hair, taking the time to *really* look at Jax and caught my breath. Jeans and a dark blue crew neck sweater never looked so good. His shirt was tucked into the front of his pants, a square, metal belt buckle holding up his jeans. I kind of hated that buckle. His eyes met mine, and held. I smiled. His lips lifted in return as I made my way across the room.

"Hey," I said, moving my hand in the direction of both men. "Charlie, this is my friend, Jax. Jax, this is my friend and the executive director of CARE, Charlie."

Jax nodded, and tilted his head toward Charlie in acknowledgment. "He introduced himself when I got here."

"How did you two meet each other?" Charlie asked, looking from Jax to me.

"He rescued me one night when She-Ra died. He works at Red's."

Charlie eyed him with interest. "I bet it's nice for Syd to have a mechanic around."

Jax lifted his shoulders slightly, almost uncomfortably, and changed the subject. "Ready to go?"

"Yep." I grabbed my coat and purse. "I'll pick She-Ra up later tonight if that's okay, Charlie?"

"No problem," he answered. "Have fun."

I followed Jax outside to his truck. This was the first time I'd gotten a look at it when I wasn't drugged. It was a metallic grey Ford with chrome accents.

He opened the door for me and pointed to the running board that I could use as a step. Once we were both settled, he turned out of the CARE parking lot and started driving.

"So, where are we going?" I was so curious about the date and what he had planned. I'd spent far too much time the previous week marinating over it, and my homework had suffered as a result. I just couldn't decide where a man like Jax would take a woman on a date. He was a mystery.

Jax grinned in response.

"Seriously? You're not going to tell me? Not even a hint?"

The corner of his lip ticked up even more. He shifted in his seat, his left leg falling open, relaxed, his body angled toward mine. "You lied to Charlie."

"What?" My brow pinched in confusion as I noted that we were now headed up into the mountains.

"About how we met. Your car was the second time I saw you. The first time was at the Soup and Spoon." He draped his arm over the steering wheel and glanced at me, eyes alight. "I guess you forgot."

Oh, I was *well* aware of that particular memory. The smirk Jax was sporting indicated he knew I hadn't forgotten, either. "It doesn't count as *meeting* when we didn't even speak."

One eyebrow went up at that. "Communication is more than just words. I thought we said plenty."

So had I. My heart sped up as I remembered it in detail: his eyes, his biceps, his dare to approach him. "Why didn't you come over and talk to me that day?" I asked.

"Why didn't you talk to me?" he countered. "I extended the invitation."

I folded my arms across my chest. "With your eyes. Eye invitations are hard to read." Really, it hadn't been. I knew exactly what he was saying, and it involved a lot less clothing than either of us had been wearing at the time.

"You missed out."

Arrogant. "So did you!" I argued back. "What if you'd never seen me again?"

"That wouldn't have happened."

"How can you be so sure?"

"Because I would have found you."

That was a little creepy. "Like a serial killer, huh? That's your get-laid strategy?"

"No, like the guy who protects the girl from the serial killer."

I nodded, wondering if he thought that kind of alpha-male assholery was attractive.

Okay.

So it was.

It really, really was.

Some primitive part of my psyche found the protectiveness insanely appealing. It was probably also the part of my psyche that thought Ragnar Lothbrok from *Vikings* was the sexiest man on the planet, and made me wish I'd been a hot Viking's wife.

"How did you get involved with CARE?" Jax asked.

I relaxed against the seat. "My mom was sick for a while. Cancer. We stayed at CARE while she was being

treated. I loved the staff, and everything they did meant so much to me and my dad." I paused, remembering how hard it was to see my mom so helpless. Even now, just the thought of going to the doctor gave me a mini panic attack. But things would have been a lot worse if we hadn't had the support of the CARE staff to help us through it all. Having other people who were going through similar problems really helped us deal with everything that was going on. And I think it helped my mom to know we had that kind of support network, too. "I wanted to be able to help people, like my family had been helped, so I decided to volunteer."

Jax was quiet for a minute. "How old were you?"

"She was diagnosed when I was nine."

"And now?"

"She's fine. I mean, she still goes in for check-ups, but they caught it early enough that she was okay. She got treatment and then things went back to normal, and we went back to moving around. I grew to love Winchester while we were here, though, and decided to come back for college."

He nodded, taking it all in. I always felt weird telling people about my mom; it felt like they didn't know how to react. Jax didn't seem uncomfortable with the information, he was just quiet. "Where do your parents live now?" he asked.

"Southern Florida. My dad's retired, but you won't convince him of that. He keeps taking on work here and there. He gets bored easily. My mom used to be a project manager at an insurance company, but she's retired, too."

That was more personal information than I'd ever given Jax…and the first time he'd ever asked. I took it as a good sign that he wanted to know more about me.

I looked out the windows and noticed the brilliantly colored leaves. Vibrant shades of crimson, gold, orange, and pink blanketed the landscape. I loved this time of year. A memory clicked in my head as I thought it. I remembered saying something along those same lines to Jax a few weeks ago when he'd been helping me clean gas off my car—before the bottle ejaculated on him. Did he remember me telling him that? Naw, guys weren't that perceptive, at least not the ones I'd been with in the past. Jax was different than other guys in a lot of ways, though, so maybe he was different when it came to being attentive, too? "Did you bring me up here to see the leaves?" I practically blurted it out, and felt like a complete fool for it.

He looked over at me, his eyes bright. "Maybe."

I stared at him. He shifted his eyes back to the winding mountain road, so I had time to study him. I couldn't figure him out. At all. "What's your deal?" I finally asked.

"What do you mean?"

We really hadn't spent that much time together, and for the life of me, I couldn't figure out what his interest in me was, or why he'd asked me out on a date. I mean, my interest in him involved a vision of him

mostly naked in his apartment, and a lot of muscles I couldn't pronounce correctly, but why would he want me when he could walk into a room and pretty much hand-pick any girl there? And it wasn't like that information was a secret. He was absolutely aware of his effect on women. "You're spending a lot of your free time with me, and now you're doing thoughtful things like taking me on a drive in the canyon because I mentioned I like the fall colors. Plus, you asked me out. With anyone else, I'd say they were interested in something more—like a relationship. But you don't do relationships."

"Maybe I'm taking you on a drive because I like the fall colors and wanted company?"

Oh. Now I felt super stupid. I stared out the window, noticing the trees, but not focused on them like I was before. He'd said this was a date, though, hadn't he? So why was he suddenly acting like it wasn't? Jax was so guarded with his feelings, it was hard to get a read on him. But I'd spent enough time with him now to know he used statements like that as some sort of defense mechanism so people couldn't go too deep. I wasn't going to let him get away with it. Especially not after I'd just shared something really personal about my own life.

I turned toward him, ready for a chat. "You might have wanted to see the fall colors, but that's not why we're here. You just don't want to admit you thought of me and made an effort to do something you thought I'd enjoy."

The muscles at his jaw pulsed. Finally, he said, "Maybe."

And that's all I got. I sat in the passenger seat getting more and more annoyed. When we got to the end of the road, he parked. We got out and climbed a hill overlooking the valley. I took a deep breath of the crisp mountain air and closed my eyes, then opened them again, like seeing the scene for the first time. The mountains made a beautiful backdrop for the gorgeous autumn colors painting them. I pulled out my phone and snapped a few pics of the scenery, then eased down next to Jax on a large rock.

We sat in silence, looking out over the area, but my mind was racing with thoughts about what had happened in the truck, and the way he'd deflected me. I had fun with Jax. He was a good friend, and he was the definition of man-candy, but true friendship requires a level of intimacy that goes beyond making jokes. And relationships require even more than that. He said he didn't want one, but I wasn't sure he really knew what he wanted at all. I knew what I wanted, though. I wanted to get to know him. The real him—not the mysterious, reserved version he put out there for the rest of the world. What was he hiding? And why wouldn't he open up?

I turned to him, unable to hold my feelings in any longer. "Look, Jax. I like you. You're funny, you're smart, you force me out of my comfort zone, and I really like hanging out with you."

"Thanks!" he said, leaning back against the rock

and resting his hands behind his head as he looked up at me. He gave me a wide grin. "I know."

I narrowed my eyes. That. It was *that* attitude that needed to go—or at least be tempered by some honesty and real moments. "But you're also hard to read because you refuse to let anyone in. You can have friendships and relationships like that, but they're surface relationships—and they don't last. Not to mention, it's a pretty lonely place to be. Who do you confide in if you have no one you trust enough to be real with?"

He looked away. "I get through things fine on my own."

I shook my head. "No one does. Everyone needs a constant. Someone who's always there for them. Someone to count on." I paused. "If you want this friendship to go deeper and mean something, you have to let me in. If you don't, we'll stay just the way we are."

He didn't say anything for a long time. "I don't mind the way we are." He paused before adding, "I mean, I wouldn't argue if you wanted to lose some clothes, but other than that, I think things are good." He was doing it again: using jokes to deflect away from the real issue so he wouldn't have to deal with deeper emotions. I shook my head and laughed in disbelief as I stood. "Well, I tried. Surface it is, then."

His brows knit together like he was trying to figure something out.

As I started to walk away, I looked over my shoulder and shot back, "But just so you know, surface doesn't help *this*—" I gestured between me and him, "—move forward. And it definitely won't get my clothes off."

I took off back down the mountain, enjoying the beauty around me by myself.

"Where's Brynn tonight?"

I sighed. I'd hoped we'd make it back to CARE without talking since we didn't seem to be too great at words today. I was wrong. We pulled into the parking lot and Jax parked next to She-Ra as I answered, "She's at a party. Why?"

He ignored my question. "Where's this party supposed to be at?"

"One of the frats."

He leaned back, watching me closely. "You're both in grad school. Why is she still going to frat parties?"

I shrugged. "We just finished undergrad in May. We still have friends at the frats."

"You don't strike me as the frat party type. In fact, I'd have guessed you'd be home studying most nights."

I was totally bugged he'd pegged me like that. That was the old Syd. "Guess you thought wrong."

He folded his arms across his chest. "I didn't."

I wrinkled my nose. Annoyed again. "Fine. Brynn

likes going to frat parties, and I don't like her going alone so I usually tag along—just like when I follow her to bars. Some of them aren't bad, though. Almost everyone there is always super drunk or stoned, so that's pretty entertaining. We know most of the guys and have friends there, so it's safer than going to a bar and hanging out with random guys. And since I'm always the designated driver, I'm one of the only people at the party who can remember what happened after it's all over, so that gives me good blackmail material." I paused, making a decision. "Plus, some of the guys are hot."

His amused expression slipped ever so slightly. His mouth formed a thin line, and a vein pulsed at his temple. I'd said the "hot" comment on purpose—not because it was the truth, but because I wanted to see his reaction. I turned away, trying to hide my own feelings. He was bothered by me looking at other guys. And I liked that it bothered him. A lot.

"I didn't know drunk, spoiled mama's boys were your type. So, yeah. I got that wrong."

I turned back around, giving him a lethal stare. "I didn't know you were analyzing my type."

He held my eyes. "You're really not difficult to figure out."

Now I was pissed. "Well, you apparently got my type wrong, so maybe you should reassess. I think you're giving yourself too much credit—and not giving me enough."

"I don't think so, sweetheart. You don't even date."

My eyebrows show up. "I date! I'm on a poor example of a date with you right now!"

He ran his tongue over his teeth, his lips ticking up slightly. "You don't date, you dally, and not well."

My mouth fell open, part shock, part offense. "What's that supposed to mean?"

He leaned against the door of his truck as he angled his body toward me, like he was getting ready for a long discussion he needed to be comfortable for. I couldn't help but notice how his pants stretched across his crotch. "How far have you gone, Sydney?"

My breath hitched. Like usual, he'd taken me completely off guard. I folded my arms across my chest, squaring my shoulders. "That's none of your business."

"That's fine. You don't have to tell me. I already have a pretty good idea."

"So now you're psychic?"

"No. I just know you."

I stared at him, completely annoyed. "Not that well you don't."

He crossed his arms over his chest, mimicking me. "You're terrified of affection and romantic relationships. You've spent your whole life with a preconceived notion of the person you're supposed to be—and the person you're supposed to end up with. You came to college a good girl, and probably decided to test your limits a bit. You might have even had sex,

but I'm guessing you were A. drunk, B. in a determined fit of stupidity, or C. trying to prove something when it happened," he said, holding up his fingers and ticking off each letter as he said it. "And I bet it's never happened more than once or twice, and it probably wasn't very memorable." I tried to keep my expression blank, but I was shaken by his assessment and didn't do a very good job of keeping the shock off my face. He'd nailed it. Completely. He smiled slowly as my reaction confirmed his assumptions. "You were either scared of the possibility of being intimate with someone, or felt guilty for betraying the person you thought you were supposed to be. So you backed off, and decided to concentrate on getting your degrees instead of on all the other experiences that are also part of college and becoming an adult."

I thinned my eyes. "Experiences you seem to have plenty of, I see."

He ignored me. "You're afraid of intimacy."

"Look who's talking," I yelled, pointing at him. "You won't open up for anyone. I can't figure out who you really are; no one can. Because you refuse to let people in."

He shook his head. "One, I have reasons for not letting people in. Two, I'm not afraid of sex—I love it—I just don't like the baggage that comes with long-term relationships."

"Exactly, you're afraid of relationships because you have to open up. What most people consider a normal part of getting to know someone, you think of as baggage. Has anyone ever gotten far enough inside your heart to really know you? To find out your hopes, your dreams, your fantasies? Have you ever—even once in your life—been vulnerable with someone? Because if you want to talk about intimacy, that's the definition. It's someone you trust implicitly. Who have you had that with, Jackson? Why won't you let people in?"

"That's none of your business," he ground out.

"I bet I could guess," I said, throwing his words back at him.

"No." He paused. "You couldn't. And don't try." His eyes held a hint of anger, but it was laced with something else, a morose sadness. The response was so stern and out of character for him that I decided not to push him on it. At least not right now. It didn't seem like I needed to add that argument to the one we were already having.

"You don't know me, Jax. Not like you think you do." I opened the door and picked my purse up off the seat next to me, grabbing my keys from inside. "When you're ready to open up and have a real conversation, let me know."

I slammed the door shut and unlocked She-Ra. Jax was still sitting in his truck as I backed out of the parking space. I didn't look at him as I roared away.

Eleven

avoided Jax for a week. It wasn't difficult. Other than Red's and the Soup and Spoon, it's not like we spent a lot of time in the same places. He hadn't even texted. After our argument, I shouldn't have been surprised. I replayed the day in my head. We hadn't said a word to each other the entire ride back to town. Which was fine. It gave me a chance to look at the beautiful leaves while I seethed about the man next to me who refused to let me in. Judging by the picnic basket that I'd noticed in the backseat of his truck, though, he'd had a more extensive date planned for us. I guess my calling him out and then storming off down the mountain on my own hadn't made him too eager to spend any more time with me. And if that hadn't sealed the deal, our argument at CARE surely did.

I shrugged inwardly. Oh well. His loss. I wasn't going to be the one to initiate further discussion. If he wanted to make things work with us, and open up, then he needed to follow through and instigate the conversation.

I grabbed my handbag and got out of She-Ra. I'd just finished at the salon, and I felt fantastic! My stylist added some warm, caramel-colored tones to my already blonde hair. I'd been feeling sassy, so when she'd asked how I wanted it styled, I'd told her Hustler-hair—big messy curls with lots of volume. She'd done exactly that. I looked like I'd just been tossed around a bed repeatedly—and had enjoyed it.

I settled into a booth in the back of mine and Brynn's favorite pizza place. We were supposed to meet for lunch, but she wasn't there yet. That wasn't a surprise; Brynn was habitually late. I usually just showed up fifteen minutes later than our agreed upon meeting time. I was still usually the first one there.

I pulled out a book to pass the time. No werewolves. Thanks to Jax, I hadn't been able to read a paranormal romance without thinking about him since August. I was pretty bitter about it. I really liked naked, naughty werewolves—the pretend kind, not the ones with piercing azure eyes who thought they were better than fiction.

Ten minutes later, Brynn floated through the door and took her seat in the booth next to me, her eyes growing bigger as she gave me a once-over. "Hey, hot

girl!" she said, throwing her bag down and picking up a small piece of bread. "Love the hair! You should wear it like that all the time."

I reflexively lifted my hand and touched it, pushing the curls up even higher. "I was feeling sassy today."

Brynn grinned, tearing off a piece of bread and dipping it in some olive oil and garlic on the table. "I like Sassy Syd. Will Sassy Syd also be doing other sexy, sassy things? Like getting naked with a hot man?"

I wrinkled my nose. There was only one man I was interested in getting naked with, and I was still annoyed with him. "Not anytime soon."

"Still haven't worked things out with Jax?"

I lifted a shoulder. "It's not my problem to work out. He's the one who refused to open up, so until he does, I guess things between us are stalled." I took a drink. "I don't even know if there *was* a thing between us."

She rolled her eyes. "Oh, there's definitely a thing. I'm surprised you haven't ripped each other's clothes off in public—or private—yet."

Frankly, I was a little surprised myself.

"How are your classes going?" I asked after we'd ordered our food. "I haven't had an update on your research lately."

Brynn clapped her hands together in front of her. "Oh my gosh! I totally forgot to tell you!" She rummaged through her bag—she frequently lost things in the depths of her purse—and pulled out her phone. "Look at this! Look!" She threw down her phone on the table in front of me. I glanced at the article on the screen. It was a study measuring dick size by state. I scrolled through it, looking at the state sizes and measurements. It wasn't the most comprehensive or scientific study, but apparently a condom company had taken it upon themselves to list the states where the largest sizes were sold.

"So, I guess you're considering a move to North Dakota?" I asked.

"Hell no! I don't want to live there, I just want to visit. I think we need to do a dick tour. Maybe a road trip of the top five states. You know…for research." Her eyes lit up and she grinned playfully.

I leaned back in my chair eying her with a smile. "I deal with enough dicks here in Winchester. I don't need to make a special trip to find more."

"You deal with every day dicks," she said, exasperated. "I'm talking about quality, Syd. The kind of penis you remember on your death bed."

I lifted a brow. "You think you'll be remembering penises on your death bed?"

She widened her eyes like she was horrified at the thought of anything else. "If I'm not, my life has taken a *seriously* wrong turn."

I laughed. She might not end up in a relationship—ever—but I guess everyone has different priorities. Brynn's were definitely more about pleasure than companionship.

I scrolled down the rest of the list. "I don't think this is a very accurate estimator. It says Colorado is number eleven. That doesn't correspond well with your findings."

She wrinkled her nose. "Or I'm just looking in the wrong places…or maybe it's the wrong ages?"

I nodded, though, considering her range of experience, I found it hard to believe she didn't have size estimating down to a science already. I guess that's why she needed to continue her research.

Our food came out and we each grabbed a slice, gooey cheese bubbling over sauce and soft pizza dough. My side had Canadian bacon and pineapple; hers had tomatoes, green peppers, mushrooms, and onions. Pizza was a treat Brynn didn't allow herself to have very often.

Brynn kept discussing her dick trip plans—which she'd put a surprising amount of thought into considering the article had just come out yesterday and she had classes to attend and homework to do.

"As much as I'd like to come along, I don't have time. I'm buried with school work, and you should be, too."

She waved me off. "We have breaks coming up for Thanksgiving, Christmas, and spring break. We could go then!"

"I am *not* spending Christmas on a quest for the biggest penis in north America."

She gave me a serious lock. "It would be a noble quest, Syd. Women everywhere would thank us."

I laughed softly and shook my head. "Maybe when I'm not so busy with school. I'm going to use any vacation we get to try to relax a little. Maybe sleep, and catch up on TV shows."

She frowned. "Party pooper." She picked up a stray pepper that had fallen onto her plate and popped it into her mouth, then immediately almost choked.

I reached over, patting her back, my expression concerned. "Are you okay?"

She took a drink of her lemon water to wash it down, her eyes directed across the room. "Hooooly shit," Brynn said when she could talk again. Her voice was hoarse from the pepper trying to kill her.

I pushed my brows together, wondering what she was exclaiming about, and what had caused her windpipe to almost close. I followed her eyes, and that's when I saw him.

Everything felt like it was in slow motion. I could barely breathe. The little girl couldn't have been more than four. She had an adorable smile and looked completely smitten with the man next to her. The stunning, busty blonde woman sitting across from her looked at Jax the same way. I was so riveted at the scene of domestic tranquility playing out in front of me, that I didn't even notice the water I'd knocked over until Brynn yelped.

I turned to her, not wanting to take my eyes off of them, but needing to clean up my mess. "Well, now I know why he wouldn't open up," I said through my teeth. "He had a wife and kid to get back to."

Brynn gave me a serious look. "You don't know that's who they are."

I watched as Jax picked up a crayon and helped the little girl with sun-kissed platinum braids color on the placemat in front of her while he leaned in next to her ear, talking and laughing. His expression was soft—loving in a way I didn't even realize he had the capacity to feel, let alone show. The gorgeous woman said something and Jax looked up at her with adoration. I'd never been so jealous. I glanced back at Brynn, my face falling. "You don't look at someone like that unless you care about them. A lot."

The woman must have felt our stares because she looked our way. She said something to Jax and he glanced up at us across the room. His eyes met mine, wide with surprise. Shock flitted across his face, but not unhappy shock. That was Jackson West. Confident even in the face of leaving his last romantic interest without a word to go back to his *real* family. He seemed like he didn't want to look away, but finally, he glanced at the super model next to him and tilted his head in the direction of our table. He said something to her, and then he looked at us, totally self-assured. I couldn't have been more furious.

"I think he might be coming over here," I whisper-hissed at Brynn.

She turned slightly, watching him stare at me like a stalker. "His eyes are on us like a laser, so I'm guessing that's a pretty good assumption."

"What do I do?"

She lifted her hands, palms up, like she wasn't sure. "Say hi?"

I frowned. "I think I'd rather punch him. In the balls."

Brynn snorted. "You could always do that, but maybe you should find out who the woman and kid are first."

This was an introduction I was totally caught off guard by, and completely unready for. I needed time to gather my thoughts. I needed time to figure out if I even wanted to talk to him now that I knew what he might be hiding. A restaurant was not the place to do that. I grabbed my purse and keys off the table. "I can't do this, Brynn."

Her mouth gaped. "You don't want to talk to him? At all?"

"Yes. No. …Maybe." I shook my head. "I can't deal with it right now. I need some time to think. I'll meet you back at the house later."

Brynn nodded. "Okay," she said, looking back at Jax. "I don't think he'll be too happy you left and ignored him."

"Good. He should know how it feels."

I couldn't get out of there fast enough.

It had been two days since the pizza incident, and he still hadn't called, texted, or contacted me in any

way. Brynn had talked to Jax after I'd so hastily run out of the restaurant. She'd made an excuse for my leaving. She said he'd seemed disappointed, but he hadn't offered any other details about what he wanted, or his love-child and model wife. I was going completely off assumptions, but without any other information, assumptions—crazy or not—were all I had. I couldn't stop thinking about it. And I certainly couldn't call and ask for an explanation. I couldn't go clinger after only one official date.

And truthfully, I had no idea what I'd say. I was still working through my feelings about the whole thing. In my head, the scenario played out with us having a civil conversation, and Jax telling me I'd totally misread the situation and if any gorgeous woman was going to have his babies, it would, of course, be me. The reality of that—and a much more probable scenario—would include a lot of yelling, and Jax disappointing me in every possible way. So, I'd chosen to avoid him until I could figure my shit out. I got the impression he was doing the same.

Operation Avoid had been going so well until Thursday afternoon—the day my fuel filter died. I cursed it, and the manufacturers who made it, then called Red. I waited for the tow truck, my stomach in knots. It was afternoon. It was a weekday. Jax was working. I briefly considered selling my car so I wouldn't have to deal with Jax anymore. New Camaros were sexy, and didn't come with the threat of constantly seeing a man my brain wanted to slap, and my hands wanted to fondle. It was a problem. I shook my head, telling myself to get a grip. I wasn't the type to run from my problems. I'd suck it up and deal.

Plus, maybe Jax wouldn't even be the one to come get me. Even as I thought it, I knew that wasn't what I wanted. I wanted him to show up, tell me the girl and kid were just friends, that he'd been wrong, and that he was ready to let me in, and do it all while fixing She-Ra. He'd sweep us off our feet and tires, and we'd live happily ever after, never fighting, disagreeing, or having another problem in the world. Ugh. Stupid Disney movies. They'd really warped my perceptions of happily ever after.

My heart started to race when the tow truck pulled up. He wasn't even out of the truck before I recognized his sexy brown curls peeking out from under the ball cap on his head.

He sauntered over to me, assessing the situation. His cocky swagger and smirk made me PMS-level annoyed—irritated enough that he probably should have brought some protective gear. The more he stood there and said nothing acting like that, the more agitated I got. We stared at each other, neither of us saying a word for a good thirty seconds, then he looked at She-Ra. "Red said you think it's the fuel filter?"

Seriously? Not even an acknowledgment of *everything* that had happened since our "date," and the lack of resolution? My annoyance was quickly turning

to pissed off. "I don't think," I said through my teeth, "I know. It's happened before."

"If you're so sure of what's wrong, why don't you fix it?"

I cocked my head to the side and narrowed my eyes. "Do you think I carry spare fuel filters in my purse? Because I don't."

"Well, if it happens this often, maybe you should consider it. You have a whole trunk with space for parts."

My hands fisted at my sides. "Or I can take it to my mechanic—who, aside from when it comes to hiring certain employees, usually has excellent instincts—and he can tell me if I've misdiagnosed the problem and fix it."

A vein in Jax's forehead pulsed. "Are we going to talk, or are you just going to stand there getting more and more pissed off?"

"So now you want to talk?" I widened my eyes. "And I'm not pissed," I ground out.

He tilted his head and gave me a look. "Why do girls do that? It's completely obvious that you're mad and probably thinking of ways to kill me with your shoe, but you lie and say nothing's wrong. How does that help the situation?"

Shock crossed my face. "This from the king of deflection and evasion?" He said nothing. "Quid pro quo, Jackson. I'll be honest when you are."

He breathed out a long-suffering breath and muttered something I couldn't understand before going around to the back of the truck and loading She-Ra. I waited until he was done, providing super helpful instructions like he'd never towed a car before, then got in the passenger seat and we went back to the shop.

The atmosphere was icy when I stormed into Red's, totally ignoring Jax following me. I plopped down in one of cushioned seats in the waiting area, and pulled out my bag, making sure to show the cover of the book I was reading. A fantasy novel with a six-pack wielding alpha male on the cover. Red was standing at the counter, watching me. "What are you reading?" Red asked, probably wondering why I was waving the book around.

I glared at Jax as I answered. "A romance novel. And you know what? This hero is WAY better than a werewolf."

Jax smirked as he rolled his eyes and turned to Red. "We have the filter in stock. I'll be done with it soon." He walked out.

Red leaned his forearms on the desk in front of him. "I assume you don't want to go out there with him and help fix it?"

I snorted. "Absolutely not."

"What's up with you two?"

I slitted my eyes again just thinking about it. Why was this pissing me off so much? I mean, aside from the fact that Jax hadn't opened up to me, he'd made no attempt to contact me for over a week, he hadn't explained his secret family, and he still wasn't admitting he was wrong or trying to do anything to fix the

problem—oh yeah, all of those things were why I was so pissed. "Absolutely nothing."

Red held up his hands in defeat. "Well, I hope you work it out. He's been moody as hell for the past week or so."

My eyes brightened. If he'd been moody, maybe that meant he felt bad for being an ass and keeping secrets. Maybe it meant he was going to apologize for his assholery.

Hmm, probably not, though, if he thought I was still pissed. I decided I'd try to be less ornery when he came back in.

The filter change took less than twenty minutes. I paid Red, then went out to the front of the store where Jax had pulled She-Ra. He was leaning against the car, his legs crossed in front of him, hands in his pockets as he watched me.

I'd spent the last twenty minutes thinking he might be willing to talk and tell me he was sorry. That gave me plenty of time to feel bad for being so mad instead of trying to talk to him in the first place. As I got to my car, I ducked my head down, unable to meet his eyes. I didn't want to fight with him. I wanted him to talk to me. I wanted whatever this was between us to get better, not worse, and the anger wasn't helping anything.

"How was your week?" he asked, completely relaxed. He exuded such a calm demeanor, but inside, I had a feeling that calmness came at the price of a carefully managed exterior—the only one he'd let people see. That kind of control must be exhausting.

I dropped my bag in the backseat, and leaned back against the car, mimicking his posture. More than anything, I wanted to ask him why he refused to open up to me. But I knew it would just get me more answers in the form of questions that led nowhere. He needed to be the one to initiate that conversation. Instead I said, "Fine. How was yours?"

He smiled, but it didn't reach his eyes. "Fine. I got to scare some girls."

I ran my tongue over the inside of my cheek. "Really? Did you threaten to take off your shirt or something?" He communicated in jokes and surface conversation, so maybe this would help me break the ice.

"If I had, they wouldn't have been running away from me, now would they?" He paused. "You didn't run when I took off my shirt. In fact, I'd say you were downright captivated."

"I was in shock that you had no problem stripping down in front of me, and wondered how many other people had been graced with the view."

He shrugged. "I don't have anything to be ashamed of."

"Again, self-confidence is definitely not an issue for you."

"Nope."

"So, why were you really scaring girls?

He looked at me sideways. "Think about it, sweetheart. This one's not hard."

I felt my heart beating faster as I immediately got defensive. "Don't be condescending to me. You could be scaring them for any reason." Was he talking about the girls at the pizza place? Why would he scare a toddler?

"It's Halloween tomorrow. Where do you think I've been scaring them?"

I widened my eyes, realization dawning. "So *now* you're going to admit you were playing Jason at the haunted mine?"

"You already knew."

That didn't matter. I wanted *him* to admit it—and tell me he'd kissed me and couldn't stop thinking about it—without my provocation. "So, you're a drama nerd? I wouldn't have pegged you for that. You're more of a throw-someone-across-a-field-and-steal-their-ball guy than a sing-dance-and-act type."

He lifted a shoulder. "I'm a mystery."

I snorted. "No shit."

He picked up a pen from his pocket and started weaving it absently back and forth through his fingers. "So, who was the asshole you were with at the mine who left you alone with a murderer holding a chainsaw?"

Ah, he had the same opinion of guys named Drew that I did. I shrugged. "A friend."

His eyes slitted as he looked off in the distance. I

kind of wondered if he was even going to respond, when he said, "Surface?"

I studied him, surprised he'd remembered the conversation in the mountains at all since we seemed to be avoiding every possible topic related to getting to know each other on a level that didn't involve jokes and inappropriate sexual references. "I'm not sure. We'd only just met. He bought me hot chocolate, so that gets him points. If he brings me Swedish Fish next time he sees me, he might be a contender."

He stopped fiddling with the pen and looked over at me. "I'd say you're low maintenance if Swedish Fish are all it takes, but considering how uptight you are, that's probably the first in a long list of things you want from a man—and life in general." He slowly licked his lips, holding my gaze. "He won't be able to measure up."

I crossed my arms over my chest. "I'm glad you think you know me even though we haven't had a *real* conversation in, well, *ever*." I could feel my anger simmering. "And as for my date, I'm not too worried. He doesn't have anyone to measure up to."

I straightened my back, standing tall, and shifted my attention to She-Ra—she needed to be washed, waxed, and detailed. I was acutely aware that Jax was still standing less than a foot away, and I could feel his eyes on me. But if he wanted to continue talking, he was going to have to lead. I was sick of always being the driver of conversation with him and getting non-answers.

A minute later, Jax's voice interrupted me. "I guess you think he'll go deeper."

I lifted my lips in a knowing smile. "It's not difficult to find someone willing to go deeper than you."

A muscle twitched at the side of his neck. I figured this was Jax's version of anger…a bit more reserved than mine since there was no yelling or throwing of things. His irises darkened like the sky right before a storm. He leaned into me, moving his head down next to mine, breath hot on my neck. "Not many can go deeper than me, sweetheart. In *any* way."

I could tell I'd hit another nerve. Maybe if I hit enough of them, he'd actually communicate with me. "What's your definition of going deeper, Jax? Because 'deeper' definitely hasn't been my experience when it comes to you," I said. "You're not even willing to dip a finger in."

He exhaled a slow breath and scrubbed his hand over the stubble on his chin, making a rasping noise that was oddly attractive. I immediately thought of what that same stubble would do to me naked, and the air suddenly felt like Phoenix in July. I unbuttoned my jacket, realizing how quickly the atmosphere had shifted from anger to sex—or some combination of the two. I looked at him, his gaze a dark sapphire, tan skin over bulging muscles and sinew. His tight expression made me wonder if he was thinking somewhere along the same lines as me: that angry sex sounded pretty damn fantastic right now, and his apartment wasn't very far away. I felt sweat starting to bead on my chest, my breasts heavy. He was so *male*. My eyes dragged over him again, getting stuck around his belt—so *very*, *very* male. An ache pulsed between my thighs as I tugged off my jacket, "It's warm today."

His eyes softened as he took in my white and grey low-cut v-neck sweater. "It's hot everywhere you are."

I held his eyes, entranced by his magnetic pull. I literally had to shake myself to stop getting hypnotized by his gaze, words, and his sexy, earthy smell. He had been with another woman and child two days ago! And now he was here flirting with me, no explanation? What the hell? This was *so* not okay, and I couldn't let myself get drawn in. "No, we're not doing this."

"Not yet, but we could be in less than three minutes if you drive fast."

I shook my head. "Sex doesn't make up for a total lack of communication in every other area."

"You only think that because you haven't had sex with me—yet."

My stomach fluttered. Comments like that weren't helping me stay on track. I wasn't having sex with Jax until he was willing to do more than just get naked. "Who was the woman and little girl, Jax?"

He sucked in a labored breath and immediately shut down. He looked away, saying nothing. We stood there in silence again. No explanation. I was pissed. "You're so good at flirting. But you're not great at emotions."

"Not true," he said, shaking his head. "I just don't see a reason to let many people in."

"Is there anyone you ever *have* let in?"

Silence stretched as he played with the cap of the pen he'd been holding.

"Even that question is too hard for you to answer." I shook my head. "You're having fun now, sleeping around, joking and being a general ass—hell, maybe even having kids—but in ten years when you're still alone and have no connections with anyone, I think you'll regret your choices."

He pursed his lips, an angry flush rising in his cheeks. "And what about you, Syd? Do you think you'll be happy in ten years with your shiny new car, various degrees, and great job, but only a dog to come home to at night? Does that sound like a fun future to you? Because that's where you're headed. You're so afraid of not meeting your goals that you're terrified to deviate at all. I might seem like I have no direction and I'm unwilling to let people in, but that's not the case. Those perceptions are based off of calculated decisions I've made. My experience informs my choices. But you," he paused, shaking his head, "you're wound so tight, you wouldn't know how to let go and enjoy yourself if you tried."

I gasped, shock and hurt warring inside me as my face fell. He'd just articulated the fears I'd kept locked so deeply inside me that I hadn't even dared write them in my journal. My goals were important—and not just to me. My parents had been through so much, and more than anything, I wanted to make them proud and become the best attorney possible—just like my dad had been before my mom got sick and he had to pull back to take care of her. I wanted my parents to see that they'd made a difference in the world, and that I'd been one of their achievements. But lately, I'd started to wonder if I would achieve everything I'd ever wanted only to regret not experiencing more while I had the chance? Was I missing the best time of my life because my grades and future were more important to me than my social life? Jax seemed to think so.

Either Jax didn't register my deflated expression, or he didn't care, because he kept going. "You're great at judging other people's lives and assuming you know what they need and how to get it, but you're not so good at examining yourself, Sydney."

My hurt quickly morphed into anger. "This is another one of your deflecting mechanisms. You're not ready to deal with your own issues, so you turn things around and make other people feel bad instead. You get pissed at the revelations about yourself, and deal with it by making snarky comments—downright rude in some cases—to push people away so you don't have to face the hard shit." I turned on my heel and shoved the car door open. This hadn't gone as expected, and had definitely taken a horrible turn from the potential angry sex. Angry sex was the last thing on my mind. I couldn't even stand to be in the same air space with Jax for one more minute. "Well,

congratulations. You've accomplished your goal. Consider me effectively pushed out of your life. I hope I don't see you around. Ever."

I slammed the car into gear and left a good amount of tire tread on Red's concrete. I refused to look in the rearview mirror to see if Jax was watching me. I couldn't handle it if he was, and I definitely couldn't handle it if he wasn't. I took a heaving breath, and almost made it to the end of the street before I started crying.

Twelve

I'd spent a long time in my room that night nursing my tears, and then drowned my sorrows in romantic comedies, chocolate, and french fries. I'd told Brynn what Jax said, including Jax's accusations and my secret fears. Like a good best friend, she'd tried to make me feel better and said I absolutely wouldn't end up alone with a house full of animals. I wanted to believe her, but wasn't sure if I could. Still, she'd been pretty pissed that Jax had hurt my feelings. She said she'd go over and twist his balls off, but that seemed a little extreme. It did make me feel better that she'd offered, however, and I knew who to go to if I ever needed any ball torture done. With her research skills, I felt like she'd probably excel at knowing exactly what would cause pain in that area.

The sulking had lasted all night and most of the morning…until Brynn mentioned a Halloween party at Ice—a bar in town. I desperately needed to blow off some steam, and let's be honest, after Jax's breakdown of what he clearly thought was my pathetic life, I now felt like I had something to prove. Maybe he was right, and maybe that's why I felt so bad. I'd decided to take charge and make some changes. My goals were still important to me, but I could reach my potential and experience life, too. If my Halloween costume was any indication, my first experience would be a draft around my rear area, and the threat of catching a cold.

"Where in hell did you get this costume?" I asked Brynn, pulling down my skirt. I hadn't worn something this short since I was a toddler.

She shrugged. "I thought you'd like it! It matches your car!"

She was right about that. The She-Ra costume was pretty authentic, complete with a white dress that fell a few inches below my ass, a gold belt, gold feather-like head band, gold lace-up boots, and a red cape. Thank the goddesses for the cape. It was the only thing keeping my butt cheeks off display. Oh, and there was a plastic sword. I really liked the sword.

Brynn, who promoted ass displaying as often as possible, used the Halloween holiday as an excuse to wear a mostly see-through red and black corset with frilly red panties in public. Someone asked her what she was and her response was, "Sexy." That pretty much summed it up. Halloween wasn't about authenticity or actual costumes for Brynn, it was about attracting the biggest specimen for research.

Ice was full of college students dressed in every costume imaginable. Well, most of the girls were dressed up, but not as many of the guys. And in general, most of the girls had taken Brynn's approach to costume picking, and just grabbed something from their lingerie drawer instead of something with a meaning. I was glad Brynn knew me well enough to pick a costume that mattered instead of another corset and panty pair. I was open to being a little more spontaneous and having more fun, but I drew the line at wearing lingerie in public.

We walked into the dark club, bright lights pulsating as music pounded and bodies flailed around the dance floor. Everything in Ice looked like ice. Decorated in hues of light blue and white, there was an entire wall of water. The wall must have been cooled because as water ran over it, it created an ice formation that was actually really pretty. We were sitting on light blue benches when the server came. Brynn quickly ordered something with enough alcohol to disinfect several wounds. The server turned to me, "What do you feel like, sugar?"

Maybe it was the "sugar," or it maybe it was Jax's words about me being too uptight to have any fun running through my head. But I did something I hadn't done since sophomore year of undergrad. I ordered a

mixed drink. Brynn's mouth dropped so far that I actually looked around to see what she was so surprised at.

"You're drinking?" she asked as the server left.

"You bet I am."

She stared at me like I'd just grown two heads. "Are you sure that's a good idea? You haven't had hard liquor in years. You can barely handle a glass of champagne on New Year's Eve."

I waved her off. "You're overreacting. I'll be fine. I just want to have a little fun."

We sipped our drinks, got up to dance, and came back to drink some more. I'd never enjoyed being dry-humped so much in my life. So this was what it was like to be Brynn. To have fun and not worry about the next test, or how grades during the first year of law school were more important than any other year, since law firms recruit during second year and are most interested in students who finished top of their class in year one.

The alcohol warmed and calmed me in a way I hadn't been relaxed in years. I took another sip of my yummy fruity drink—the good kind that are so sweet you can't even tell how much alcohol is in them. I gazed out across the room and noticed a guy who looked a bit like Jax. That pissed me off. And I didn't want to be pissed. Drinks were fun! I was having fun! And I was not going to end up alone with only a dog as a companion. Nope. Nope. Nope. I was going to start letting loose, and Jackson West could go to hell.

"Hey, hot stuff," Collin said, coming over and smacking Brynn on the ass. There were so many panty frills in his way that I doubted she could even feel it. Collin was wearing a giant cow costume, complete with udders hanging in the area around his waist.

"What's with the cow costume?" I asked. "Sudden interest in farm animals—not that it would surprise me."

He grinned. "Asking a girl to milk me is a great conversation starter."

Brynn thought that was hilarious. She was also probably drunk. I might be a little bit drunk, too.

"That's so stupid," I said, taking another drink.

"What? It helps me see their technique so I don't waste my time with girls who have no clue."

I rolled my eyes. No wonder he and Brynn kept each other around for booty calls. They shared similar completely inappropriate methods when it came to picking partners. "I can't believe you've been successful getting a woman to even talk to you, let alone take her clothes off for you."

His lips curled up. "Believe it, baby."

"'Baby' from you always sounds wrong, but it sounds even worse when you're using your cow costume as a sexual audition."

He came over and started giving me a cow lap dance. I pushed him off, mildly amused by it. Collin was funny, I'd give him that. Funny, but annoying.

One of Brynn's favorite songs came on and she got up, shaking her hips and ass as she curved her index finger at Collin in a 'come here' motion. He was up before she even had to pull out her "screw me" eyes. She gave me the same finger wiggle. I laughed, and followed her and Collin onto the dance floor.

We were dancing in a big group, though I was mostly focused on Brynn—like most of the guys dancing around us. I was so caught up in the moment, that I wasn't paying attention to anything but having fun. Collin was an ass, but I knew he and his friends wouldn't let anything happen to me or Brynn. I felt safe with them, unlike our previous club experience with the strangers Brynn had picked up.

We repeated the cycle of dancing, taking a break for drinks, and dancing again for hours. I felt a little light headed, but nothing too crazy, and I'd been alternating my mixed drinks with water so I wouldn't have the hangover from hell in the morning. By last call, I was sweaty, exhausted, and didn't have a care in the world. It felt fantastic!

Brynn and I walked out to She-Ra. She stumbled, but Collin held her up and helped her into the car. "Are you sure you're okay to drive?" Collin asked me.

"Drive?" I said, "Oh yeah! I'm totally fine!" Even as I said it, I felt a little fuzzy. Maybe I'd had more alcohol than I thought. Driving probably wouldn't be good. We probably needed a cab instead. I started digging through my purse for my phone. I could find a cab company there. My head was down, so I didn't see it coming.

And by it, I mean Jax's fist. It slammed into the side of Collin's face so hard that I actually heard cracking. What the…?

"What the hell are you doing?" I yelled, pushing Jax. His sudden appearance was a shock, and his attitude was helping to clear my mind of the alcoholic haze.

"Stopping you from making a huge mistake," he said. Collin was rolling on the ground, writhing in pain. Jax turned to me, grabbing my purse. He reached inside and found my keys, palming them into his pocket. "Get in my truck."

I was leaning down, checking on Collin. "Who the hell do you think you are? You get in your truck, and leave me alone! And give me my damn keys back!"

His eyes were blazing with fury. "There's no way in *hell* that's happening. You won't be getting your keys until you can stand, and see, straight."

Collin sat up, rubbing his jaw. "That hurt, man!"

"You were about to let two drunk women *drive* home. I hope to hell it hurt, and if I could make it hurt worse, I would."

"I wasn't about to drive, you asshole!" I shouted. "I know I had too much to drink. I was looking for my phone to call a cab."

Surprise crossed Jax's face, and then something that looked like relief. "Well, now I'm here. It will save you the cab fare."

"We don't need your help." I wasn't in the mood to argue with him. We'd had a rough couple of weeks, and I didn't imagine spending any time together would make things better. And riding home with him when I was drunk and more likely to speak my mind was an even worse plan. No. That wasn't happening. I looked around and noticed a few idling cabs at the front of the club that I hadn't seen before. "Will you help me get Brynn, Collin?"

He stood up, moving his jaw back and forth. It would probably be sore, but it looked okay. Collin lifted Brynn out of She-Ra, and then I locked the car and set the alarm. I didn't like leaving my car in a parking lot in the middle of town on a weekend, but I didn't have another choice. We started walking toward the waiting cabs.

"Where are you going?" Jax asked, falling into step next to me. He still looked angry, but he seemed to be maintaining a semblance of control.

"To get a cab, you jerk."

"I told you, I'm taking you home."

We got to the cab and Collin opened the back door, helping Brynn inside. "And I told you I don't need your help."

He scrubbed a hand over his face. "Going out to a club and getting drunk like a teenager was really mature."

I laughed outright. "You're the one who told me I needed to stop being so uptight. Remember?"

His expression went rigid. "I didn't mean do something that could have gotten you killed."

Lines formed across my forehead. "That's kind of a worst case scenario, don't you think? I didn't drive. I just didn't realize how much I had to drink until we got out of the club. When I did, I was going to call a cab until you came over and assaulted my friend."

He pressed his lips into a thin line.

"What the hell is your problem?" I yelled. "You won't open up to me, you haven't contacted me in weeks, and you have a wife and a love-child! Why don't you go be with them and leave me alone!"

His brow pinched in confusion. "Wife? Love-child? What in the world are you talking about?"

"The model and kid you were sitting with at the pizza place!" I yelled. "You didn't even call to explain why you'd decided to use me to cheat on her, and at Red's you refused to answer my question about her. You're a douchebag of the highest order, Jackson West. And you can go to hell!"

I pushed Collin out of the way and got in the backseat of the cab. I was about to tell the cab driver our address, but Jax leaned down through the passenger seat window and told him instead, then handed him twenty bucks. He looked back at me, holding my gaze, his expression full of determination. "This isn't over," he said, then backed away and the cab took off.

Thirteen

I spent the next morning nursing a wicked hangover. The water trick hadn't helped as much as I thought it would. Brynn, who was used to this kind of liquor consumption, recovered much better than me, and brought some special hangover cure potion to my bedroom. I nursed the unpleasant tasting drink for a couple of hours, but it did the trick. By mid-morning, my head and stomach were feeling significantly better; my heart was another issue entirely.

Jax had been at Ice. How did he even know I was going to be there? It seemed a pretty big coincidence for him to show up out of the blue at the same club as me. Maybe that's all it was, though, a coincidence.

After my shower, I made my way down to the

kitchen and found Brynn sitting at the table with her laptop and books. It was rare to see her actually doing homework. "There's a mocha coffee from your favorite café . You might need to warm it up."

"Thanks," I mumbled. I grabbed the coffee cup off the table and put it in the microwave. It came out piping hot and perfect. I sipped it as I crossed my legs under me in the chair across from Brynn. "Thanks for the coffee." I was grateful one of us was capable of functioning this morning, and considering how much Brynn had to drink, it probably shouldn't have been her. Then again, I wasn't actually sure how much *I'd* had to drink.

"Don't thank me," Brynn said, highlighting something in her textbook. "Thank your boyfriend."

I furrowed my brow. "What boyfriend?"

She gave me an exasperated look. "Jax. He was outside this morning and brought us breakfast. He sat there all night."

No. Way. "He did not."

She nodded her head. "He did."

I couldn't believe he'd really sat outside like some sort of security guard. What? Was he afraid I was going to try to walk back to Ice and get my car? "What the hell? Why?"

"Because he's in love with you. Why else?"

I rolled my eyes. No. He wasn't. He had a wife and child. "That's ridiculous. He does not love me. He doesn't even like me."

She looked up at me from under her brow.

"Listen, I love you, but if you really think that, you're a complete idiot."

I scowled at her. "Are you forgetting about the woman and kid at the pizza parlor?"

She shook her head, grabbing a piece of dried fruit from a bag on the table and popping it in her mouth. "You're making assumptions. You have no clue who they were."

"I've asked him about it twice now, and twice he's refused to explain. I'm pretty sure that means it's someone he doesn't want me to know."

Brynn frowned. "I don't think he's the type to have a kid and leave them high and dry. He seems overly cautious and responsible...like he's constantly looking out for people—including us. He wouldn't bareback it. I bet he has a Costco sized box of condoms."

I took another sip of the delicious coffee. Not too bitter, or sweet—perfect. "You know, the other day when he hurt my feelings, you offered to twist his balls off. Now you're defending him," I pointed out.

"Because he made you feel bad. But that doesn't mean he's a bad guy, it just means he made a mistake."

"So now you suddenly think you know him?"

"Better than I did when we met him in August."

I shook my head, lips tight. "No, you don't. That's the trick. He keeps everyone at arms-length and doesn't let anyone get close. No one knows Jackson West. Not me, you, or anyone else."

She paused and took a drink of her detox lemon water. She set the glass down slowly and said nothing for a while, like she was using the time to collect her thoughts. She rested her arms on the table, folded over each other, and looked at me. "I've watched you with him on a couple of occasions, Syd. I've seen how you've changed because of him, and I think he's been changing, too. Do you really think he'd be so protective of you if he didn't have feelings for you? He cares about you, and the things that are important to you— me included. Honestly, of everyone who has ever been in his life, I think you were getting the closest to knowing him."

I stared at her, dumbfounded. "That's ridiculous. I told you what happened on the fall drive, and then at Red's garage. He doesn't want *anyone* to know him. He won't open up enough."

"He wanted to get to know you. He was seeing if you'd be vulnerable first. I think he'd started to open up with you—"

I gave a derisive snort.

"—or at least, he was trying. When you've been one way for most of your life, it's difficult to immediately change—especially when it's something that's ingrained in your psyche, and has become such a big part of who you are as a person. You should understand that more than anyone. You're trying to change and become—" she paused, searching for the word, "more spontaneous. It hasn't been easy for you,

and it probably won't be easy in the near future. You have to understand how hard this is for him, Syd. You're asking for a lot more than some personal information. You're asking for the key to who he is. I get the feeling it's not a key he gives many people—if anyone."

I stared at her for a long time. Something was up…and I thought I might know what it was. "Is this you playing psychotherapist, or is this something he told you while he was hanging out on our front porch delivering coffee and apologies this morning?"

She smiled. "A little of both."

I quirked a brow. "Which parts did he actually say?"

"That he's careful about who he lets in, and you caught him off-guard. He knows he has to make changes if he wants you in his life—in whatever capacity that ends up being. But it's going to take some time, and you'll have to be understanding when he keeps things close to his chest."

I blew out a breath and took a long sip of my coffee, thinking. "It's not that easy, Brynn. He's impossible to relate to because he refuses to give me anything to connect with. Relationships require both people to open up. I get that he's trying to change, but it's really frustrating to spend time with him when everything is so one-sided."

"I know. And he knows, too. He's working on it. The question is whether you'll give him the time to figure it out. I hope you do."

I took another sip of my coffee, the smooth chocolate and java gliding over my happy taste buds. It was nice of Jax to think about me, and take the time to bring me a drink. "I'll think about it." I wanted to give him the benefit of the doubt and be the person he chose to talk to, but I wasn't sure how long I could wait. I hadn't been successful at getting him to let me in yet, so it seemed futile, and felt like a waste of time. But I did like being with him, and felt like there was a strong connection between us. Only time would tell whether anything would eventually develop from it. It felt wrong not to at least give it a chance, though, and see what would happen.

Brynn watched me puzzling it out and then smiled widely. "Admit it," she said, grabbing another piece of dried fruit. "You like him."

I smiled. "No, I won't admit it."

"That's all right," she said, breaking a piece of the fruit in half and taking a bite. "You don't have to, I already know."

I sighed, conceding. I wrinkled my nose, unhappy with what I was about to admit. "Like doesn't cover it. My ovaries tremble in his presence."

She laughed out loud. "Then you should hang out with him more often."

"I like him, Brynn. Maybe too much." I played with the coffee sleeve, dropping it down to the table and pushing it back up for several minutes before coming to a decision. "Here's the deal. I'll hang out

with him when I have time, and see what happens," I shrugged and looked down at my coffee, "but he's just another friend."

She shook her head, laughing softly to herself. "Did you see the way you looked down at your coffee when you said that? You couldn't meet my eyes because even you don't believe he's just a friend—and *friendship* is definitely not what you want."

I really hated having a best friend majoring in psych. Her body language class alone was going to kill me. I couldn't hide anything—not that I could keep anything from her anyway, but before the class, I could at least disguise my emotions better. I closed my eyes and leaned my head back against the chair. "It's hard. I feel something for him, but I don't have a lot of experience with this kind of thing, either. Are my feelings real, or is it my hormones? I don't know. It's not black and white, and I can't find the answers written down for me somewhere. He's not a book I need to study to get a grade. If he was, I'd probably be a lot better at this."

She smirked. "I bet he'd enjoy the studying part. You both would."

I glanced up at her. "It doesn't matter if I'd like it or not. If I let myself get involved with someone, it will screw with my head. Even Jax as my friend has screwed me up six ways to Sunday. Relationships are hard, regardless. They're even harder when the man you're interested in refuses to tell you his history. I need to focus on school. It's a lot easier to do that if I'm just his friend."

She leaned back and put her feet on the chair next to us before taking a deep breath and looking at me. "I'm going to say something that might not make you happy, but it's because I love you, so don't throw your coffee at me." I was officially intrigued. She continued, "It's easier, but while you're busy planning for your future, you're missing out on the present. You're going to look back at this time in your life, and wish you'd experienced more than straight A's."

That sounded a lot like what Jax had said, only less harsh—or maybe it seemed less harsh because it was coming from someone I knew loved me and had my best interests in mind. I knew Brynn was probably right, but I didn't know how to change. I was the type of person who decided to do something, and threw everything I had into it. I wasn't sure I was ready to throw that into Jax when I didn't know if I could trust him to give it back. Commitment and communication weren't his strong suits.

Brynn watched my thoughts play out and shook her head. "You want him, and it's obvious he wants you."

"Does he? Or does he just want the challenge? I'm afraid once he gets what he wants, he'll be done with me. If it happens, then I've lost a relationship, a good friend, and my grades will probably be shot to hell. It's a high risk to take."

"Everything worth having is risky, Syd. You just have to decide if you're willing to jump in." She got up from the table and grabbed her books. "Nothing is guaranteed. If I were you, I'd march over to his apartment, strip off my clothes, get some answers, and stop wasting time."

She grinned as she left me at the table, feeling more confused than ever.

Fourteen

Though tempting, I hadn't taken Brynn's advice. I was pretty sure having sex would make Jax even less likely to tell me how he really felt. Sex was one of the ways he deflected. It seemed wise to wait on the naughty bits until we'd at least had a slight progression in the emotional department. I knew I wanted more than friendship from him. The question was whether Jax and I could both handle it. It meant I'd have to let love take a pretty big space between all of my other goals, and Jax would have to learn to let me in.

I walked out of the house the next morning and almost tripped over a book-sized white box sitting on our doorstep, a red ribbon wrapped around it in a bow.

My name was on a tag glued to the box. I untied the bow and opened the box. A notecard sat on the top. I picked it up and saw a crap-ton of Swedish Fish underneath. I smiled, opening the card. It read: *I'm sorry...for a lot of reasons. I'll try to measure up. —Jax*

I smiled again, thinking that maybe this might work out after all. I wasn't sure what would happen as far as a romantic relationship went, but I'd missed Jax as my friend. I was willing to forgive him and move forward so I could get some questions answered. I was excited to see where things might go, and happy he'd be back in my life.

I put the box on the table and grabbed some Swedish Fish on the way out the door. They'd make a great snack between classes, and an even better breakfast. Better tasting...not healthier. I smiled every time I thought of the gift during the day, and a warm feeling rushed through me when I stopped for gas and saw Jax. He came out of the work bay and met me as my car filled up. "Using candy to apologize. Smart man."

He smiled shyly, putting his hands in his pockets and looking down, like he was worried about the conversation, and how I'd react. "You said Swedish Fish were the way to your heart."

I lifted a shoulder. "Most guys wouldn't have even listened, let alone remembered what I said. So thanks."

He gave me a sidelong glance, his gaze more intense than usual. "There's not much you say that I forget."

I inhaled a shallow breath. This was a different Jax than the one I'd always talked to before. He seemed more...*real*. "Good to know." I noticed dark circles around his eyes. He looked a little tired. "So...have you punched any strangers in parking lots since the other night?"

He smiled slightly. "No. And I want you to know I did apologize to Collin after you left, and made sure he was okay."

I was surprised to hear that. "That was nice of you since you probably dislocated his jaw."

"You're giving me too much credit."

I disagreed with that. I was sure the credit I gave him for a plethora of things was well deserved.

"I apologized to Collin, but I didn't apologize to you—in person, at least. I'm sorry for what happened. After the haunted mine shut down, I went to Ice with some of the other actors to celebrate the last night of scaring people. I noticed you in the club, and realized you were drunk. Then when I saw you at your car and reaching in your purse, I just lost it. I couldn't let you get hurt—or hurt someone else. Even the thought of it made me crazy." He paused and looked away, then turned back. "The bottom line is I should have given you a chance to explain yourself, and not flown off the handle. I'm sorry, Syd."

I stared at him, eyes wide and stunned. This was more emotional development than I'd gotten from him in months. He seemed genuinely remorseful for what

he'd done, and like he actually wanted to have a conversation instead of directing the topic to something else, or making a joke. "Thanks," I said, pleased he'd opened up a little bit. "I really appreciate you talking to me and saying you're sorry."

He rubbed a hand over his chin. "That's not the only thing I'm sorry for. I'm sorry I said those things to you about being alone and having your priorities in the wrong place. You were right. I don't open up to people. There's a reason for it, but I've spent a lot of time thinking about what I want from life, and I've realized I don't want to end up alone, Syd. If that means I need to learn to be vulnerable, I'm going to have to do that. And I'd like you to be the person I'm vulnerable with."

My mouth was on the ground. I couldn't have been more shocked if someone had just handed me ten million dollars.

"I...I don't know what to say." I stuttered out. "I mean, I'd like that, too—at least, I think I would. I don't know how it will work, and it will probably be difficult for both of us. You were right, too. I need to stop being so rigid. Between the two of us, we have a lot of baggage to deal with...but maybe we can deal with it together?"

He looked over at me, his lips widening in a smile, his eyes bright. "This isn't going to be easy, Syd, but I want to try. I need you to be understanding, though. I have feelings for you...feelings I never thought I'd have. You've single-handedly rearranged my outlook on relationships, and I'm terrified. I don't know where this is going, and I can't make you any promises, but I want to be with you. More than anything. And I'll do whatever it takes."

He reached over and took my hand. Sparks shot through me as my heart raced. He was saying all the things I dreamed about him saying. It was everything I wished he'd said in the past, and it was exactly what I needed to hear to commit to this…whatever it was. "You're the only one who matters to me, Syd. I couldn't do this without you."

That triggered a thought in my head. A question I needed answered before I could completely agree to a relationship with him. "Wait," I said, holding up a hand. "Who was the gorgeous woman and cute little girl at the pizza place? Because it looked like you cared about them a lot, and if you have a wife and family, this—" I said, motioning between us, "—really isn't going to work."

He laughed out loud. "So that's where the wife and love-child question came from."

"What are you talking about?"

"Before you went home from Ice, you were pissed because of my wife and love-child. I couldn't figure out what you were talking about."

I crossed my arms over my chest. "Yeah, well, now you know. Who the hell were they?"

He smiled slowly. "Two people I hope you'll meet.

I would have introduced you that day if you hadn't run out of the restaurant. She's heard a lot about you, and really wants to meet you."

Now I was getting annoyed, and it was quickly morphing into pissed. He must have read it on my face, because he answered, "She's my sister, Courtney. And that was her daughter, Paige."

Ooooooooohhh. His sister. I wanted to smack myself on the head. I'd jumped to conclusions just like Brynn had warned me not to do. I hated when she was right. "Well, that makes me feel better. She was so pretty and you looked so taken with her that I kind of wanted to punch you both."

He laughed again. "She'll be happy to hear you stopped yourself."

"Me, too, since that probably wouldn't have made us the best of friends. Does she live here?"

Jax shook his head. "She was just visiting."

"Does she come to see you often?"

"Sometimes." He paused again and toed some gravel on the ground. I felt like there was more to the story, but I didn't want to push. I was surprised when he went on without any provocation. "She needed to talk to me about some family stuff. I love her, and Paige is my favorite kid in the world, so it was really good to see them both."

His eyes lit up when he talked about his sister and niece. I knew this was a huge step for him, and I was glad he felt like he could talk to me about it. "Is Courtney married?"

His jaw set in a firm line and he looked like he'd stopped breathing completely. "No. She's not. And thank God for that."

"You don't like Paige's dad?"

"No. I don't. He'd be at the bottom of a lake if I had my way."

A potential murder seemed pretty serious and I waited for him to elaborate. He didn't. "Let's talk about something else." The angry lines on his forehead smoothed as he leaned back against my car, and blew out a breath. "How was your day?"

I could tell he still had a lot on his chest, but I felt relieved he'd decided to talk to me about it, even if he hadn't gone into a lot of detail. I wanted him to realize talking could help him work through things better than holding it all in. Hold too much, and you eventually explode. I understood he was still getting used to opening up about things, though, and felt like this was a lot of progress so I didn't mind the subject change.

"It started out pretty damn excellent when I found some Swedish Fish on my doorstep. One of my classes was canceled so I had time to do some research in the library, and then I got to hang out with you. So, I'd say it's been a win."

He laughed. "Only you would think having class cancelled so you'd have more time to study is a good thing. I bet most of the other students went home and took a nap."

"They're probably not getting the grades I am

either." I still had a few of the fish I'd stuffed in a sandwich bag on my way out of the house this morning. I grabbed one before offering the bag to him.

He grinned and took one, too.

I bit the head off as he watched me. "You like to kill them quickly."

"No point in prolonging their pain."

He nodded, purposefully biting the tail first.

"Torture isn't very nice," I said.

He smiled slowly, a glint in his eye. "I'd say it depends on the type of torture and who's doing it."

A flush crept up my cheeks, and my mind immediately went to bondage devices—I wasn't sure how I felt about that. "It was probably too much to think the sexual references would go away?"

"Yeah. You should lower that expectation."

"Noted."

I took the gas pump out of the car and put my gas cap back on before grabbing my receipt. As I turned and met Jax's eyes, there was something behind them I hadn't seen before, but recognized from men I'd seen with Brynn. It was a combination of desire and intrinsic need. I stilled, stunned Jackson West might feel something like that toward me.

"Come see a movie with me on Saturday."

I widened my eyes. Considering the way he was looking at me, a movie wasn't the thing I'd expected him to suggest. "A movie?"

"Yeah."

"Like—another date?"

He grinned conspiratorially. "That is what people in relationships do, right? Date?" He bit his lip, looking up at me knowingly. "I'll pick you up at six."

My stomach suddenly felt like butterflies were rioting. I was anxious, excited, and flat out terrified all at the same time. "Oookkaay."

"You seem a little nervous."

"Should I be?"

He grinned again, his cheeks dimpling. He was sexy on a whole different planet than I was used to. "Always." He tucked a piece of hair behind my ear and leaned into me, then kissed me lightly on the cheek. "I'll see you Saturday."

I watched him walk away, wondering what I'd gotten myself into. I knew this was more than just a little date. This was a massive step into the relationship zone. It was exactly what I wanted, now I just had to be sure I was ready for it.

Fifteen

The theater wasn't crowded. We had the top three rows to ourselves, but chose the back row in the corner where we could put our feet on the bannister in front of us. The pink, knee-length cotton skirt I was wearing made that a bit difficult, but we were shielded in the corner enough that I didn't think I'd flash anyone.

"I can't believe we're seeing a horror movie," I said. "It's so cliché."

"What do you mean?" Jax asked, reaching for the popcorn I was holding.

I looked over at him. "Horror movies were made for guys. They're scary, so the girl jumps or grabs your arm all through the movie. Pretending to be her valiant protector, you put your arm around her to keep her safe." I rolled my eyes. "It's the perfect opportunity to show how alpha you are by protecting us from fake monsters on a movie screen that can't really hurt us anyway. In real life, you guys probably wouldn't even protect us from a spider. But still, the protective aspects are appealing to both women, and men, in the situation. It's an illustration of how even if we think we've evolved as humans, primitive nature still has a level of control."

He smiled slowly. "I can see you've really thought that through. You should consider a dissertation deconstructing horror movies and their connection to the evolution of humans. I'm sure it would be a fascinating read."

I glared at him. "Say what you want, but I bet you take all your dates to scary movies for that *exact* reason."

"I'm not gonna lie," he lifted the armrest so there was no barrier between us, "it does keep them occupied, and me…entertained." His mouth slid up into a coy smile.

I lifted my head and gave him an I-told-you-so look. He grinned.

The trailers started; more horror movies. Probably meant to be just as scary and primitive as the movie we were about to see. I knew about their wizardry, though, and I would not be tricked.

At least, that's what I told myself for the first

twenty minutes until a giant horned demon with bright red eyes and fire breathing from his mouth jumped out from the darkness with the single-minded intention to take the soul of everyone on the screen and in the theater.

I jumped, grabbing for Jax instinctively—and totally against my will. When a demon is coming for you, any bicep will do, though his were extremely well-defined. The demon on the screen was terrifying, and getting closer. It was about to breathe a fire-filled death on its next victim. I felt hot air on my neck. I was the next victim!

I screamed.

Jax laughed.

I slugged him in the shoulder. He laughed some more.

Totally annoyed, I folded my arms across my chest and moved to the right—as far away as possible. He reached his arm behind my shoulder, pulling me back into him. A shiver ran through me—which upset me because I was positive the shiver had nothing to do with demons, and everything to do with Jax's arm around me, holding me, protecting me.

Another scary part had me grabbing Jax's leg because his bicep was currently occupied with my shoulder.

"Your hand makes an excellent tourniquet," he whispered after a few minutes.

I hadn't realized I was gripping him so tight. I released his leg immediately. "Sorry."

He reached over with his other hand and grabbed mine. "I didn't say I wanted you to move your hand. I like it there."

Halfway through the movie, he shifted, his leg falling down, opening wider. His whole body angled in toward me. Electricity pulsed between us and my heart was thumping out of my chest. His eyes latched to mine as he reached down and started pulling my hand…up.

I forgot to breathe as I watched my fingers drag over the inner seam of his jeans. I only remembered to gasp in air when I was almost ready to pass out. As my hand moved, I hazarded a glance at his face. His sapphire eyes were dark and fiery with need and anticipation.

And he kept moving my hand. Slowly.

When we reached the crease at the top of his thigh, he guided my fingers to the large mound at the left. Still holding my eyes, he started to stroke the mass, back and forth, up and down. Light at first, and then a little harder. I broke my glance away and watched him move my hand over him. I was so turned on watching him touch himself—teaching me how to touch him— that I almost forgot we were in the middle of a theater. I'd forgotten the movie, and demons, and other movie goers long ago. He spread my fingers out, splaying them over him. I could feel the mound getting bigger, harder, and wondered what he looked like out of his boxers. He let go of my hand. I kept rubbing. He held

my eyes as he moved his fingers. I felt the button on his pants come undone, then heard the zipper.

My heart raced as he took my hand and slipped it under the waistband of his boxers. Our fingers slid down, down, down, until I—we—hit something hard—and big. I gasped at the feel of him, thick, smooth, and huge. He wrapped my hand around him. And then, he started to stroke. Up and down, guiding me. My breasts were heavy and my core was burning. I'd never been this wet, or felt so wild. I wanted him to take me, right there in the middle of the theater. I didn't care. I needed to have sex with Jackson West, and I needed it to happen immediately!

It was that single thought that shook me out of my lust induced haze, and made me realize I was losing myself. I was stroking his dick where anyone could see. Would we get thrown out? Arrested for indecent exposure? What would this do to my potential law career? Would the girl in the movie get away, or would the demons win? My mind was racing and I couldn't stop it.

Abruptly, I pulled my hand away. I got up, whispering a hasty excuse that I needed to use the bathroom. I had to get out of there. I was burning up. I pushed through the bathroom doors into a stall and quickly locked the door. I leaned against the cold metal of the stall door, staring at the beige tiled bathroom wall, and tried to catch my breath. My breasts were swollen and I ached—everywhere. When I finally felt composed enough, I opened the stall and gasped.

Jax was leaning against the sink, palms on the counter, showcasing his bulging biceps. A piece of his tattoo peeked out from under his shirt. His bright blue eyes were sparkling with a wicked gleam. I attempted to move, but it didn't go well. I stumbled. He gave me a wolf-smile as he caught me. "Slippery, eh?"

Yeah. And that's not all that was wet.

I blew out a breath, immediately thinking of discarding our clothes. I spent the next full minute trying to get the thought of his hard abs and my naked breasts pressed against them out of my mind. "If we're both in here, neither one of us will know what's happening in the movie."

He tilted his head to the side. "I'm sure neither one of us cares."

I tried to take some of the edge off with a joke. "Did you make a wrong turn and not see the girl wearing a dress on the door?"

"The girl I want to see out of her dress is in here."

I sucked in a breath as he pushed me up against the wall. Every part of me wanted to be claimed by him, taken. His lips pressed into mine, the kiss as frustrated as I felt. His length was long and hard against my thigh, tempting me to unzip his pants again and pull him out. I wanted to see him in the light—all of him— and find out what I'd been missing. My hands raked down his hard abs, and stayed there as his tongue slipped over my lips and into my mouth, licking, caressing, tangling with my own.

Several of the buttons on my black shirt were now undone, my lacy black and white bra peeking out beneath my top. One hand ran over my breast, stroking the hard tips of my nipples through the lace, while the other pushed my skirt up, running light strokes over my thigh. I sighed and he broke away, moving down my body to take my nipple in his mouth. The combination of his tongue and teeth on the fabric scratched over me in a torturous way. My hands went to his jeans and I popped the button, slowly sliding the zipper down. My hand was poised over the waistband of his boxers when the door creaked open. I scrambled away from Jax like he had a disease. A teenage girl walked in the bathroom, surprise written on her face when she noticed Jax's presence.

Jax flashed her his winning smile, putting her at ease. He was excellent at that. I wished I had the same talent, or that his comforting smile would work on me at the moment. Noting her confusion, Jax said, "My date was sick. I came in in to check on her."

I glanced at him, suspicious. He sure had that excuse handy. I wondered how many times he'd used it before.

The girl gave me a once over, taking in my unbuttoned, disheveled clothes, smeared lipstick, and snarled hair. Then she did the same to Jax, stopping on his half untucked shirt, unbuttoned pants, and kiss swollen lips. She rolled her eyes. "Yeah, right," she said. "You know, they have stalls for that." Then she stepped into a stall of her own and locked the door.

Jax bit his lip and held back a laugh. I put my hand over my mouth to try to hold in mine. We both quickly rearranged our clothes and hair. Then Jax came over and took my hand. He held the door for me as we walked out of the bathroom together.

No longer interested in the movie, Jax and I started toward his truck. On the way, I realized that had just been mine and Jax's first *real* kiss. "Thanks for making out with me in the light this time," I said, my tone teasing.

His lips slid into a slow smile. "I thought about killing your date that night, but decided I'd much rather kiss you."

I lifted a brow. "It was an incredible kiss. You should have claimed it. Drew got credit as the ninja kisser for a while."

Jax snorted. "He wouldn't have been able to find the broad side of barn in that dark hallway, let alone your mouth." He wrapped his arm around my waist and leaned in to whisper in my ear. "And Syd, if we hadn't been interrupted in the bathroom just now, I would have found a lot more than your lips."

A thrill ran through me as I thought about what Jax had been doing, and what he had planned for the rest of the night. Being with him let me lose myself…even if only temporarily. And I couldn't wait to do it again.

Sixteen

"So, how did things go with Jax last night?" Brynn asked as she grabbed her detox lemon water from the fridge. "What did you do?"

I shrugged, a smile playing at the corner of my lips. Brynn hadn't come home until I'd been on my way out the door that morning. We'd made plans to catch up later in the day. I'd attempted to study, but had a really hard time concentrating when all I could think about was my hand in Jax's pants. So, I'd sat on the couch and spent some quality time with the HGTV channel until Brynn got home instead.

Brynn watched me for a few minutes, then her eyes went wild as she bounced on the couch. "Shut up!

What did you do? And I hope the answer is Blue Eyes!"
Again, the combination of her psych classes and being
my best friend was making it impossible for me to keep
secrets.

"We went to a movie."

"And?"

"And it was scary."

"*And?*"

"And I jumped and grabbed his arm and leg."

Her voice was getting higher now, her impatience
showing. "AND?"

"And I kind of gave him a hand job in the
theater."

She shoved me into the throw pillows. "Shut.
Up!" She was breathing so fast I thought she might
hyperventilate. "Oh. My. Shit!!! I'm so excited for you!
You hit third base with Jax! How does it feel? Wait!"
she said, moving to the edge of the couch and waving
her hands. "More importantly: how did *he* feel…you
know, for my research."

I giggled at the excuse. "Pretty amazing," I
admitted.

"What did it look like?"

I shook my head. "Not sure. It was really dark in
the theater and I couldn't see it. But he felt pretty damn
big in my hand." I'd thought Jax was just being
arrogant when he made all the comments about being
better than a werewolf, but now, I wasn't so sure.

She blew out a breath. "I bet! He looks like he'd

have a lot going on down there since he *is* a mountain man with a big ass ax."

I snickered and rolled my eyes. She'd never let the mountain man thing go. "It was a little scary, actually. I know I've only been with a couple of guys, but none of them were *that* big. I nicknamed it *the Beast*." Because it seemed about as big as a werewolf's. "I'm a little scared for actual sex."

She grinned, and took a sip of lemon water. "You just need a guy who knows how to get you there. I have a feeling Jax won't have any problems in that department."

I frowned, thinking of all the experience he surely had. "Thanks for reminding me."

She shook her head. "No, you should be happy about that. Seriously. You want a man who knows what he's doing."

I didn't want to think about his past experience at all, regardless of whether it would make sex better for me. "I'll try to remember that when I'm a raging ball of jealousy."

She waved me off like it wasn't a big deal. And to her, it wasn't. I was positive she'd slept with more people than Jax. "Tell me more! I want details!"

I gave her a step-by-step summary, cataloging everything from my hand sliding into his pants, to me running away to the bathroom, Jax finding me, and both of us getting caught—in various states of undress—making out, by a teenager. Brynn thought that part was very funny.

"What happened after you left the theater?"

"We were both pretty worked up. He brought me back to the house and we kissed a lot more in his truck. My shirt got unbuttoned again before we broke apart and I said I needed to go."

She slapped me across the leg. "Why didn't you invite him in?"

I shook my head and breathed out a sigh. "I need to take this in steps, Brynn. I haven't been with a guy for a *long* time. I need to get back in the headspace that says it's okay to be in a relationship with someone again without it distracting from my goals. And I need Jax to be in a place where he's willing to be vulnerable and intimate with me, not just have a booty call buddy. This all started because he said he wanted to try to make a relationship work, and he somehow got me to agree to it. Having sex too soon could screw that up. Foreplay is good for building that intimacy before we go all the way."

Brynn leaned back against the arm of the couch. "Okay, I see your points, but part of me thinks you were just freaked out because losing yourself in a moment—and a man—is something you haven't let yourself experience before. You won't freak out next time, and when it comes to the actual main event with Jax, I think you'll be kicking yourself for waiting so long."

I thought about what she'd said. I was freaked out, but I knew this—Jax—was what I wanted. We both

just needed to be patient with each other while we worked through our personal demons. "I hope so. It was scary losing control like that. It felt like my whole world was revolving around him, and the potential to have him inside me. For that brief moment, I was lost. I would have done anything to have him. I didn't care about the consequences, or about anything else. I was want, need, and nothing more. It scared me. It's never been like that before. With other guys, sex was the next logical step. It wasn't...*this.*"

She nodded, smiling like she was remembering some happy moments of her own. "It's like being drunk, but without the hangover."

I frowned. "The aftereffects might be even worse."

"You're just scared. Stop talking yourself out of this before it's even happened. Blue Eyes is going to be an *excellent* sex partner."

"I'm sure he is, but I'm not worried about the sex. I'm worried about what comes after. I'm afraid I'll get even more emotionally invested because of it, and he won't."

She reached over and put a hand on my thigh in a comforting way. "I don't think you have to worry about that. I'm pretty sure he was invested long before you."

I spent a lot of time the next week thinking about Jax and what had happened between us. Part of me felt like things were progressing too fast. We were moving forward, but the physical aspect of our relationship was moving a lot faster than the emotional one. I considered telling him we needed to stop everything, but I knew that was a cop-out. Brynn was right. I was scared. Scared to let go, scared to trust someone else to be my partner, scared of the distraction of a relationship—and, to be honest, I was nervous about my lack of sexual experience compared to Jax's. But sex was how Jax communicated, so meeting him halfway wasn't necessarily a bad thing. Slowing down might not be a bad idea either, though. And that's what I'd decided to tell him. Then he'd called me and asked if we could hang out tonight.

I had an idea of what his version of "hang out" meant, and it wasn't going to happen, at least, not yet. Foreplay. We were going with foreplay from now on— for a while, at least.

When I heard him knock, my breath immediately quickened. I took one last look at myself in the mirror, checking my warm, blonde hair, neutral makeup, and rosy cheeks and lips. I took a deep breath, willing myself to calm down and not look like a girl who suddenly felt like a virgin. I was even more nervous now than I had been when Jax and I first started spending time together. Maybe because we'd done something intimate—that countless other girls had

also done with him. I groaned. That reminder helped my nerves quite a bit, and I opened the door.

So much for my commitment to foreplay.

He was wearing a black leather jacket over a red and black striped shirt. His jeans hung off his hips, tight around his thighs. He looked mouthwatering. His gaze went over me like a physical touch, holding on my hips, and then my chest, before coming to rest on my face. His eyes were dark with unspoken promises.

I couldn't hide my desire, and a knowing look flashed in his eyes. "Hey, sweetheart. Hungry?"

Hungry? That didn't even cover what I was for this man. Obsessed, rapturous, lustful. I mean, hungry fit in there somewhere, too, but what I felt required so much more than one word. And a lot of actions. Actions I'd like to try right now, and might end up initiating on the porch if he didn't get in the house soon. I bit my bottom lip, pulling it back with my teeth. "You could call it that."

He grinned. "Good." He pushed past me into the house. It wasn't until that moment I noticed he was holding bags. "Because I have dinner."

"Dinner?" I asked, totally dumbfounded as I followed him into the kitchen. "Like, food?" I'd really thought he was about to be my main course and dessert.

He put the bags on the counter. "Food is usually required for dinner." He shrugged out of his coat, hanging it over the back of one of the kitchen table chairs, and then started taking things out of the grocery bags. "We're having pasta and chicken. I hope that's okay."

"Are you kidding? I've been cramming for tests and living off of crackers and candy for the last few days. Anything that doesn't involve energy drinks sounds good to me."

His lips lifted as he preheated the oven, and then started preparing the food. "Good."

"Can I help with anything?"

"Yeah." He handed me a bowl. "Can you make the breading mix for the chicken?"

I stood next to him at the counter. "What do I need to do?"

He put water on the stove to boil for the pasta. "Crack the eggs in the bowl, then lightly spank them."

I burst out laughing. "There's no way your recipe says to 'spank' the eggs."

"Lightly spank. Lightly beat. Same thing."

I raised an eyebrow. "You have a thing for spanking?"

He bit his bottom lip and cocked a brow. "Wouldn't you like to find out?"

The trouble was, I really did want to. I knew, without a doubt, that sex with Jackson West would be mind-blowing. And I got the feeling he had an adventurous streak when it came to carnal activities. That made me excited—in more ways than one. I'd never had a partner like that before.

I eyed him over the mixing bowl. "Are you going to turn all of the instructions into innuendo?"

He grinned. "I might. I have a gift."

I laughed as I beat the eggs and added milk. "You didn't tell me you were going to bring dinner. And I definitely didn't know you were a chef."

"I'm a mystery," he said, pouring the pasta into the pot. He grabbed a glass pan for the chicken.

"Yeah, I thought we were going to fix that."

He didn't say anything as he dipped the chicken in the egg mixture and then coated it all in bread crumbs. When he was done, he put it in the oven and set the timer. He checked the pasta, and then leaned against the countertop, his palms pressing into it, making his biceps bulge.

"What do you want to know?"

I was pretty captivated by his arms—and body in general—so it took me a minute to remember what I'd been asked. "Oh, umm…where did you grow up?"

"A small town in Arizona. There wasn't much to do there. I left as soon as I could."

"Where did you go?"

"California.""For work?" I could easily see him booking a job as a model. And he'd acted in the haunted house…maybe he'd tried to get a job in Hollywood.

He took a sauce pan off our pan rack, and started mixing the red pasta sauce on the stove. "No. For school. I studied mechanical engineering."

My eyes went wide. With a mechanical engineering degree, he should be doing a job that was far more complicated than fixing blown tires and radiator hoses. "Then how did you end up in Winchester?"

"I like to move around. A job I enjoy and life experiences are what matter to me."

Oh. My stomach felt like it dropped to the floor, and I tried not to let the disappointment show on my face. So even though he was here and we were in a relationship for now, he probably wouldn't be staying long. Maybe that was for the best, though. I could move forward in the relationship with the knowledge that it wasn't long term. It might help me become less attached.

He drained the pasta and poured the sauce over the top. He sprinkled bread crumbs and cheese on top of it, then put the pan in the oven with the chicken. "This is almost done. Do you want to grab some plates and wine glasses?"

I opened the cabinet and put everything on the kitchen table. I went back to grab napkins and heard the front door open. "Damn! That's a hot truck in our driveway. I'm almost not pissed that it's taking my spot and I had to park on the street." Brynn sauntered into the kitchen leaning against the counter and smiling playfully. "Hey there, Blue Eyes."

Jax raised a brow at the nickname. I was surprised she hadn't used it in front of him before.

I rolled my eyes. "Jax, you remember Brynn— from all of the times you've rescued us. Brynn, Jax."

She slowly shook her head. "Nope. He'll be Blue Eyes forever." She inhaled deeply, noticing the

heavenly smell coming from the oven. "Oh. My. Shit!" Her mouth fell open. "Blue Eyes can cook, too? Jesus, Syd! Marry him!"

Color rose in my cheeks. She didn't seem to care. "Actually, better let me taste it first. Then we can decide if you should make a run down to the courthouse tomorrow."

Jax grinned and pulled the food out of the oven. He opened a bag of fresh rolls, and put it next to a salad on the counter.

I shook my head at Brynn. "You're ridiculous."

"I thought you had higher standards than just a man who can cook," Jax said to Brynn. "I remember the conversation from Soup and Spoon. There seemed to be a size requirement."

She grabbed a cherry tomato from the salad bowl and took a bite. "Yeah. Well, I'm pretty sure you've got that covered."

"Brynn!" I yelled, completely humiliated.

Jax's lips lifted in an unapologetic smile. "Yeah. I do."

"But you're dating my best friend. So, it doesn't matter to me. I am, however, looking out for her, and have decided you're one in a million," she turned to me mouthing the word 'million' again, "And she needs to get on you immediately."

Jax slid me an inviting glance. "I couldn't agree more."

I rolled my eyes at Brynn. "I might regret this, but do you want to eat with us?"

She grabbed another tomato, popped it in her mouth, and answered around it. "Can't. I have a date."

"Someone new?"

"Yep. Nothing better than combining research and pleasure."

I pushed my brows together, concerned. "Where did you meet him?"

"In class. We've done some projects together. He's nice." She glanced at the clock. "I better go change or I'll be late." She leaned down and gave me a hug. "Have fun. And definitely do something I wouldn't do…if you can think of anything."

I shook my head. She had no filter.

"Good luck," Jax said. "I hope he's everything you're looking for—you know, for the sake of research."

She flashed a devious smile. "Me, too," she said, skipping out of the room.

Jax and I sat down. "She's a little hyper," I said, spooning food onto my plate.

"I like her."

"Most men do," I answered as I cut my piece of chicken.

"Well, I like her personality."

I frowned, thinking that Brynn was not someone I could compete with when it came to men. If Jax wanted her, or someone like her, I'd never be able to keep his attention. "And she likes pretty much *everything* about you."

"Syd." His voice was deep and soft. I looked up at the change in his tone. His gaze locked with mine, his attention totally focused on me. Like he'd read my mind and knew my insecurities. "There's only one woman I'm interested in having a relationship with. And she's sitting across from me."

A warm feeling spread through me, and I grinned like a kid on Christmas. I couldn't help myself. "Good answer." I took a bite. "The food is fabulous! Where did you learn to cook like this?"

He shrugged. "I've been on my own for a long time. I knew I'd have to learn to cook if I didn't want to eat stuff from the frozen or canned food aisles for the rest of my life. So I took some cooking classes."

We continued eating as we talked. "How long is a long time? I don't even know how old you are."

"Twenty-seven. And you're what, twenty-two, twenty-three?"

"Twenty-three."

"What do you plan to do after law school?"

"Become a successful lawyer. I'd like to do pro bono work for non-profits on the side, though."

He took a drink of his wine. "You have a big heart."

I shrugged, not liking attention being drawn to me. "I just try to help where I can."

The food was amazing, but I didn't know what Jax's plans for the rest of the night were. If they included me naked, I didn't want to look like I was growing a food baby. So, I sat back and sipped the rest of my wine. "You've met my friends," I said, "so when do I get to meet yours?" I remembered him telling me he didn't have many friends, but there had to be *someone*.

He pushed his plate away and relaxed back in his chair, rubbing a hand over his stomach. I wasn't sure where he was putting all the pasta because it wasn't showing up on his body. I'd kill for his ability to eat carbs. "I don't have a lot of friends. Well, that's not really true. I have a lot of *surface* friends," he said, emphasizing surface. I doubted he'd ever let the surface/deeper conversation we'd had go. "I'll admit," he said, "it's been really nice having you in my life. You're the first person in a long time that I've wanted to get to know."

I looked at him, eyes wide. I wasn't expecting that confession. "Thanks, Jax," I said sincerely. "That means a lot."

The room fell into silence for a few minutes and Jax seemed to be thinking. I got up and grabbed our plates, and took them to the sink before bending down to load them in the dishwasher. As I stood, I felt his presence behind me. His arm wrapped around my waist and I leaned my head against his strong shoulder, my hand resting on his. I'd anticipated that he'd try to make a move and finish what had been interrupted at the theater. Instead, he just held me. Tight. Like he needed the touch and the connection, but not in a

sexual way. He leaned down and kissed my cheek, his lips soft against my skin. "You're unraveling me, Syd—" he paused. "—and I like it."

Seventeen

"So, I hear you're dating Jax," Red said, as I pushed open the door to his shop the next day. She-Ra was due for an oil change.

Jax was such a private person, I was surprised he'd told Red. "Yeah. Having a free mechanic on call was too much temptation to resist."

Red laughed and grabbed some papers out of the printer. "He's a good guy, Syd. I'm happy for you. You'll both be good for each other."

"I think so, too." I smiled, and put my keys on the counter. "I'll be back in a while."

Red's eyes went wide. "You're leaving She-Ra here?"

"Yeah. I'm meeting Brynn for coffee."

He nodded his head, as he leafed through the papers. "See, that's how I *really* know you care about Jax. You're leaving your car and not supervising."

I laughed. "Jax knows he'll be in serious trouble if he screws something up."

"He should be terrified," Red said. "We'll have it done in about an hour."

I glanced over through the window on the door, my eyes searching the garage. I found him leaning over a large metal tool box. He looked great from every angle, but especially this one. I couldn't get enough of his shoulders, back, and ass. I sighed as he crouched down, muscles bunching in his legs. Red chuckled and I looked over at him. He shook his head. "You should go see him…before you hyperventilate watching him and pass out."

I fought a grin as I gave Red a playful glare and pushed through the door. I flashed Jax a huge smile as he turned around.

"Hey," Jax said, his voice husky. He looked me up and down, taking in my dark wash jeans, white sweater, and light blue scarf. "You look hot. I missed you."

I smiled as I melted into his arms. I liked this new, open Jax. A lot. I felt like he was trying really hard to communicate with me, regardless of how hard it was for him. That made me care for him even more. "I missed you, too."

"Are you going to wait here while I work on your engine?"

I smiled slowly, my eyes raking over him. His gaze

darkened to a deep sapphire, the desire between us palpable. "I like the sound of that," I said, licking my lips "but I'm meeting Brynn for coffee across the street. I'll bring you something back."

He picked up a wrench from the tool box. "So that's what I've been missing out on by not having relationships. Coffee runs."

I smacked him on the ass. "Just for that, I'm not getting you the whip cream."

"That's okay," he said, bending over the hood of the car he was working on and giving me a sidelong glance, "I have some at home for us later."

I blushed as I walked back through the door, avoiding Red's knowing gaze.

I walked across the street to my favorite café. Brynn was waiting for me in our spot. She already had her drink—something low fat, with fake sugar for sure. Brynn had calorie issues. I picked up a chocolate chip cookie, then ordered my coffee—with full fat, real sugar, and chocolate—and met her back in the corner where she was sitting in the comfy overstuffed leather chairs. I was eager to hear how her date went.

"Hey!" I sank into the empty chair next to her. "How was last night's research?"

"Disappointing," she said with a frown. "He had the right equipment, but he was a piss-poor operator."

I unwrapped my cookie and took a bite. "Maybe your standards are just too high?"

She wrinkled her nose. "Or maybe I'm dating the wrong guys." Her eyes lit up and she gave me a

conspiratorial smile. "Speaking of men perfect in every way—or at least the important ones—how was dinner last night?"

I grinned, replaying the night in my head. After he'd told me he liked that I was unraveling him, we'd moved to the couch and lost some essential pieces of clothing. I'd also found out that Jax is partial to lacy, slightly see-through bras—I figured most men probably were. "Fantastic." I took a sip of coffee and winced, burning my tongue. "He's an excellent cook. Apparently, he took lessons."

She cocked a brow. "I'm sure he's excellent at a lot of things. How was dessert?" She brought her cup to her lips, hiding a smile.

I grinned, and took another bite of cookie before answering just to torture her. "Even better than dinner."

Her other brow shot up. "Did it involve chocolate sauce?"

"No, but there were a lot of wandering hands."

She narrowed her eyes. "Hands? *Only* hands? *Nothing* else wandered?"

I shook my head.

"Jesus," she breathed out, totally offended. "You're killing me, Syd! Killing me!"

I rolled my eyes. "I told you, we're taking it slow."

She cursed again. "Slow is an understatement. You're moving at snail speed! Have you *seen* the man you're dating? You could wash clothes on his abs! He cooks! And he has a gigantic c—"

"Syd?" I looked up at the deep voice that had interrupted Brynn's list of Jax's attributes. It was Cade, my friend from school.

"Hey, Cade!" I gestured between my two friends. "Cade, this is my best friend, Brynn. Brynn, this is Cade from my criminal law and torts classes."

"Hi," Brynn said, dragging out the "i." Her eyes traveled over his face, to his broad shoulders, large chest, and held around his waist.

"Nice to meet you," Cade answered back. Brynn tore her eyes away from his musculature and traveled up. Their gazes met—and held. I stared at them both for a minute, unable to ignore the vibe. I knew Brynn, and I could tell she was attracted to Cade. I didn't know Cade as well, but judging by his inability to look away, he seemed pretty interested in Brynn, too.

"Are we still studying in the library after class tomorrow, Cade?" I asked, trying to break the silence and remind them I was still there.

Brynn acted like she was coming out of a fog as she turned her attention back to me.

"Yeah," Cade answered. He seemed reluctant to turn away and focus on me, but he finally did. "That sounds good." He noticed my cookie sitting on the side table between my chair and Brynn's. "They have the best cookies in town."

"Yeah, and coffee. It's our favorite place," I said, nodding toward Brynn.

His gaze settled on Brynn again, and he seemed

completely ensorcelled. "It was nice to meet you, Brynn. I hope I'll see you both again soon."

"You'll definitely see me this week," I said, reminding him of the study date I'd just reminded him about thirty seconds before. "The exams before Thanksgiving break seem like they'll be brutal."

"We'll study hard and do fine." Music started playing and Cade reached a hand into his back pocket, pulling out his phone. He checked the screen, and then glanced up. "I have to go, but have a good day, ladies." He walked toward the counter to wait in line.

Brynn leaned over, her voice whisper low, expression serious. "Who. The. Hell. Was. That? And why have you been keeping him a secret?"

"I wasn't!" I said, my voice defensive. I'd stopped trying to set Brynn up years ago. "He was in my law school prep class, and now he's in a couple of my other classes. We sit by each other a lot and study together. He's really nice."

"I don't care how he acts, have you seen how he looks?"

My gaze traveled to where Cade was waiting for his order. I looked at him through Brynn's eyes. Wheat colored hair, strong upper body and a nice ass—not as nice as Jax's, but really, even Michelangelo's *David* couldn't compete with that perfection. I could definitely appreciate Brynn's perspective. "He's attractive. He's not dating anyone that I know of. And he *is* nice. Maybe the problem you've been having lately is that you're just going after appearance instead of heart." She bit the corner of her lip. "You should ask him out."

"Hmm," she said, sitting back with a thoughtful expression. "Maybe."

I shrugged. "I think you'd hit it off."

Cade walked by with his coffee and waved as he went out the door. Brynn and I both waved back. She tapped the side of her coffee cup with her forefinger and I could see the wheels turning in her head. "I'll think about it."

Brynn and I talked for another hour or so and then I left to go pick up She-Ra.

"Jax washed her and parked her in the back lot," Red said as I walked in the door.

"Thanks! You're the best, Red."

His eyes brightened as he smiled. "I know."

I paid for the service and went out into the bay to find Jax. "Hey," I said, grinning as I walked up to him and handed him the coffee I'd promised. He took a sip. "Mmmm, that tastes good. Like you."

I blushed, thinking of the parts of me he had tasted—and the parts he hadn't, yet. "You're going to give me an ego," I said with a smile.

"You deserve it," he answered back.

I smiled wider, liking this whole relationship thing, and that Jax felt comfortable with me. "Red said you have my keys."

"I do." He took them from his pocket and dangled them in front of me.

"Can I have them?"

He dragged his bottom lip back with his teeth. "I'm holding them hostage."

I quirked a brow. "In exchange for what?"

"Your obedience in all things."

I burst out laughing. "Oh honey, you've really got the wrong girl if that's what you're looking for."

He ran his tongue over the inside of his cheek like he was amused and assessing me at that same time. "We'll see about that."

I could feel the color rising in my cheeks and marveled that he could still make me embarrassed considering all the foreplay we'd done.

"Tell you what. I'm about to go on break, so I'll give you your keys if you go to lunch with me."

That was all he wanted? I was hoping for something more scandalous than a sandwich. "Done."

We stopped by a local deli. I ordered a veggie sandwich with chips and grabbed a bottle of iced green tea. He ordered something with a lot of meat. I looked at his food as we sat down. "You're either trying to have a heart attack, or get color cancer."

He laughed, and took a sip of his soda. "I'd rather live a short life I enjoyed than a long one eating lettuce."

"Well, I know where you stand. You might want to get life insurance while you still can. In a few years, they won't issue you a policy." A serious look crossed over his face, but it was gone as fast as it was there.

We moved to a booth near a window that overlooked a creek, the trees above it bare of leaves. The water was still moving despite the cold air. It hadn't started snowing yet, but I knew the frigid temperatures were just around the corner.

Jax sat next to me in the booth. I loved that he sat beside me instead of across from me. It made me feel protected, and like he wanted to be close to me. I was glad, because I really wanted to be close to him.

We ate our food and talked until Jax's break was almost over. "Are you ready to go?" I asked, worried he'd be late getting back. I didn't want to get him in trouble with Red, though Red wasn't the type to get upset easily and would probably let it slide.

"Almost." He grabbed his coat. "I have something for you first." He pulled a bright blue box out of his pocket…and I almost hyperventilated. It took me a good thirty seconds to realize it wasn't Tiffany blue. I'd just agreed to a relationship, anything more than that right now would probably make me apoplectic. He handed the box over to me.

"A gift?" I didn't realize we were at the gift giving stage. I also worried that in the midst of my focus on school, I'd missed some sort of relationship milestone and was about to look like a total ass for not getting him anything. "Did I miss an anniversary?"

His lips tilted up. "Nope. I just wanted to give this to you."

I took the box from him, gently pulling the lid off the top. I opened it and parted the tissue paper inside. My mouth fell open when I saw it. It wasn't something I'd usually wear, but I loved it. "You got me a bracelet!" I said, staring at the dark material and beads. The material looked like hemp, but it was multicolored, alternating between black, dark blue, and lighter blue. It had three beads. A large, black oval bead was in the center, surrounded by a smaller black bead on the right side and the left. As I tilted it in the light, I caught a glimmer of color, but I couldn't make out what color it was exactly—it kept changing. From blue, to purple, to a hint of pink. The beads, and the craftsmanship of the hemp, were absolutely stunning. Jax's voice pulled me from my bracelet admiration.

"I made it for you."

My gaze flashed to him, his eyes soft and his expression a little vulnerable. He'd stunned me wordless. If there was anything I thought Jackson West might do as a hobby, bracelet making would have been dead last on that list—right next to dressing in drag. When I was finally able to form words, I said, "You make bracelets?"

He shrugged. "It helps me focus and relax."

I wanted to know where this particular hobby had developed. "When did you start making jewelry?"

He didn't answer for a long time; instead, he took

my wrist, and tied the bracelet on with a complicated knot. His thumb gently rubbed back and forth on my pulse point. "About eight years ago." His eyes met mine. "You can't ever take this off. It has to break and fall off instead." He leaned over, his breath warm on my neck. "That means my mark could be on your wrist for years."

My whole body tingled. "Is that some sort of bracelet making rule?"

His lips slid into a soft smile. "No. It's just bad luck if you do, and all of your hair will probably fall out." He leaned back lazily, resting his arm around my shoulder. "But go ahead and risk it if you want."

I frowned, not liking that threat—fake or not—at all.

I looked down at the beads on my wrist. The colors were beautiful, and I couldn't believe he'd actually made something for me. My attempt at learning to knit had almost cost my mom an eye, so I understood the time it took to learn a skill like that, and learn it well. Jax had, and I was honored he was willing to share his talent with me. "It's beautiful, Jax. Really. I couldn't love it more." I reached across his lap and grabbed his free hand. "Thank you!"

His lips formed a wide, relaxed smile, and he exhaled a breath. I could tell he was happy I was pleased with the gift. "The colors reminded me of She-Ra."

I laughed, examining it again. "I can definitely see that."

I looked over, noticing his bracelet as well. The dark matte beads were strung together, side by side, and held with some sort of plastic. I'd always wondered about it, but I'd never mentioned it. I tilted my head toward his wrist. "Did you make your bracelet, too?"

"I did."

I looked at it a little more. It was masculine, and sexy. The matte color reminded me of something Batman would drive. "I like it."

"Me, too." He kicked a leg out, stretching. The movement, combined with his arm around me, made his shirt ride up, showing off his incredibly cut abs. I was so distracted, I almost didn't hear his next sentence. "If you're good, maybe someday I'll tell you what your beads mean."

Wait. What? "The beads mean something?" Like, he'd taken special care to pick out the right ones? Now I was fiercely curious about them.

"They do."

I looked down at the beads again, like I might be able to divine their meaning with my stare. Unfortunately, the beads weren't in the mood to chat. "When will you tell me?"

He looked at me and grinned. "When you go out of town with me during your Thanksgiving break."

My jaw dropped. I might have stopped breathing. I'd told him I was staying in Winchester during Thanksgiving break this year. I was going to order pizza and celebrate the holiday by watching movies,

House Hunters, and eating junk food. I'd planned to invite Jax, and thought he might be able to help me burn off the junk food. "Seriously? An out of town trip? That's…serious." I immediately thought of all the things that could happen on a trip like that. Alone. In a romantic location with just the two of us and probably a lot of alcohol, soft bed, flower petals, and bubble baths. I swallowed. Hard.

His expression was a combination of seduction and mischievousness. "Are you up for it?"

I looked over at him and glared at the challenge. "I think that's a better question for you, Mr. Werewolf."

He licked his lips. "Oh, that won't be a problem." He smiled slowly. "Will you come with me?"

I held his eyes. "Repeatedly."

He threw his head back and laughed. "Good, it's settled then." He stood and we walked back out to his truck.

"So, where are we going?" I asked, thinking about the romantic bed and breakfasts in Colorado that he'd surely researched and reserved for us. I hoped he hadn't booked the Stanley Hotel. Everyone seemed to love the place because of Stephen King, but it just creeped me out.

What he said next made me stop in my tracks and almost fall over. "We're going camping."

Eighteen

"C-c-camping?" I stuttered out.

"Yeah." He must have noticed my look of utter horror, and inability to stand upright. "Don't give me that look. It will be fun, I promise."

Jax and I had seriously different definitions of the word "fun." I suddenly had an idea and turned to him, my eyes glimmering with hope. "Like camping in cabins? Is that what you mean?"

He gave me a funny look. "No."

My bottom lip went to the side in a worried frown. "So an RV?" I'd camped in RVs before. They weren't ideal, but they had running water, and toilets that didn't make you feel like one wrong move would make you fall into a horrible, smelly, bacteria infested abyss. Yes,

I thought, nodding my head inwardly, I could handle an RV with minimal trauma.

He grinned. "Nope."

Dear goddesses. I closed my eyes. "Please tell me there will be showers and flushing toilets."

"There are toilets, but not flushing." My breath staggered. "And no showers, but the lake we'll be camping next to is nice, and we can hike to some hot springs."

That sounded…unhygienic.

Jax laughed again at my distress. "We're going to pitch a tent—in more ways than one—and spend the weekend together."

I'd just remembered something very important and smiled, thinking it was definitely my way into a hotel. "Can't pitch a tent in winter. Soooo, I'll start looking up hotels? Do you want one with a pool? Because I *really* like heated pools. And jacuzzis. "

He looked at me sideways and grinned. "Actually, you can put a tent up. People camp during winter all the time."

"They do? Why?" I asked, genuinely baffled. "Are they all asylum escapees?"

"No," he said, blue eyes bright and teasing. "They just enjoy being outside."

They were bat-shit crazy is what they were. But since Jax seemed like he might be one of them, I refrained from saying so out loud. "So we're camping in the cold? The lake won't matter! It will be freezing!"

He chuckled. "You know, I think this proves what a nice guy I am. A jerk would let you go ahead and think we were spending the holiday camping in the tundra. But, since I'm not a jerk—and because I want you to pack a bikini—I'll tell you the truth."

"Thanks," I muttered, not happy about the direction of the conversation, or our potential trip straight to hell.

"We're camping in Arizona. Nice and warm. Nothing to worry about."

Six hours in a car with Jax should have been wonderful. And it would have been, if I didn't feel like we were about to spend the next four days smelly, uncomfortable, and as possible food for wild animals. We'd left right after my classes finished. I'd spent most of the drive studying—since my professors were sadists who didn't believe the law took holidays. We'd arrived in time to see the sun set. I had to admit, the amethyst, fuchsia, orange and crimson hues over the Arizona sky were breathtaking. They would have been even better if we'd walked into a nicely equipped hotel room and gotten busy on an actual bed after the romantic scene. Instead, we were setting up camp.

"Here." I said, handing Jax some papers as he pulled stuff out of the truck. I'd printed the information out before we left just in case my phone didn't have service and I couldn't access them in my cloud. Good thing, because I didn't have service and my only way to connect with someone was to yell across the canyon.

He glanced at them as he took the papers from me. "What are these?"

"Research. Dangerous plants and animals we might encounter in the park."

A laugh started deep in his chest. And didn't stop. I punched him in the shoulder. "Hey! It's not funny! Some of these things can kill us. We need to be aware."

He shook his head and handed me the sleeping bags. "Sweetheart, I've been camping in this area for years. I know about the potential dangers."

I pressed my lips together. "How fantastic for you. But I don't. So I need to be prepared. I'm glad one of us thinks things through." I took the sleeping bags to the tent. I'd offered to help him set it up, but after I broke two tent pegs, he said he could take care of tent preparation on his own. That offered me a valuable lesson about how if I didn't want to do something, I just had to do it poorly.

"You'll at least be a little safer from bears. Winter and all. They're hibernating."

I shook my head. "Not yet they aren't. I checked. They're filling up to prepare for hibernation. Which means they're hungry. And we're probably the perfect size."

He gave me a sidelong glance as he took more stuff out of the truck. "You're being a little dramatic."

"Oh, you'll see drama when a bear comes into camp. You just wait. And I'll also say I told you so as I'm running away—faster than you." I stopped thinking about bears, scorpions, and rattlesnakes when I saw what he was holding. "You brought an airbed?" My mouth fell open in shock.

"I thought I'd have a better chance of getting your pants off with a comfortable work space."

I blinked. "Good thinking. You'd have an even better—I'd dare say excellent—chance at that if we packed up right now and went to a nice hotel. I saw plenty of them on the way here."

He grinned. "Eh, I like a challenge."

By the time we finished organizing the camp site and made, then ate dinner, I was exhausted. I wanted to fall into bed and sleep for days. I yawned and stood up. "Where do you think you're going?" Jax asked.

"To crawl onto the airbed and try to sleep. Wake me up if a bear tries to eat you."

He grabbed my hand and pulled me onto his lap, his lips pressing a light trail of kisses down my neck. "I want to show you something first."

I narrowed my eyes. I had a feeling I knew what that something was. And it involved him removing his pants. He read my look. "No, not that. You're too tired to handle it."

"That doesn't sound like something better-than-a-werewolf Jax would say."

He grinned. "I'm the gentlemanly werewolf type."

He put his arms around me and I snuggled into his chest, enjoying the feeling of his warm embrace. I'd complained about the trip a lot. Really, a long road trip and camping were the last things I wanted to do after an exhausting weekend of studying and then three days of exams before the Thanksgiving break. I was hoping for a chance to relax, and didn't think I'd get it in the current environment. But as I breathed in the earthy smell of pine needles and fresh air, and listened to the sound of animals and the water from a creek near the camp, I realized I *was* relaxed. I didn't need a fancy hotel or a spa. I really enjoyed just being here. Together, in Jax's arms, and without other people around.

The campsite was deserted, probably because of the holiday, and the fact that it was winter and not many people ventured into the wilderness at this time of year...not even in Arizona. The night was unpolluted by man-made lights and sounds. There were no distractions; just me and Jax. For the next three days. I sighed at the thought and held him tighter.

"Hey, don't fall asleep on me."

"I'm not."

"Are you too tired to walk a little?"

I frowned. I wasn't too tired, but the bears in this area were black, which meant I couldn't see them coming to eat me in the dark very well, either. "No, I'm not too tired. I just need to get something first." I went

to the tent and grabbed a can from my bag. I felt much better about wandering at midnight now that I was prepared.

Jax furrowed his brows as he noticed my hand. "What is that?"

"Bear spray. I rented it. That way if we need it, we'll have it, and if we don't have to fight off any angry nine hundred pound animals, I'll be able to get my deposit back."

He laughed out loud and shook his head. "You're kind of nuts."

"You say that now, but just wait until a bear's on your ass. You'll be eating your words."

"There's not really even proof that bear spray works."

"Tell that to all the people who had it and didn't get eaten by bears."

"If it makes you feel better, that's what matters." He took my hand. "Come with me."

We walked on a trail near the campsite that wound its way up a hill. When we came to the top, I could see what seemed like fog. Fog in movies was always the catalyst for something horrible happening. Ghosts, zombies, and beastly monsters always came out of fog. I looked at Jax, concerned. He smiled reassuringly, pulling me onward. As we rounded a corner on the trail, I noticed pools and pools of steaming water.

Jax released my hand and bent down, taking off his shoes. "What are you doing?" I asked, shifting my gaze between Jax and the pools.

"Getting in. I told you there were hot springs."

I'd been pretty traumatized by the entire camping discussion and had tried to block it from my memory. I brought it back and vaguely remembered him saying something like that. "Oh, yeah."

He lifted his shirt, his abs rippling with the movement. I lost all train of thought.

"Come on, get in."

I shook myself out of the haze his naked upper body had created. "Is this what you had to show me?"

He smirked. "Part of it."

I stared at his wide chest then let my gaze trail to his arms. His tattoo caught my eye. There was something so sexy about a man with huge arms and tattoos. The number seventeen was sky blue, and the tribal design wrapping around it was grey. I'd noticed the tattoo before on the day he'd started to strip in his bedroom. It was the only ink he had. "Does the other part involve you naked?"

"I can keep my shorts on if you want. It might make you more comfortable."

It didn't. I was a fan of Jax naked. Big fan. Huge.

He undid his belt. "I can't show you until you get in the water with me."

"How often are these things cleaned?" I asked, eyeing the water and waving my hand in the general direction of the pools. It looked like spring break for microbes.

He froze, staring at me. "You're kidding, right?"

I pushed my brows together, confused. "No. Who knows what animals or other disgusting things are in there. Do you know how many germs thrive in warm water like that?"

He came toward me, his abs flexing as he walked, belt hanging off his shorts, the top button undone. Putting his arms around me and leaning down, he pressed his mouth against mine. His tongue ran over my lips and between them as his hands moved over my white tee shirt and inched it up. He moved from my lips to my neck and I sighed, tilting my head back. He lifted the shirt over my head, and I heard it drop on the ground. I felt his warm hands on my back as he trailed his mouth over my chest, where he lingered between my breasts, before continuing down near the waistband of my navy blue shorts. As he kissed my stomach, he popped the button on my shorts, slowly sliding the zipper down as his lips went lower with it. He tugged my shorts, and before I knew it, I was standing in the middle of an Arizona campground half naked. I opened my mouth to protest and Jax chose that exact moment to drop his pants. And he'd lied about keeping his boxers on. He wasn't wearing any.

Oh. My. Hell.

I gaped at the Greek god standing in front of me in the moonlight, with steam rolling into the sky behind him. I'd seen Jax almost naked before, but never in full glory like this. I was positive I'd never get tired of the view. And naked in this setting—good hell, he looked like he'd just stepped out of an ad for all things hot and wonderful. His sculpted abs tapered into a lovely V— the kind that athletes always seem to have, but never real men. Well, Jax had it, and wasn't shy about showing it off. The V directed my eye straight down to his crowning glory—the Beast. Jax was an incredible male specimen, and I couldn't stop staring. He moved his arms back around me, and kissed me again, then bent down, picked me up, and took me straight into one of the bubbling pools.

"Hey!" I said, fighting him a little. Naked Greek god or not, I still hadn't gotten an answer about the germ issue.

"They're natural hot springs, sweetheart," he said, reading my mind. "They don't get cleaned. And you won't get a disease or anything else from them." He sat down and settled me on his lap. I could feel his hard length pressing against me, and suddenly I didn't care much about microbes. Not. At. All. "Relax."

"So, this was a ruse to get naked and seduce me in water?"

The corner of his lips lifted. "No, that's my plan for tomorrow."

I gave him a playful punch in the arm.

"I wanted to show you this." He turned me in his lap and tilted my head back so it was resting against his shoulder. I looked up and gasped. I'd never seen so many stars. It was like the sky was sprinkled with glitter. I could even see the Milky Way threaded across it like a wispy cloud.

"Oh my God! It's breathtaking, Jax. I've never seen so many stars!" I immediately found the Big and Little Dippers and pointed them out to him. It was a habit I had anytime I looked up at the night sky.

"And there's Orion," Jax said, pointing at the three stars lined diagonally like a belt.

I noticed Jax's tattoo, framed by the stars, as he lifted his arm. "You know what I love?" I said, turning my head to look at him. "Tattoos. They just do it for me. I'm really glad you have one."

He smiled, but it didn't reach his eyes. "The artist did a good job."

"How long have you had it?" I asked, wondering why he suddenly seemed more somber.

"Years," he answered. "It's hard to remember a time when I didn't have it."

I nodded, thinking about it. "I've always wanted one, but I'm afraid I'll regret it."

Jax held me tighter. "Just make sure it has meaning to you, then you won't."

"I don't know if there's anything I'm passionate enough about to put on my skin permanently."

His lips ticked up in a smile. "You could always get one of a werewolf."

I blushed. Jax chose that exact moment to slip his hand inside my bra. The lace above the cups scratched against my sensitive skin, and my nipples tightened immediately as he rubbed his fingers back and forth. "Do you like that, Syd?"

I nodded, my breath ragged as I felt his hardness straining against my back.

"So do I." His voice was a husky whisper in my ear. "I can't keep my hands off of you." He moved his hands lower, teasing the top of my panties before he pushed under them, spreading his palm out as he reached my center. My breath came in gasps as he slipped a finger into my slick heat. Pressing in—"I want you." –pulling out. "All the time." He curved his fingers, stroking the exact right spot, the rhythm changing as he added another finger. His pace quickened and I writhed in his lap.

"Jax," I said on an exhale. I tried turning around, but he held me firm.

His breath was scorching on my neck. "I've been thinking about what you'd feel like since I met you."

I squeezed my thighs tighter, not caring whether I hurt—or even broke—his hand in the process.

"I've been fantasizing about you, too," he said, his teeth nipping at my ear.

I could barely get a breath—I was almost there.

"I can't wait to act some of them out." His words sent me screaming over the edge. It was the best orgasm I'd ever had. As he held me close, I got the feeling that unless someone had a mold of his fingers, Jackson West had just ruined sex toys for me. And I was totally okay with that.

We'd been hiking all morning. After Jax had made me a yummy breakfast of ham, eggs, and toast right over the fire, he'd told me we were going out. "Going out" means a lot of different things depending on the context. In some cases, it could require nothing more than a pony tail and a tee shirt; in others, it required a little black dress, or even a pair of skinny jeans and a sexy top. I'd needed more information.

"Where *exactly* are we going?"

He gave me a look. "It's a surprise."

"What should I wear?"

His lips slid into a seductive smile, voice husky, "Something you can get dirty in."

I'd blushed fiercely and then pulled on some shorts, a tee shirt, and hiking boots.

We hiked through beautiful canyons with red rock. Some were so narrow I didn't think Jax's shoulders would be able to make it through them. We didn't see anyone the entire afternoon, and the solitude was extremely peaceful. We hiked mostly in silence, taking in the beauty surrounding us.

When we finally stopped, it was to eat lunch overlooking a stunning sixty foot waterfall. "I love waterfalls," I said, taking a bite of my peanut butter sandwich. Jax had used white bread to make them, and the peanut butter was crunchy—my favorite.

"Me, too."

"The sound of rushing water is soothing. I used to want to get married with a waterfall in the background."

He gave me a sideways glance. "It would have to be a quiet waterfall, or you wouldn't know what you were agreeing to when you said your vows."

I pinched my brows together. "Good point."

He looked at the waterfall for a minute before turning back to me. "So you're one of those girls who have their wedding all planned out?" he asked, taking a bite of his own sandwich. "Actually, that doesn't surprise me. You plan everything."

I gave him a playful glare. "As a matter of fact, I do not have my wedding planned, because I don't want a wedding."

His eyes widened, and he almost choked. I patted him on the back and he took a drink to wash it down. "You don't believe in marriage?" he asked. "Did your parents get divorced or something?"

I ate the last bite of my sandwich. "No, my parents are really happy. One of the few couples I've seen make it work—through the good times and the really bad times." I leaned back against the rock. "I think it works for some people. I'm just not sure if I'm one of them."

"I don't think I've ever heard a girl say that. *Ever.*"

I shrugged. "Marriage has serious consequences."

He tilted his head, interested, and waited for me to go on.

I took a drink of water to wash down the sandwich that was sticking to my throat. "I don't like what marriage does to people."

"What does it do?"

"Changes them."

"How?" He seemed genuinely curious.

I stretched my legs out in front of me and crossed them at the ankles. "The person you choose as a partner has a huge affect on the person you become. You have to compromise and change with the person, or the relationship doesn't work. You're no longer making decisions for yourself. You're making them for two people, and if you have kids, you're making them for an entire family, and God knows, it's easy as hell to screw that up. I don't want the responsibility."

He watched me for several moments. "What you really mean is that you don't like the loss of control that relationships require."

I lifted a shoulder as I grabbed a granola bar from my lunch bag and opened it. "I admit that. Watching my mom go through cancer changed me. I couldn't control the disease. Nothing was more frustrating than knowing someone I cared about was going through something horrible, and there was nothing I could do to fix it. Ever since, I've tried to be as in control of situations as possible. It's hard for me to let go."

"Interesting."

I narrowed my eyes, annoyed that he was analyzing me. "Why is that interesting?"

"Because no one can be in control like that all of

the time, Syd. Yeah, marriage—and relationships—are hard. They're a flat out bitch sometimes. But being alone isn't any easier—trust me, I should know. You live your life by this carefully chosen set of rules, thinking nothing will ever happen to make you deviate from it." He paused, his eyes downcast and his expression falling into sadness. He sat like that for a few seconds before tilting his head to me. "I wonder what will happen when you meet the person you want to break all of your rules for."

I shifted, uncomfortable. Though he didn't seem to know it, I was pretty sure I'd already met that person, and didn't know how it was going to affect me in the future.

"What about you?" I asked. "You don't like relationships, either. It's taken me months to get you to open up at all. I wouldn't have pegged you for the marrying type. If relationships are so hard for you, how do you think you're ever going to find someone you can be with forever?"

A muscle worked at his jaw. "I never said I didn't like relationships. They just haven't worked for me in the past."

I stared at him, my heart beating faster as I got more upset. "You're such a hypocrite! You just argued that I was wrong for not wanting to get married, but you feel the exact same way!"

He didn't respond for several seconds. When he did, the eyes that met mine were intense, his voice

even. "I said relationships haven't worked for me in the past, Syd. I'm trying to change that with you." He paused and then continued, "The difference between us is that you want to be alone because you're scared of giving up control, and living your life putting someone else's interests before your own." He took a deep breath. "I want to be alone because I don't like disappointing people."

What the...? "What the hell does that mean?"

"Exactly what I said." He stood, putting his water bottle back in his pack. "We should start back before it gets too late. We don't want to be out here in the dark—bears and all."

I would have rolled my eyes, but I was still too annoyed at our conversation, and frustrated he'd refused to go into detail and answer my questions...again.

We didn't say much on the way back down the mountain, and back to camp. Jax cracked some jokes as we were making dinner, clearly trying to lighten the mood. I wasn't ready for it to be lightened. I wanted to know what his comment about disappointing people had meant, and why he believed in marriage, but didn't think it was for him. I needed him to explain why relationships were so hard for him, and why he'd decided to try with me. I knew being vulnerable was an issue for him, and I was willing to wait, but I needed him to give me *something*.

He must have picked up on my mood—which wouldn't have taken Sherlock Holmes to figure out—because as we were lying in the tent on separate sides of the airbed that night, his deep voice startled me. "I believe in marriage, Syd. I just think it means being willing to give every single part of yourself...and that's not easy to do. Love for each other needs to be cultivated every day, and it needs to come before everything else, even kids. It takes work and prioritizing, but that's how relationships last. That's the kind of relationship I'd settle down for. I'm holding out for something like that. And—" there was a long pause. So long, I thought he'd stopped talking and fallen asleep. But suddenly I heard his voice again in the darkness, "And I hope you're the person I get to have that with." He turned over and wrapped his arm around my stomach, pulling me close to him, spooning me.

I stared at the side of the tent, stunned. I had no idea what to say. I hadn't seen this side of Jax often. He didn't let people in easily, and we'd fought about it over and over. The fact that he'd just told me he wanted me to be the person he settled down with was a huge step. And the fact that I hadn't run screaming from the tent surprised me. Jax wasn't the only one benefiting from our time together. I was growing, too.

As I drifted off to sleep, I had the thought that maybe Jax was finally dismantling the wall that kept people out, and in the process, he was dismantling mine as well. Even if it was just a brick at a time, I'd take it.

Nineteen

I stretched as I got up the next morning and looked around the tent. Jax was already awake. I pulled some shorts and a tee on, and opened the tent. The sun was low on the horizon, the sky still streaked with pretty pastels from the sunrise. I found Jax loading the truck. I pinched my brows together, confused. We were supposed to be here for another day. Had I done something to make him mad and shorten the trip? "Hey…what are you doing?"

He smiled widely when he saw me. "Packing up. Get your stuff, we need to get on the road."

"Where are we going?"

He came over and took my face in his hands, kissing me deeply. When he pulled back, he bit his

bottom lip as he smiled. It was so sexy I wanted to kiss him again, and go back to bed—with him. "It's a surprise," he said, putting the cooler in the back of the truck. "Get your stuff so we can go."

Another surprise? The first one had resulted in me going on a camping trip. I was worried what the next surprise would bring. I really didn't like being kept out of the loop—which was probably the main reason Jax kept surprising me. He enjoyed making me step outside my comfort zone. I went to the tent and packed up my stuff, let the air out of the air mattress, and rolled up the sleeping bags. I put everything in the truck, and then helped Jax take the tent down. We were done and on the road within the hour.

Two hours later, we were pulling into a hotel overlooking Lake Powell. "Come on," Jax said, getting out of the truck and opening my door for me.

I looked at the meticulously landscaped grounds and the beige stucco building done in a southwest style. It looked expensive...way more expensive than I was willing to spend on a night in a hotel. I'd have been ecstatic with Motel 6. I followed Jax inside and waited in line with him as he gave the front desk clerk his name. She was pretty, with dark hair and tan skin. She smiled widely at Jax as she handed him a key card and explained the location of the room. I got the distinct feeling she wanted to join him in it. That annoyed me. When she was done, I slid the key card off the desk and made a point to wrap my hand around Jax's bicep.

"Thanks," I said, the woman's eyes fluttering to me for the first time. "We've been on the road for a while and I just can't wait to get him out of these clothes." I winked at Jax and he laughed outright. He thanked the clerk and we made our way out of the lobby.

"You didn't tell me you got a hotel."

"Because I didn't want you to know. I thought it would be a nice way to end the trip, especially since you were so averse to camping in the first place."

I looked over at him, still holding his arm. "That was thoughtful of you."

He grinned. "I know."

We got to the room and he opened the door. It wasn't even really a room, more like an entire wing. The suite was gigantic! The main area had light variegated hardwood floors, covered by a beautifully woven white rug. Modern black leather couches sat on top of the rug and a huge flat screen TV was across from them.

A gigantic flower arrangement in various shades of blue and white was on the dining table. "Jax, it's amazing!"

"That's not the most amazing part." He took my hand and led me down a hall. Hardwood floors continued into the bedroom, where another white woven rug lay under a sleigh bed with a soft, white blanket on top of it. He led me into the bathroom with modern brushed steel fixtures and a large open shower. A soaker tub sat in the middle of the room.

I was taking it all in as Jax gently pulled me toward the far side of the room, and opened the curtains and a sliding glass door that was flush with the wall when opened. I gasped at the stunning view. A jacuzzi sat outside the door, surrounded by hedges on both sides for privacy. And the jacuzzi overlooked the beautiful lake, the pretty red and orange rock clear from where we stood.

I'd been too stunned to speak as we moved from space to space. Now, looking over the calm water and incredible canyon, I found my voice. "Jax…this is…I mean, I don't even know what to say. This is absolutely beautiful. It's the most amazing thing anyone has ever done for me!" I reached up, wrapping my arms around his neck.

His eyes were soft as he leaned down and put one arm around my waist, and the other hand on my cheek. "I wanted you to know how much you mean to me." He paused, like he was choosing his words carefully. "I haven't let myself feel this way for a very long time." He leaned down and kissed me, his lips pressing into mine, his tongue tracing my lips. I was completely lost in the moment, in him. I knew he was trying, and that meant the world to me. I wanted him to know exactly how much it meant. My hands moved from his neck, traveling down to his ass. I slowly moved them around to his belt buckle and started to undo it. He smiled against my lips, and said, "Nuh uh."

I stopped kissing him and pulled back. "Nuh uh?" I lifted my brows. "Why nun uh? Because I'd *really* like to let you know how much I appreciate your thoughtful planning and this beautiful hotel. And I *really* don't think you want to miss out on that."

He ran his tongue over his lips like he was seriously considering the offer. "And I'd *really* like to let you show me, but we're going to be late if I do."

I stared at him. "Late for what?"

He smiled slowly. "You can shower before me if you want. Wear something you can layer." He pulled away from me. "I'll be back. Oh, and the flowers on the table are for you."

I stared, dumbstruck, at the door as it shut. I had a thousand questions running through my head, and no one here to answer them. If he'd wanted to take me out of my comfort zone, he'd definitely accomplished the task.

I walked over to the table and admired the beautiful blue and white flowers. A card was sticking out of the arrangement. I opened the envelope and read the note: *For the woman who surprised me, in every way.*

My lips curved in a smile and I took the card into the bedroom, tucking it into my luggage. The flowers might not last, but his card would, and I wanted a token to remember this weekend.

I went into the bathroom and peeled off my dirty clothes, enjoying my first warm shower in three days. I was just finishing my hair and makeup when Jax came back. He stopped, his eyes darkening and traveling over my tight jeans and low cut dark purple top like a

predator. My body immediately reacted to his expression and my heart started to race. If this kept up, we wouldn't be going anywhere except straight to the bed. I was absolutely fine with that. I took a deep breath and managed words, "Where did you go?"

He didn't answer for a full thirty seconds. Finally his eyes flitted to meet mine. "To take care of something." He stripped off his shirt and my breath staggered. His tattoo flexed with his arms as he threw his shirt to the side of the room. I wondered if I'd ever get used to how perfect he was, and how much I wanted him. I had a feeling the answer was no.

He moved into the bathroom and before long, I heard water running. It took him less than ten minutes to walk out of the bathroom looking like a model. It took me at least an hour to be acceptable for public viewing. I was a little bitter. He grabbed my hand and we walked out of the hotel, down a long dirt path.

When we got to the bottom, there was a huge, white boat. It looked like a pretty fancy boat…maybe a yacht. We stepped on board and met the captain and a few other staff members before Jax guided me toward the back. There was a long bench with a chocolate brown leather seat cushion under an awning. We sat, and a server came over to take our drink orders. Since I wasn't driving, and I was in the mood to let go of my inhibitions a bit, I got a mai tai, and Jax ordered a beer. It wasn't long before the boat shifted and we started to move. I looked around, confused. "Aren't other people boarding?"

"Nope. This is just for us."

The nicest suite in the hotel and a private yacht? What had he done, robbed a bank? "How did you manage a private yacht?"

He smiled behind his glass. "I know people."

I took a sip of my drink. "I'm sure of it. I don't want to know what you did to make this happen."

He cocked a brow. "I told them I'd offer a detailed account of what I'm going to do to you later."

My heart sped up again, and I suddenly wished we were off the boat and back in the hotel room right now. I spent the next few minutes daydreaming about all the things I wanted him to do to me. But as we turned a corner on the lake, we were suddenly surrounded by high canyons on both sides of us; colors in orange, red, pink and even some black were woven together in stunning patterns. I'd heard of Lake Powell before— I'd even seen it in movies—but being there in person was a stunning sight. We spent the next few hours drifting through the canyons, passing by other boats, some docked, some floating around the lake like us. I laughed at a few kids jumping off one of the rocks into the water. "That looks pretty terrifying," I said.

Jax smiled and seemed to be lost in thought for several minutes. "It's really not that bad. Like jumping off a high dive."

I widened my eyes. "A high dive times three you mean? That's *really* high."

He pushed his bottom lip up like he was thinking. "We'll try it some time."

"*You* can try it sometime. I'll stay back on the ground with the sane people."

He leaned over and whispered in my ear, his breath hitting my neck like warm breeze. "I'll just have to think of a way to convince you."

I shivered at that, and Jax wrapped his arm around me, pulling me closer. Jax pointed out areas of stone that were popular, like the incredible tapestry wall on a sheer face of rock in one of the canyons. It was clear he'd been here many times before, and knew the area well.

"You know a lot about Lake Powell."

"My family used to visit. It's one of my favorite places. My brother and I used to jump off the rocks like those kids were doing. One time, he hit something when he jumped and tore a ligament in his arm. He was so drunk he didn't even notice until the next day. He was also underage, so we didn't tell anyone he'd been drunk when he did it. We made up a story about him having a high tolerance for pain and not noticing it right away." Jax laughed at that memory, a light dancing in his eyes. "We always had a good time."

This was one of the first times Jax had volunteered information about his past or his family. I felt like I was being included in a very selective club, and I didn't want him to stop talking. "Do you still come here a lot?"

He paused before answering, "This is the first time I've been here in years. I'm glad I came with you, though. I've missed it."

One of the staff members walked over and informed us dinner was ready. I looked at Jax, sincerely surprised. He'd put so much thought, planning, and money into this. It was hard not to read into it. I knew he really cared about me, which was nice because even though it scared me, I truly cared about him.

We got to the front of the boat and found a beautifully set table with more flowers and China dishes rimmed in platinum. The servers brought our appetizers, and we ate the delicious food as we watched the sun set over the lake. The colors of the sky rivaled the colors of the gorgeous rock. It was serene and romantic. I understood why this spot held a special place in Jax's heart. It now held one in mine.

We were finishing up dessert as I noticed the lights from our hotel. I looked at Jax and held his eyes. "This was the most magical night I've ever experienced, Jax. No one has ever gone to such detail, or planned something like this for me. I'll remember this for the rest of my life."

He took my hand as the boat docked. "Wait until we get to the hotel and I'll give you something to really remember."

A flutter started in my stomach, and quickly moved lower. I couldn't wait to get back to our room.

The glow of candlelight cast pretty shadows over the suite as we entered. Jax smiled seductively and took my hand, guiding me into the bedroom. Rose petals were sprinkled all over the floor and the bed. "I had housekeeping come in while we were gone and set it up."

I took in the romantic room, and slowly stepped out of my shoes. I turned around, holding Jax's gaze. His eyes darkened as I unbuttoned my shirt. "It's a little warm in here," I said, letting the shirt fall far enough open that Jax got a clear view of my cleavage, "don't you think?"

He licked his lips like a man who was stranded in a desert and hadn't had water for days. "I think you need to lose your clothes. That's what I think."

I smiled coyly. "Oh, do you?" I didn't move.

"Take them off, or I'll tear them off."

I lifted my eyes in playful surprise. "My, my. Someone's aggressive tonight."

"Syd—" a warning tone carried in his voice as I slowly unzipped my jeans and stepped out of them, then dropped my shirt. The tone quickly turned to a groan as he took in my red, see through corset, two red satin bows strategically covering my nipples, and matching red panties.

"I'm going to rip that off, too."

He stalked over to me and pressed his lips to mine in a deep, breath-stealing kiss. I was burning inside, and had never wanted anything more than I wanted him.

I'd been waiting for this moment with Jax for far too long. I could barely catch my breath as he picked me up, and laid me gently down among the rose petals on the soft bed. I leaned back and watched as he practically tore his own clothes off. In record time, he was naked, his sculpted body a hulking mass over my own. He reached down, and slowly pulled the corset string. It loosened, and he immediately pulled the corset off me, then took one side of my panties in his hands and pulled, leaving them in tatters. I'd never been more turned on.

His breath caught as he took me in. I wished I could see myself through his eyes. I'd never felt so beautiful—or wanted. He kissed me again, moving a hand over my breast. But it wasn't just his hand; there was something in it. I jumped at the sensation, and looked down. Jax's bracelet was no longer on his wrist—instead it was doing some very nice things to my chest. He reached out, dragging the bracelet beads across me, pressing into my nipples with the smooth, round stones. My nipples pebbled at the feel of the cool, smooth rocks.

"I have an even better idea for these," he said, replacing the beads on my nipples with his mouth. The beads in his hands continued a trail downward, creating a path over my stomach. Skirting the juncture of my core, the beads hit my thighs instead, taunting and teasing me. I wriggled, wanting him more than anything. "Please, Jax," I begged. My eyes were

unfocused and I couldn't think of anything but the need he was creating inside of me.

Jax's lips lifted slowly, enjoying the game. "What do you want, Syd?" he asked, his voice gravelly as the beads went back and forth over my mound. I was swollen and aching. I wasn't sure how much longer I could take this torture. And then his fingers found the bundle of nerves that were about to drive me insane.

I moaned.

"I bet I know what you *really* want," he whispered. My breath was short, barely contained as I waited for his next move. He wrapped the beads around his fingers, and without warning, pushed into me. The new sensations of the cool, smooth beads moving deep inside me made it difficult to breathe. Every shift of movement sent me into a new state of bliss. With each twist of Jax's fingers, the beads hit another spot that threatened to take me over the edge. I didn't want to lose myself like that tonight, though. Tonight, I wanted my first orgasm to be with him inside me.

I reached down and grabbed his hand, willing myself to make him stop moving his fingers and the beads. It was the hardest thing I'd ever done. "I need you, Jax. Now. Inside me."

His eyes darkened and he slowly pulled the beads out, one by one, each pull threatening to send me further over the edge. He laid the beads on the mattress, then moved between my legs, towering over me. His sapphire gaze raked my body, taking me in with intense focus. "God, you're beautiful." He reached down to position himself, and then took my mouth with his as he thrust into me, and I lost every sense I had. His thickness filled me completely. There was nothing but this moment, these sensations, and Jax. Jax was what I needed. In every way. He pulled back slowly, and pushed in harder. I tugged him down to me, needing to hold on to him. To be as close to him as I possibly could. My hands scraped over his back as he rolled his hips. Sweat slicked our tangled bodies. He grimaced, "I can't stop, Syd."

"Then don't." I took his mouth with mine like it was oxygen. He bucked inside me as I pulsed around him, basking in the ecstasy. His body relaxed and he breathed out a deep sigh. He lay on top of me for several seconds before moving off to the side. Putting his arm under my shoulders, he pulled me half on top of him, so that my head rested on his heart. And that's how I fell asleep. Listening to Jax's heartbeat, feeling like the luckiest woman in the world.

I woke up a couple of hours later, still on Jax's chest with his fingers trailing lightly through my hair. I gave a contented sigh at the relaxing tugs. That was the best sex of my life. Jax was as focused and passionate in bed as he was out of it. I hadn't been disappointed.

No wonder Brynn loved sex enough to make it a research topic. She'd had experience with men like Jax. If I'd known what I was missing out on all these years, I wouldn't have waited so long to find someone who knew what they were doing. I was glad I hadn't done that, though. I liked that the best sex of my life had been with someone I truly cared for.

Jax shifted and I groaned. I didn't want him to move. "I'll be right back," he said, leaning down to kiss my head. He was gone for a minute and then leaned over the side of the bed and picked me up, carrying me outside. It was the middle of the night and the air held a chill, but Jax put me down in the Jacuzzi and I wasn't cold for long. He stepped in behind me, holding me between his legs, the warm water and jets relaxing us both. Moonlight was shimmering off the glassy surface of Lake Powell, and stars shone above us. The entire night had been perfect. I never wanted to leave.

I turned my head against Jax's chest, looking up at him. "You're pretty incredible, you know that?"

His lips ticked up. "Of course I do."

I put my hands over his, and realized his bracelet was back on. "You told me I couldn't take my bracelet off."

"You can't."

"But you can take yours off?" I asked, rolling my fingers over the beads, drops of water shining on them. I'd never look at the bracelet again without thinking of tonight. Even the thought of them, and what they'd done to me, made me wet all over again.

"I said *you* couldn't take yours off. Mine has no rules."

I laughed. "I think that statement applies to your whole life."

He held me closer, his hands tracing my breasts. "The bracelet did its job."

I lifted one corner of my mouth and nodded in agreement. "Damn straight it did." That was better than most of my sex toys. And it didn't even require batteries, or a special box to hide it from my mom.

"No. I mean your bracelet worked."

I knit my brows together. "What?" My bracelet hadn't done anything but shift on my wrist while I was writhing in pleasure. "What are you talking about?"

"Your beads. They're rainbow obsidian. They're supposed to help you let go of fear and dissolve barriers. Considering you let me in—in more ways than one—I'd say you've conquered your fears, and dropped quite a few barriers."

I snorted. "Well, let's hope the barrier keeping me from getting knocked up stays nice and sturdy." Really, I wasn't worried. We'd used a condom, and I wasn't anywhere close to ovulating. But, since sex with Jax was something I wanted to happen at least once a day, I'd have to go see my doctor about getting a new diaphragm. My old one definitely needed an upgrade.

"Did you choose those beads because you thought they'd make me less uptight?"

He cocked a brow. "You bet I did. I was

desperate, and willing to use any help I could get—even metaphysical."

I gave him a playful glare and pinched his thigh. "So," I said, glancing at his bracelet, "do your beads have a meaning, too?"

His expression fell and he was quiet for several seconds. "They do."

It seemed like the meaning was pretty important. I waited to see if he'd tell me what it was.

After about a minute, his expression changed. He smiled and said, "They promote healthy egotism."

I rolled my eyes. "Well, you should take them off then, because you certainly don't need any more of that."

He pulled me closer into him, his body pressing against my back. I could feel his length against me, ready and willing. "You think my ego is sexy. I bet you'll even dream of me tonight."

"See," I said, "you have no problems in the self-confidence arena."

"I don't mind admitting when I'm good at something."

Oh yes. He was sooooo good. I shifted forward off his lap, turning around to face him. I let my gaze trail over his perfect body, my eyes hooded. I slowly licked my lips, thinking of everything we'd already done together, and everything I still wanted to try. Jax's brows pinched together, a look of wary desire crossing his expression. "Syd—what are you doing?"

I stood, moved closer, and then straddled him, rubbing myself against his hard length. Back and forth. Back and forth. "What do you want, Jax?" I asked, my voice breathy.

His eyes were latched to my breasts, watching me as I moved. "What I've wanted since the first day I saw you. To make you mine." He reached behind him and grabbed a condom. He'd come prepared. He sheathed himself quickly, and then lifted me up, positioning himself at my entrance. In one quick movement, I came down on him, hard. He groaned so loudly, I thought he'd probably woken up the rest of the hotel. And I didn't care. I moved—slowly at first, teasing, just like he'd teased me. He drew circles around my nipples with his tongue until they were taut, then took them in his mouth, laving them gently at first, and then adding a little bite. The combination of pleasure and pain overcame me. I couldn't go slow. I wanted to feel him again, to know I'd given him that pleasure. My pace quickened as we moved together, a perfect fit in every way. Our eyes met as I reached my peak, and Jax quickly followed. I fell against him, my breath ragged. "If we're going to keep this up, I'm probably going to need a personal trainer."

Jax's lips lifted. "I'd be happy to help."

I had no doubt about that.

We got out of the Jacuzzi and cleaned up, then got back in bed. He wrapped his arms around me and I snuggled into his nook, my head on his chest again.

After a few minutes, his breaths lulled into the slow and steady rhythm of sleep. I lay awake for a long time, analyzing everything that had happened, and especially the conversation we'd had in the Jacuzzi. I couldn't stop thinking about his somber reaction when I'd asked about his beads. I knew there was more to the meaning than an improved ego. He'd chosen them for a reason, and the reason was something he still wasn't comfortable sharing. I wondered if he ever would be.

Twenty

We slept in and ordered room service. Jax even served it to me in bed, naked. We quickly forgot about the food. When we finally got around to eating, the meals were still surprisingly warm thanks to the plate covers.

We checked out of the hotel around noon. On the way out of town we stopped for gas, so I went into the store to grab some snacks and drinks for the drive. They had coffee with an entire bar of flavors and creamers to choose from. I smiled, making myself the perfect cup of dark chocolate coffee, and Jax a toffee coffee mix. I was at the counter paying for everything when I heard yelling outside the store and turned to look out the window. The person yelling was Jax. He

was standing in front of a guy almost as tall as him with light blonde hair. Jax was working his jaw and looked like he was struggling to stay calm. I finished paying quickly, my eyes still on Jax as the clerk handed me the bag and I raced out the door.

I cautiously made my way toward them. I could hear their conversation, though. Everyone could. Other people had stopped to watch the altercation.

"Look, I just wanted to say I'm sorry, that's all," the blonde guy said.

I could see the veins pulsing at Jax's neck. "How dare you even talk to me?"

The guy held up his hands. "I know. But when I saw you here, I couldn't believe it. I couldn't let you leave without telling you that I think about it every single day. I'll never forget, and I'll always feel bad for what happened."

Jax was breathing harder now, his chest rising and falling fast. "Feel bad. You'll *feel bad,*" Jax said through his teeth. "That's nice to know. I'll make sure to tell Ryan." Jax moved toward the guy, his fists curling.

My eyes were wide with shock. I didn't know what was going on, but I couldn't let Jax hit the guy, especially when the stranger seemed truly sorry for whatever had happened. Jax started to lift his arm when I called out to him, "Jax!"

My voice pulled him out of his anger enough to stop him from following through on the hit. From the murderous look in his eyes as he glanced toward me, he probably would have done more than just punch the guy, and he'd have spent the day in the county jail on assault charges. Jax slowly lowered his hand and took a few steps back. He directed his attention at the guy again. "Don't speak to me ever again, Wilson. Ever."

Jax got in the truck and I hurried to the passenger seat. I wasn't sure he should even be driving as worked up as he was. He leaned his head back against the headrest and closed his eyes. Then he took several calming breaths.

When it seemed like he'd calmed down a little, I reached over, lightly putting my hand on his leg. "Jax, are you okay?"

He took another deep breath, opening his eyes. "Yeah," he said. He buckled his seat belt, and twisted the key in the ignition. "Yeah, I'll be fine. Just as soon as I get the hell out of Arizona. I never should have come back here."

We drove in silence. Jax was clearly working through something, and I had no idea how to help him. He didn't seem like he wanted any help, either. But, after an hour, the things left unsaid and unexplained hung in the air like thick soup. I couldn't stay quiet any longer, and it was clear Jax wasn't going to be the one to start the conversation about why he'd almost beaten some guy at a gas pump. "Jax, what happened back there? Why were you so angry?"

Jax pursed his lips and stared at the road, like I wasn't even there. He didn't answer for a long time.

When he finally did, his answer let me know exactly where I stood in his life. "What happened doesn't concern you. It's none of your business."

My mouth fell open. Considering how far we'd come, I couldn't have been more shocked. This was not the Jax I'd spent the last three days with. Hell, this wasn't even the Jax I'd spent the last few months with. This Jax was even more closed off than when I'd first met him. All vulnerability, all romance, all emotions that he'd had toward me seemed to be gone completely. Maybe he was just mad, but it was like he'd flipped a switch and turned his feelings off. And I was pissed. "None of my business? You looked like you wanted to kill the guy! What the hell do you mean it didn't concern me? I care about you. That makes it my business!"

He shook his head. "Not this time."

I was getting madder by the second. "Are you kidding me?" I yelled. "You constantly analyze me and tell me I need to step out of my comfort zone. And when I don't want to do it, you force me. And you know what? I love you even more for it." I was so upset, I didn't even realize I'd just told him I loved him for the first time. "Your influence on me has made me a better person. But when I try to do the same thing for you, you shut me down and refuse to even think about changing. How is that fair?"

"Life isn't fair, sweetheart. You're delusional if you think it is."

"You're missing the point," I ground out. "You could be a better person, too. We could be better together. We're good for each other Jax, but you have to talk to me. You have to let me in."

"We're not doing this."

I blinked, pissed as hell that he'd just tried to shut me down—again. "Not doing what?" I hissed. "Not talking, not getting to know each other on a *real* level? Because if that's what you're talking about, you're right—we're not doing it."

A muscle near his temple pulsed. "I've given you as much as I can."

I stared at him, speechless. I couldn't believe what I was hearing. After all the steps forward we'd taken, after we'd started to really build something together and had a decent foundation, he was willing to throw it all away because he wasn't ready—or willing—to communicate. I couldn't live like this. I couldn't be in a relationship with someone who was always holding back. Relationships scared the crap out of me, but I was at least willing to try and to change. To do the things that terrified me so that we could come to a compromise and make things work together. But I couldn't do it if I was doing it alone. "I need to know if this is just a phase you're going through. Because I thought we'd taken a lot of steps forward. I felt like you were opening up to me more and more. Was this just a setback and you'll stop being an asshole once you calm down?"

He didn't even hesitate as he answered, "No. And no."

I glared at him, stunned and hurt at how quickly he'd shut me out. I wasn't going to be in a one-sided relationship. If he wasn't willing to work through the rough parts, there was no point to continuing this. "Communication is the most important part of a relationship. If you won't open up to me, I can't be with you anymore."

Jax's lips pulled tight. "I don't do ultimatums."

I shook my head. "It's not an ultimatum. I just need to know where we stand, and where we're headed. If you can't let me in, the answer to that is nowhere."

His grip on the steering wheel tightened. He was silent for several agonizing minutes. I sat in the passenger seat, rubbing one hand over the other in a soothing gesture as I waited for his response. My gut feeling told me it wasn't going to be good. He pulled into a parking space at a rest stop and turned to me, meeting my gaze. I could practically see the fire burn out. Somewhere between the romantic weekend alone together and the almost MMA tryout, he'd decided whatever this was between us, it wasn't worth fighting for. My heart started to race. I knew what was coming. "My life isn't as planned out as yours. The only thing I can offer you is right now. I can't—I won't—make any promises. That includes opening up like you want me to. If you can't live with that, then I think you're probably right. We're not going to work."

He got out of the truck and didn't look back.

Nothing is worse than ending a relationship—badly—and still having to spend six hours in an enclosed space together. I turned away from Jax, my knees pointed at the door and my head tilted against the back rest, looking out the window. I pulled out my phone and earbuds, and listened to music and audiobooks to try to take my mind off of the weekend catastrophe.

The rest of the ride back was completely quiet—and agonizing. We didn't say a word to each other. Sitting next to the man I wanted more than anything—the man I'd fallen in love with, but who clearly didn't love me—made it the longest six hours of my life. I cycled through every emotion I had. Crying silently in the truck of the boyfriend who'd just dumped you is a pretty low place to be. However, it gave me a lot of time to think, and I came to some conclusions in my solitude. It was during those six hours of reflection that I realized I'd wanted him more than anything in the world. I would have given him my whole self, regardless of what he'd asked—but he didn't feel the same way about me. He'd basically told me I wasn't important enough to change for. That hurting me was easier than dealing with his demons—demons he certainly wouldn't let me help him fight.

My heart broke.

And more tears slid down my cheeks.

The shoulder of my shirt was soaked with salty tears by the time Jax pulled into my driveway. I got out of his truck, grabbing my bag, and then went to the back to get my suitcase.

"Here," he said, taking it from me.

I couldn't handle him trying to be nice. Not after how he'd acted, and the way we'd ended things. Even if he'd calmed down and felt bad about it now, it still wasn't okay. I was hurt. Deeply. And I needed some time away from him. "I've got it."

"Syd—"

I lifted watery eyes to look at him, daring him to apologize. To own up to the royal ass he'd been, and say he was wrong and wanted to start over. He stopped in front of me, taking my face in his hands. My stomach clenched at the contact, at the feeling of his touch that I'd only recently become accustomed to, and would no longer have. He leaned down, and his mouth crushed against mine in a bruising kiss.

I kissed him back, putting all my anger into the movement. All of the emotions I'd felt for the past six hours came rushing back to me in a tsunami of pain. I punched at his shoulder as he deepened the kiss, my feelings warring inside me. I wanted this, and wanted him, but the memory of him telling me our relationship was over was too fresh. It clouded everything. I didn't think I could put myself out there for him to destroy again. I needed time to put myself back together. I needed to think—and the kiss wasn't helping. As I pulled away, angry tears trailed down my cheeks. I stumbled back to get away from him, from everything we were and might have been. I turned, looking at him one last time over my shoulder; his expression was completely deflated. I ran into the house, as fast as I could. There was a canyon between us, and I didn't think either of us had the tools to build a bridge.

Twenty-One

The piles of tissues in our trash over the next few weeks could have supplied a small country. The only good thing that had come from the breakup was that I was more focused on school than ever. Jax had distracted me for a few months, but now I had nothing to do with my time except study—and I was killing it. My grades were fantastic, and I'd ended the semester near the top of the class. In a few days, I'd be going home for Christmas to see my parents. They were thrilled, and I was happy to be getting away from a place that reminded me of everything that was causing me pain. I hoped being home, surrounded by love, would help me snap out of my emotional rut. At some point, I realized I'd become numb to the pain from my failed relationship with Jax. Like a wound trying to protect itself, the numbness was how my heart was dealing with his disappearance from my life.

He hadn't just broken my heart, he'd broken me.

Luckily, I hadn't had any car problems since the breakup. I thanked the goddesses for that. I knew I wouldn't be able to handle seeing him. Not now. Maybe not ever. I'd filled Red in, and he'd said I could call before coming in to make sure Jax wouldn't be there. I was so grateful for that. I'd been getting gas early in the mornings when I knew Jax didn't work. So far, I hadn't had to deal with him.

I knocked my bracelet against the top of the counter while I was making cookies to take to CARE. I stopped and stared, realizing I was still wearing it. I wasn't sure why. It seemed like it should have fallen off or broken when our relationship did. I grabbed some scissors to take it off, but just as I was about to cut, something stopped me. I couldn't do it. I'd let the man go; I couldn't let this go, too. It was the last representation of our time together.

I made a pot of coffee and took a mug to the living room to drink while I watched TV. *Property Brothers* was on and it was just as addicting as *House Hunters*. I was on my third mug of coffee when Brynn came through the front door, her phone to her ear.

"Look, if you want me to go out with you, I'm gonna need some proof." I narrowed my eyes, trying to figure out who Brynn was talking to, and what she was talking about.

"Well, that's not my problem. If you don't want to do it, then *we* don't have to do it."

She was silent while the other person on the phone responded. Then she smiled. "Well, if you change your mind, you have my number."

She ended her call. "What was that about?"

She shrugged off her coat and hung it in the closet. "New dating rule."

I widened my eyes. "And that is?"

"I got sick of dating cocktail weenies, so now, if a guy wants to go out, he has to send me proof."

My mouth fell open. I had no words. She filled the empty space instead. "It's a great method. I'm cutting down on a lot of time I would have wasted being disappointed. It also makes my research *much* more efficient."

My eyes got even wider. "Are you telling me guys are actually complying with this?"

She shrugged and plopped down next to me on the couch. "For the most part." She thumbed through the pics on her phone, and held them up for me to see. There were at least five. They were all well-endowed, and they all showed full body shots from the neck down. Their bodies were attractive...and immediately made me think of Jax. My stomach knotted and I pushed the thought out of my head. Brynn slid her phone into her pocket and kept talking, "Some are a little shy, but those guys are usually the cocktails, and I'm not interested in them anyway. It's pretty fail-proof. Most guys who have big dicks like to brag about it. And asking for pics seems to turn them on."

I had so many questions I didn't even know where to start. "How do you even know they're the guy's dick and not some porn pic they found online?"

She lifted her finger to her temple and tapped her head. "See, you're good. You thought of that right away. It took me a few days and one really disappointing encounter to figure out I needed to ask for some form of dick identification."

I threw my hands in the air. "How do you identify a dick?"

"Isn't that the million dollar question."

"I mean in the pic! How do you know it's his?"

"I make him send me something I can use to identify him. Most use their student IDs or license. I had one guy use his social security card. He had a nice dick, but I ruled him out as too stupid to sleep with."

I shook my head. "Men are idiots."

"Yes, they are. But they can be a lot of fun in bed, so I'll keep them around—provided they have the right equipment."

"If a guy asked a girl for naked pics before going out with her, he'd be lambasted as a misogynistic asshole. But a girl asking for them just gets the guy more excited?"

"Gotta love those double standards. Sometimes they work in our favor."

I sighed. "I literally can't think of one person who could get away with this except you, Brynn."

She grinned. "I know."

Brynn had a long history of bad guy-related experiences. Her past had helped her become what she was today: a woman who loved sex but could care less about the guy giving it to her. I couldn't blame her considering what she'd dealt with from guys in the past, but I couldn't help thinking that eventually, she'd feel like she'd missed her chance at a relationship. She was scared about what it would do to her head and her heart, though. She was already bruised, and the constant string of one-night stands helped keep her from becoming beaten. I looked at her. "I think you're the one who needs your head examined."

She lifted a shoulder, owning it. "Probably."

I was happy for the reprieve, though. If anything could take my mind off of my failed relationship with Jax, it was Brynn. The first couple of weeks after our breakup, I'd alternated between anger and sadness on a regular basis. But, for the past few days, Jax was all I could think about. I felt like there were things left unsaid. Whatever had happened with the blonde guy in Arizona had been traumatic for Jax. He'd reacted out of anger and emotion. Now that we'd had some time apart, I wondered if he regretted anything he'd done, or leaving our relationship in pieces. I felt like I needed to talk to him to be sure. If his actions had just been the result of his emotions, maybe he'd be ready to talk now and we could move forward. If not, I'd at least get some closure. But I wasn't sure how to broach the topic, or even start a discussion. I'd tried—unsuccessfully—in Arizona. And I wasn't sure I was big enough to make the first move again.

Brynn had been watching my closely. "You need to go talk to him, Syd."

I pulled my knees into my chest. "I know. I just don't know if I'm ready."

"Don't wait too long. Sometimes distance is good, but other times, it's just an open wound left unattended. Open wounds don't heal themselves, and they tend to get worse."

I nodded. "Maybe I'll stop by his apartment this weekend."

"You should do it in a trench coat, with nothing underneath," she said with a wink.

I rolled my eyes. "I don't think that would help the discussion."

"Are you kidding? You'd get whatever you want."

I laughed. "You're going to be a shitty counselor."

She shook her head, unoffended. "Effective. An effective counselor."

"*Rapunzel* again?" I took the book from Macy and settled into the soft bean bag chair. Her brother had had a bad day at the hospital and I wanted to do anything I could to take her mind off of it.

She nodded her head and smiled widely.

"Okay." I settled her on my lap and read the book. Then read it again. And again. We were halfway through our fourth reading before her mom came in.

"There you are!" Macy's mom, Patti, came over and picked her up, kissing her hard on the top of her head. "I've missed you." I couldn't help but notice her mom's red-rimmed, tired eyes. I understood why. She'd been at the hospital all day, and according to Charlie, she'd been spending most of her time there for the past week.

"Thanks for taking care of her, Syd," Patti said. "It helps to know Macy has people who care about her when I can't, and a place to feel normal." I smiled at her in understanding. It wasn't just Macy who needed that.

"No problem. She's my favorite person to hang out with."

Macy's smile spread across her entire face. "You're my favorite, Syd!" She jumped out of her mom's arms and came running over to give me one last hug. "Will you bring cookies next week?"

I bopped her on the nose. "Only if you promise to help me bake them."

She nodded her head excitedly, her face beaming as Patti took her down the hall to go to bed.

I bent down, picking up some toys that Macy had left scattered on the floor. I was putting away the last of them when Charlie came into the room. "How are things going, Syd?"

I smiled, but knew it didn't look authentic. "Okay. Just a lot going on."

He narrowed his eyes, watching me with the intuition of a man who spent a lot of time with people who were hurting. "I hope whatever it is, you're okay. You know I'm here to talk if you need anything."

Tears pricked my eyes. I was so emotional ever since things happened with Jax that it felt like I was wearing my feelings on my sleeve. "Thanks, Charlie. That means a lot."

He sat down on a chair next to me. "I hope this doesn't make things worse, but I wanted to tell you something."

I furrowed my brows, concerned. I didn't know if I could handle any more surprises or bad news. "What is it?"

He took a deep breath. "Well, ever since Jax picked you up from CARE a few months ago, I've felt like I recognized him from somewhere."

I nodded, remembering the two of them together. "I got the impression he knew you. I figured it was through Red's garage or something."

Charlie shook his head. "No, I met him the day he picked you up—at least, I thought I did. I'm good with remembering people and faces, and I've been racking my brain trying to figure out why he looked so familiar."

I froze. Charlie recognized Jax from before I introduced them? Why?

Charlie continued, "I finally remembered. I met him about eight years ago at the hospital."

I pinched my brows together. "The hospital? What was he doing there?"

Charlie rubbed a hand over his chin. "His whole family was there, actually. I offered to let them stay at CARE while the doctors tried to help his brother."

I'd only heard Jax mention his brother one time. At Lake Powell, when he was talking about jumping off the cliffs. "What was wrong with his brother?"

Charlie took a deep breath. "He'd been in a really bad car accident. They brought him to Winchester because the orthopedic surgeon is one of the best in the country. They were able to fix his injuries, but he went into a coma. He never came out."

My eyes went wide and I forgot to breathe. Jax's brother had died? Why hadn't he ever told me? My mind started to race. This had to be why he hadn't opened up to me. And I was sure it was the reason for all of his commitment issues, too. I grabbed my purse. I couldn't wait until the weekend. I needed to see Jax *right* now. "Thank you so much for telling me, Charlie. I didn't know."

"You're welcome," Charlie said. He put his hand on my shoulder as I started to walk past him. "The reason I remembered Jax was because he took the death so hard. I've seen a lot of people deal with grief in different ways. Most come out of it eventually, but Jax just shut down. One day he'd been smiling and saying hello to me in the hospital hallways, the next, he just went into a daze. He barely acknowledged the people around him, and was severely depressed. But that day he came to pick you up and I talked to him, the light was back in his eyes and he seemed genuinely happy. He was the same man I remembered from before his brother passed away." Charlie paused. "I think you might have had something to do with that."

I wasn't sure if that was the case, but I knew we'd been making progress before Arizona. I needed to talk to Jax before another night went by. I leaned in and hugged Charlie. "You have no idea how much you've helped me."

I left CARE and took She-Ra straight to Jax's apartment.

Twenty-Two

knocked on the door. No answer. I wondered if he was screening his visitors and just didn't want to see me. Maybe I should have texted him or called before I came over, but after Charlie had told me about Jax's brother, I couldn't get to Jax's apartment fast enough. My heart ached for him, and what he must have gone through.

I rang the doorbell this time, just in case he hadn't heard the knock. It was several minutes before I heard footsteps padding toward the other side of the door. I waved and smiled so if he looked through the peephole, he'd see I wasn't wearing combat gear. I heard the click of the deadbolt, and the door knob turned. I lifted my head to meet Jax's eyes with my best smile possible, and my face fell.

Pretty blue eyes stared back at me, but they weren't Jax's. They were a woman's—and I recognized her from the pizza place. It was Jax's sister. She was as stunning as before, her hair pulled into a ponytail. She was wearing a red, cashmere sweater, and bootcut jeans. "Hi," I said with some trepidation. "I'm looking for Jax."

Her smile widened and her face lit up. "You're Sydney! I'm so glad I finally have the chance to meet you!" She hugged me like we were old friends, and suddenly the awkwardness I'd felt when she opened the door fell away. "I'm Jax's sister, Courtney. Jax has told me so much about you."

I pushed my brows together. "He has? Recently? If so, you probably shouldn't believe a word of it."

She smiled again. "Yes. Recently. Jax is out right now, but you should come in. I'd like to talk."

I stepped inside and she motioned for me to sit down on one of Jax's leather couches. "I'm sorry, I didn't realize he had family in town."

"I've been staying with him for a while. He's had a rough couple of weeks." She paused, taking in my face. "I imagine you have, too."

I gave a tiny nod and looked down at my hands. I'd never met her before, and didn't want my first discussion with her to be about my fight with her brother. I wanted her to have a better first impression of me than that.

"I was just pouring a cup of coffee. Do you want some?"

I perked up at that. "That would be great."

She went to the kitchen and came back a few minutes later, handing me a steaming mug. "I put some milk and chocolate sauce in yours. Jax mentioned that's how you take it."

My eyes widened. "He talked to you about how I take my coffee?" Sheesh. Clearly they were close. What else had he told her? Images from our night in the hotel over Lake Powell flashed through my head. I shifted in the chair, uncomfortable. I hoped they weren't *that* close.

"He's told me a lot about you. More than any other girl he's ever been with." She sat on the couch across from me. "Actually, you're the first real relationship he's had in years."

I took that information in. "It's not much of a relationship at the moment."

"Well," she said, taking a sip of her coffee, "that's because Jax needs to get his head out of his ass."

It's a good thing I hadn't been drinking my coffee at the time, because I would have spit it across the room. I laughed out loud. "That was…unexpected. I thought you'd defend him."

"Oh no," she said, shaking her head. "I have a low tolerance for idiocy. And the way he acted was a prime example of stupid."

I laughed again. "I like you."

She grinned conspiratorially. "That's good, because I like you, too."

I wasn't sure what to say next, and was happy I had the coffee to fill the silence.

Courtney crossed her legs on the couch and looked at me. "He told me what happened and that you broke up. I know he didn't give you any details, or tell you why he reacted the way he did at the gas station. Instead, he let his past cloud his judgment and he pushed you away like he always does with people he loves. It was a dumbass move and he almost lost you over it." She paused. "At least, I *hope* it's still an almost. Please, give him the chance to explain. Between you and me, when you left, it destroyed him. I've only seen him this depressed one other time. He can't lose you, Syd—and he knows it now. He needs you. And Jax doesn't need anyone."

I stared at her, completely stunned. Given how he'd acted and that he hadn't tried to contact me for three weeks, I didn't think he cared at all. I opened my mouth to ask for more details when I heard a tiny voice say, "Mommy?"

The adorable little blonde girl I'd seen at the pizza parlor with Courtney and Jax came stumbling down the hallway, rubbing her eyes. Her pink sweater had a dog on it, and her black pants had pink paw prints printed on one leg. Courtney stood, a huge smile on her face as she swung her daughter up into her arms. "Hey, baby! Did you have a good nap?"

She nodded, putting her head against Courtney's chest.

"Do you want to meet a really good friend of Uncle Jax's?" Courtney asked.

She lifted her head a little, eyeing me suspiciously. Finally she gave a tiny nod and Courtney said, "Paige, this is Sydney."

I smiled and waved. "Hi, Paige." I'd noticed toys on the table and saw some Disney princesses I recognized. "Is this Ariel?" I asked, holding up her doll. Paige nodded her head. "I always wanted hair just like hers. It's so pretty!"

She smiled and jumped down from Courtney's arms, coming over to me. "Want to help me brush it?" she asked, her expression full of innocence.

"Sure!"

She went to a box next to the coffee table and got a brush out, then came back and sat on the couch next to me as we combed Ariel's hair together. As soon as she was done, she decided she wanted to watch a movie. Courtney took her back to the bedroom and put the movie on, then came out again.

"She's a beautiful little girl," I said.

Courtney smiled. "She's the light of my life."

"I can see why."

"You're good with her."

I shrugged. "I work with a lot of kids at the place I volunteer at."

She nodded, like that wasn't a surprise. Jax must have told her about CARE, too. "Did Jax tell you about Paige's dad?"

I took another sip of my coffee. "Not really. He just said he wished the guy was dead."

Courtney frowned. "Well, that's not very nice. We didn't work out, but I got Paige from it, so I think it was worth the pain."

I heard a lock click in the front door. Courtney glanced over at me as the door started to open.

Jax looked up as he stepped in the apartment, his gaze landing first on Courtney, and then on me. His eyes met mine and I held my breath. He looked like he was holding his, too. There were so many things unsaid between us, and it was like all of the words hovered in the air as we stared. I couldn't read his expression. He wasn't mad, or upset. In fact, he almost seemed…relieved. Our eye contact was broken by Paige's voice yelling, "Uncle Jax! Uncle Jax!" She ran to him with her arms spread wide.

He smiled at her, scooping her easily into his arms. "Hey, Paigey-poo."

She wrinkled her nose. "Eww. I'm not poo."

"You're not?" he asked, acting surprised.

She let out a high-pitched giggle. "Nooooo."

Courtney stood up. "Paige, do you want to go get some ice cream?"

Her eyes lit up and she nodded her head vigorously.

"Go grab your coat, then."

Courtney picked her purse up and put her own coat on, then helped Paige with hers. "It was nice to

finally meet you in person, Syd. I hope to spend a lot more time with you." She put her hand on Jax's arm and held his eyes as they had some sort of wordless conversation. "We'll be back later," she said, taking Paige's little hand and closing the door.

Jax dropped a bag on the floor and I realized he was wearing gym clothes—shorts and a sleeveless shirt. He looked like he'd put on even more muscle in the last three weeks. The gym must be his way of dealing with emotional issues—mine involved studying, and eating a lot of candy. Jax's head was down, eyes on the floor. He ran a hand through his hair and slowly inched his eyes up to meet mine.

"Hi," I said, my voice barely a whisper.

"Hey."

I couldn't read his expression, and wasn't sure if he even wanted me there. "I didn't mean to surprise you. I came over. To talk. Courtney was here and invited me in."

He nodded. "I'm glad she did."

I watched him closely. At first I thought he might be glad I was there, but now his face had gone back to a blank mask and I didn't know what to think. "Are you glad? Really? Because you don't seem like it."

"And you're an expert on how I seem?"

"I used to think so."

He took a deep breath. "I've had a rough few weeks, Syd."

"Do you think you're the only one who's had it

rough?" I asked. "Do you know what I went through when you left? I felt like my heart had been ripped out. I cried for days, Jax."

He pressed his lips together. "It wasn't easy for me, either."

I stared at him, furious that he wasn't even acknowledging what he'd done, or how he'd hurt me. It was all about him. "Oh, it wasn't? It was just so freaking hard to pick up the phone and say, 'Sorry, Syd. The guy on the trip made me fall back into old habits and shut you out. I'm trying to deal with it all, but I'm going through a lot of shit. I need some time to figure out how to talk to you, but when I do, I want you in my life. Wait for me'."

A muscle worked in his jaw. "It's not that easy. And I'd never ask you to wait for me. That's asking too much."

"Too much what? Too much emotion? Too much commitment? Because that's what relationships are. Intimacy, commitment, emotion. *Love*. It's being there for each other, especially during the times that are so shitty you feel like it would be easier to have your heart torn from your chest. I could have been there for you, but you didn't even give me a chance."

He shook his head. "It was stuff that didn't concern you. Stuff from my past that you shouldn't have had to deal with at all."

My heart was pounding through my chest; I was furious. "That's not how relationships work, Jax. I

would have been there. I *wanted* to be there for you. Everyone has issues. Everyone has baggage. You go into a relationship knowing those things will come up, and willing to work on them because you care enough about the person to take on the hard stuff."

He snorted. "After your ultimatum, I don't think that would have been the case."

I shook my head, even more pissed. "It wasn't an ultimatum. I was just trying to understand where we stood. What I meant to you. I wanted to be there for you. I wanted you to talk to me. You didn't even try."

He put his hands on his hips, pacing from one side of the room to the other. "Do you think it was easy for me? You were the one person I wanted by my side. The one person I thought understood me. The one person I'd let in. But by the time I was ready to talk, you'd already decided you couldn't be with me. It was too late."

I shook my head. "That's been your problem all along. You keep your emotions at bay instead of dealing with them. I just wanted you to tell me when, or even if, you'd be ready to talk. If you had, there wouldn't have been a problem. I would have been there for you, Jax. And it was a douchebag move not to let me."

His eyes latched on mine, and for the first time, I finally felt like he'd *really* heard me. He stopped pacing and moved closer. "You're right. It was. And I'm sorry, Syd. We've been through a lot together, and we've been through a lot in the last few weeks. But now you're here, and I'm not willing to let you walk out of my life again." He closed the distance between us. "If you want me, you have me. And this time, I won't hold back. I'll give you everything I've got." He sat down next to me, grabbed me around the waist, and pulled me close. "I'm yours, and I always will be."

Blood pounded through my veins like liquid heat as he crushed his lips into mine, pushing his way into my mouth with his tongue. My need for him was raw, intense, and primal. I grabbed at his hair, my fingernails scraping over his back, pulling at his shirt. The kiss deepened even more, and I'd never wanted him more than I did in that moment. I couldn't get enough of him. I'd never be able to get enough. I stayed lost in the kiss, in the earthy scent of him. But a nagging in the back of my mind made me slow the kiss down. I needed questions answered and having sex on his living room floor wasn't going to get me those answers. I broke away and scooted back, breathing hard. I smoothed down my hair and licked my lips, still holding his eyes. "Did you miss me, Jax?"

A muscle worked in his jaw and he was breathing as hard as I was. "Every damn day."

"I was at CARE today," I watched as realization flashed through Jax's eyes. "Charlie told me he'd been trying to figure out where he knew you from, but couldn't place you. He finally figured it out. He told me about your brother, Jax."

Jax face fell as he scrubbed his chin. He reached down and took my hand, then pulled me closer on the couch. He was silent for a long time as he stared down at the carpet. Whatever he had to tell me had been a defining moment in Jax's life, and I knew it wasn't going to be easy to relive. I rubbed his hand, letting him know I'd be here for him—whenever he was ready.

His voice was low when he started speaking, "I was home from college, visiting. Ryan was a couple of years younger than me and still in high school. He wanted to go to a party with some friends; idiots from the football team. He asked if I wanted to go, but I was in college, and wasn't interested in reliving high school. He said he'd be gone for two hours. Two hours came and went, then four hours. My parents thought he'd just lost track of time, but I had a sinking feeling in my stomach. At five hours, I left to go look for him, thinking maybe the car they were in broke down or they didn't have cell service or something." He stopped talking and looked at the wall like he was gazing off in the distance, seeing the memory all over again.

"I drove to the party and found out they'd left two hours earlier. I searched all over town, looking for him at popular hangout spots. Each time I didn't find him, the pit in my stomach got deeper. Finally, I decided to try an old abandoned building that some kids used for drinking, drugs, and sex. It wasn't really Ryan's scene, but he wasn't driving and he was with a bunch of assholes. I was halfway down the road when I saw the lights." He paused for several seconds, swallowing. His voice was rough when he went on, "The car was upside down, the lights shining on wheat in a field. I got out and started running to the car. That's when I found the first body." His expression wavered. I reached my other hand over, holding both of his hands in mine, trying to comfort him any way I could. "I immediately dialed 9-1-1 and kept looking for Ryan. He was still in the car and had been wearing a seatbelt, but the top of the car was completely crushed—"

He stopped, his eyes welling up.

I put my hand on his back and rubbed it, pulling him closer to me as tears dripped from my own eyes. I hadn't known Jax's brother, but I couldn't imagine having to see anyone I loved like that. The images would haunt me for the rest of my life. "The ambulance came," Jax said, his voice unsteady. "They had to use the Jaws of Life, but they were able to get Ryan out. He was still alive and they airlifted him to the hospital in Winchester because the doctors there were the best for his injuries. For a while, we thought he might pull through. But he never came out of his coma. I never got to talk to him again."

He rolled his bracelet between his thumb and forefinger, and took several minutes before he was able to speak again. "I was depressed for a long time. I felt guilty, and blamed myself for not going with him that night. If I'd gone, I would have driven and it wouldn't have happened. I was also livid at the guy who'd been

driving the car—he was so drunk he couldn't see straight. That asshole is the one who lived. Ryan and the two other guys in the car didn't."

My heart sank and I felt a combination of sadness for the needless deaths, and anger at the boy who had caused them. No wonder Jax had been so upset the night he thought I was going to drive drunk. He probably thought the same thing would happen all over again, and he'd lose someone else he cared about.

Jax paused, then took my hand and met my eyes. "The guy who lived was the one who came up to me at the gas station in Arizona. Maybe it makes me a bad person, but I'll never be able to forgive him for taking Ryan away from us. It was such a stupid mistake to make, and it cost the lives of three people. Seeing him again that day was like reliving the entire scene in my head. I was furious, and I just shut down—like I did after Ryan died. His death taught me that there are no guarantees. It doesn't matter how much you love someone, it can't stop horrible things from happening to them, and taking the people you care about. Until you came along, the only people I'd let into my heart in the past eight years were Courtney and Paige. And even that scares the hell out of me. I don't want to ever feel the pain of loss again—and I don't want someone to have to feel it for me. I couldn't stand the thought of having someone I care about be scarred the same way I was when Ryan died."

He looked at our entwined hands. "That's why I

have such a hard time opening up, Syd. It's not because I don't care. It's because I care too much."

It was like the wall in Jax's head had fallen, and a flood of emotions was finally coming through. I was shaken at all of the information Jax had just trusted me with, and deeply moved. I knew this was a huge step for him, and my heart was bursting that he'd wanted to let me into a memory that was so difficult for him to go back to. "Oh, Jax. I'm so sorry," I put my arms around him, and held him tight. "I'm sorry I wasn't more understanding in Arizona, and I'm sorry this happened to you and your family. I wish I'd had the chance to know Ryan."

Jax smiled at that. "He would have liked you."

I gave him a watery smile back, and we spent the next few minutes just holding each other.

"How did you come out of your depression?" I asked.

I felt Jax's fingers on my head, moving absently through my hair. "Counseling. And figuring out ways to deal with my anger. That's how I started making jewelry." He pointed to his matte, black beaded bracelet. Memories of Lake Powell were suddenly very vivid in my mind.

"The bracelet that helps your ego?"

He smiled. "It really does do that, but the stone is supposed to take away negativity and help you deal with grief. I've worn it for years. On the one year anniversary of Ryan's death, I got my tattoo." I looked

at the number seventeen and the tribal design under it. I'd always wondered about the meaning, but never asked. "Ryan died when he was seventeen."

I hugged him tighter. I just wanted to hold him forever, and make the pain go away. "Oh, Jax. I can't imagine going through something like that. I think you're the strongest person I know."

He shook his head, adamant. "No. I'm not. Someone strong would have told you everything in the beginning, and never let you leave. That was one of the biggest mistakes of my life. I've been beating myself up over it ever since. I just didn't know how to say I was sorry and explain things to make everything right. Thank you for being the person who wasn't afraid."

My lips lifted. "That's what partners are for, Jax. We support each other."

He took my hands and met my eyes. "I realized something after you left. I know I can't keep shutting out people I care about just because something might happen to one of us. If I still have the chance, I don't want to live without you. I love you, Sydney Parker. I love your crazy phobias and your stubbornness. I love how driven you are and the goals you set for yourself. I love that you eat pizza and chocolate with a fork and knife, and how you keep me on my toes. I love your friends, your reading preferences, and I definitely love She-Ra. I want to make us work—if you'll still have me. I can't guarantee it will be easy, but I'll try harder than I've ever tried before. I need you, Syd. Forever."

I started to cry and wrapped my arms around his neck. I could see the future with this incredible man, and it couldn't be brighter. "I love you, Jax. And I want to spend every possible moment with you. The last few weeks without you have been hell. You make me a better person, and I never want to be apart from you again."

His eyes shown with unshed tears and love. He leaned in and kissed me, his lips soft and the kiss tender. "I'm damaged goods, you know."

I trailed my hand down his chest. "Not damaged. Experienced, compassionate, and a better person because of what you've been through. That makes me pretty damn lucky."

He reached a hand up and cupped my cheek, his eyes full of love and promises of our future together. "You saved me, Syd. I don't know what I did to deserve you, but I'm the luckiest bastard in the world to have you in my life."

My lips stretched in a wide grin. "Me, too. There aren't many girls who get to have sex with someone better in bed than a werewolf."

His eyes brightened as his arms tightened around me, and his lips pressed hard against mine, sucking in my bottom lip. My hands raked through his hair. I couldn't get enough of him; I knew I never would. He broke away from the kiss, his eyes hooded and his expression wanting. It mirrored my own. He bent down, wrapping one arm behind my back, the other

under my legs and lifted me, cradling me on his chest. His voice was husky as he started down the hall to his room, "I'm about to show you how much better I really am."

I couldn't wait.

Tempting Sydney Theater Scene
from
Jax's Point of View

The theater wasn't crowded...which was exactly why I'd decided to take Syd to a four month old horror movie at the oldest theater in town. I'd also chosen a scary movie on purpose. I'd seen her jump at the haunted house. This time, I'd be the one she was grabbing onto. We had the top three rows to ourselves, but I chose the back row in the corner where we'd have more privacy. She lifted her legs, resting her feet on the bannister in front of us. With her legs up, the pink, knee-length skirt she was wearing was practically an invitation.

"I can't believe we're seeing a horror movie," she said. "It's so cliché."

I glanced at her, suppressing a smile as I reached for the popcorn she was holding. I had no doubt she suspected my motives. "What do you mean?" I asked, feigning innocence.

She looked over at me, and I could tell it was taking a lot of effort for her not to roll her eyes. I popped some of the buttery snack in my mouth, waiting for her to tell me exactly what she thought— which she did, often. "Horror movies were made for guys. They're scary, so the girl jumps or grabs your arm all through the movie. Pretending to be her valiant

protector, you put your arm around her to keep her safe." This time, she did roll her eyes and the corner of my mouth ticked up. "It's the perfect opportunity to show how alpha you are by protecting us from fake monsters on a movie screen that can't really hurt us anyway. In real life, you guys probably wouldn't even protect us from a spider. But still, the protective aspects are appealing to both women, and men, in the situation. It's an illustration of how even if we think we've evolved as humans, primitive nature still has a level of control."

I smiled slowly, half amused, half turned on. She was so damn smart—and passionate. If she was this fervent about movie genres, it made me wonder how she'd be in bed. I just needed to convince her that sex was more fun than her homework. I was wearing her down, though. It had taken some time, but I could tell she wanted me almost as much as I wanted her. "I can see you've really thought that through," I said, leaning my head back against the chair and looking at her sideways. "You should consider a dissertation deconstructing horror movies and their connection to the evolution of humans. I'm sure it would be a fascinating read."

She glared at me, her bright pink lips forming a frown. All I could think about was where I wanted those lips. "Say what you want, but I bet you take all your dates to scary movies for that *exact* reason."

She was absolutely right. It was one of the reasons

we were here. The other was to engage in a little public foreplay—she just didn't know it, yet. "I'm not gonna lie," I lifted the armrest so there was no barrier between us, "it does keep them occupied, and me…entertained." I let my mouth slide up in a brazen smile.

She lifted her head and gave me an I-told-you-so scowl, but the frown lingered. Syd was pretty easy to read, and I got the distinct impression that she didn't like the thought of me being with other women. I couldn't blame her. I'd certainly thought of the other men in her life. I wanted to kill every one of them. She had nothing to worry about, though. No woman in my past had ever affected me like Sydney Parker. She'd gotten under my skin and into my blood. I'd fought my feelings for a long time, but you can only fight the inevitable for so long. Syd had cracked my carefully constructed wall, and no amount of patching could fix the fissure. She was exactly what I needed, even if it had been a hard road to figure that out.

The trailers started; more horror movies. So far, she didn't look too scared. I was counting on that changing soon.

It did.

Syd kept herself fairly controlled—because that's how she always was, controlled—for the first twenty minutes of the movie. I watched out of the corner of my eye as she squirmed during suspenseful parts and even half-closed her eyes. I couldn't help but notice her

chest, rising and falling at a rapid rate, her breasts straining the fabric of her shirt. The buttons would be so easy to rip off. I tapped my fingers against my jeans, trying to get my mind off of where I wanted them to be instead—gently caressing her perfect, round chest. It was all I could think about...until Syd jumped, gasping as she grabbed for me I shifted my eyes to the screen and saw a giant horned demon with bright red eyes and fire breathing from his mouth.

I looked at her hands wrapped around me and smirked. For someone with such strong opinions on horror movies and feminism, it certainly didn't look like she was seeking protection against her will. This was exactly what I'd hoped would happen. She squeezed my bicep and kept squeezing. My mind immediately wandered to all of the other parts of me I wanted her to touch. The demon on the screen was getting closer, and Syd's eyes were glued to the movie. I could see the demon about to breathe a fire-filled death on its next victim, and an evil thought crossed my mind. I leaned over, took a deep breath, and exhaled on her pretty, creamy white neck, her sexy blonde curls tickling my face as I did it.

She screamed.

I gave a deep laugh that started low in my stomach. Okay, so it was childish, and maybe I shouldn't have done that, but it was an excuse to get my lips an inch away from her neck, and I couldn't pass that opportunity up.

Syd's eyes narrowed immediately and she slugged me in the shoulder. I laughed some more and lifted my hands in mock surrender. She wasn't amused. She couldn't see the flirting behind my teasing—or maybe she didn't understand it—which seemed strange since I knew she'd been to elementary school. Regardless, she needed to let go of some of her focus and have some fun. But based on her folded arms and sudden movement as far away from me as possible, I needed to apologize for scaring her first. I stretched my arm out behind her shoulder, pulling her back into me. She held herself frozen at first, not willing to trust me, but as I ran my fingers lightly back and forth over the silky soft skin of her upper arm, she slowly thawed and melted into my chest. I liked her there. A lot. And despite my past, and what I thought I'd wanted, the truth was I wanted Syd next to me, holding onto me. Forever.

My gaze moved over her features as I took in every beautiful angle, thinking about the woman in my arms who was slowly changing my life. It still shocked me that I could have feelings like that for someone. Letting someone in, letting them care for me, and me caring for them, was not something I thought I'd ever do. Up to this point, my family were the only people I'd let in like that—and even that had been a major concession. I'd vowed never to allow anyone else a spot in my heart. But Syd had changed me. Even Courtney had noticed it when she and Paige were in

town visiting me. She hadn't even met Syd and was already having Team Syd shirts made.

A sudden pain shot through my thigh, breaking my introspection. Syd had grabbed my leg instead of my arm this time when the demon showed up. Good hell! Her hands were like a vice. I'd look like a grade-A pansy if I asked her to release my thigh, but I didn't know how long my leg could survive without blood. I finally decided I better say something. "Your hand makes an excellent tourniquet," I whispered, trying to keep the mood light.

She released my leg immediately. Well, shit. That's not what I wanted. I mean, yeah, I wanted blood flow back—to my leg, and other places—but I still wanted her hand there. Actually...I wanted her hands *everywhere.*

Her cheeks went a pretty shade of pink, almost the same color as her lips, as she ducked her head down. "Sorry."

A slow smile spread across my face as I thought of the ways she could make it up to me. I reached over with my other hand and grabbed hers. "I didn't say I wanted you to move your hand. I like it there."

And I did, but it was damn distracting. I wasn't paying attention to the movie in the first place, but now all I could think about was that I had my arm wrapped around the sexiest woman on the planet, and she had her hand about six inches south of third base. I lasted another five minutes before I glanced around, making sure we still weren't in anyone's line of sight. We weren't, and I shifted, my leg next to her falling down, opening wider. I turned, my whole body angled toward her. I could feel the electric pulse humming between us. She looked up at me from under her long, sooty lashes, lips parted and her expression full of shy anticipation. My heart felt like it was determined to drum its way out of my chest. The strain against my jeans was becoming more noticeable, and I shifted, adjusting to the growth. I met her eyes, locking mine with hers as I reached down and started gently pulling her hand up.

Her breath caught and held as she watched my hand drag her fingers over the inner seam of my jeans. My own breath was shallow as I thought about where her hand was headed. I wanted her—more than anything—but her nervous excitement made me want to yank down my zipper, rip of her panties, lift her skirt, and sit her right on my lap. She glanced at me, and it was all I could do not to follow through on my thoughts as I kept moving her hand…slowly, right to the spot I wanted it.

When we reached the crease at the top of my thigh, I guided her fingers straight to my crotch. Syd's hands were on my dick. I'd had fantasies about this moment, and couldn't wait for us to act out some of the others. Still holding her eyes, I used her hands to stroke me, back and forth, up and down. Light at first, and then a little harder. God, that felt amazing! She

broke her glance away, her long lashes fluttering down as she watched me move her hand over myself. Damn, if that wasn't one of the hottest things I'd ever seen. Syd watching as she massaged me, learning how I wanted to be touched.

I spread her fingers out, splaying them over me. I'd been hard the minute I saw her in that little pink skirt, but with her hand and total attention focused right where I wanted it, I felt harder than I'd ever been in my life. I needed to feel her on me, skin on skin. I let go of her hand, and she kept rubbing, just like I'd taught her. I held her eyes as I popped the button on my jeans and the zipper teeth clinked as they unlatched.

Her face was flushed, breasts swollen with need, and that just made me want her even more. I took her hand and slowly slipped it under the waistband of my boxers. Our fingers slid down, down, down, until we both hit my cock. She gasped, her eyes blinking up to me. A jolt of pleasure ran through me at her touch, and her response. This was what I wanted—for both of us to stop thinking, and lose ourselves completely in each other. I inhaled a rattled breath as I took her soft hand and wrapped it around my length. And then, I started to stroke. Up and down, guiding her. And then I had to immediately start thinking of sports statistics, because after less than thirty seconds of a hand job, she'd made me so hot I was ready to explode. Syd's breath was ragged as she touched me, her eyes flitting back and forth between my face and my pants. I'd never been this turned on, or wanted anyone so much. Against all manners and my own better judgment, I was ready to take her right there, in the middle of the theater. Judging by her flushed cheeks and shifting in her chair, she was ready to let me.

And just like that, I saw her face shutter. I took a deep breath, inwardly shaking my head. She was thinking too much. Shutting me out. Abruptly, Syd pulled her hand away. She got up, whispering a hasty excuse that she needed to use the bathroom. I watched her sexy little ass all the way down the stairs, and didn't miss her eyes flit back up to me as she exited the theater.

Bathroom my ass. It was either that, or have sex on the theater floor. And Syd was way too controlled for that kind of spontaneity. I shifted in my seat, trying to readjust for the situation still going on in my pants. No help there. The only thing that would remedy this problem was currently hanging out with toilets. I knew Syd was freaking out. She kept her life carefully organized, and planned for all contingencies. But she hadn't planned for me. I wasn't going to let her run away from this—us—just because she wasn't prepared for it. I stood up, and walked down the stairs.

The hallway was deserted thanks to the lack of attendance at the old theater. I opened the door to the women's restroom and looked around. The space was empty except for one closed stall, and that's where the person I wanted was. I leaned against the countertop,

my palms resting behind me, and watched the stall, and Syd's heels. I had no doubt she was leaning against that door, trying to calm down. As soon as she came out, though, I'd make sure calm was the last emotion she'd be feeling. I wanted her to feel as crazy as I did.

The lock on the door clicked. Syd looked up as she exited the stall, then froze when she saw me. Various emotions crossed her face, but the flush across her chest and darkened eyes let me know she was interested in more than going back to watch the movie. Good, because movies were the very *last* thing on my mind. She attempted to move, but stumbled. I knew how much I unnerved her, and I liked it. I flashed a wolf-smile as I caught her. "Slippery, eh?"

I wasn't talking about the floor.

She blew out a breath, and seemed to be doing some serious contemplation as she stood there, trying to decide what to do next, no doubt. She had that problem with me frequently. "If we're both in here, neither one of us will know what's happening in the movie," she finally said.

I tilted my head to the side and cocked a brow. If she thought a movie plot was more interesting than her, she needed an education. "I'm sure neither one of us cares."

I could tell she was still anxious, and she tried to take some of the edge off with a joke. "Did you make a wrong turn and not see the girl wearing a dress on the door?"

I held her eyes as I answered, "The girl I want to see out of her dress is in here."

I held her gaze as I took two long steps toward her, and she sucked in a breath as I pushed her up against the wall. I wanted to take her, claim her, in every way. My lips pressed into hers, the kiss hard and deep. My dick felt like granite against her thigh, and I wanted nothing more than for her to unzip my pants and pull it out again. I wanted her to look at me, *see* me, and find out what she'd been missing. Her hands raked down my stomach, and stayed there as my tongue slipped into her mouth, licking and caressing.

I'd managed to undo several of the buttons on her black shirt. Her lacy black and white bra peeked out beneath her top, threatening to drive me insane. I wanted to watch her strip it off, and leave it with the rest of her clothes on the bathroom floor. I cupped one hand over her breast, stroking the hard tips of her nipples through the lace with my thumb, while the other hand pushed up her skirt, running light strokes over her thigh. I was so close to being able to slip inside her. I wanted to touch her, feel her silky warmth. She sighed as I broke away, moving my lips down her body to take her nipple in my mouth. The rough fabric and soft skin was an intense combination on my tongue. Her hands went to my jeans and I moaned as she popped the button, slowly sliding the zipper down.

Yes.

This.

Syd.

She was exactly what I wanted. What I needed. In every way. Her hand was poised over the waistband of my boxers when the door creaked open and a teenage girl walked in the bathroom, surprise written on her face when she noticed my presence. Well, fuuuuck. Of all the damn times to be interrupted! I looked down, taking a deep breath to try to calm down, and contain my annoyance. Syd scrambled away from me faster than I thought anyone could even move. I almost laughed. Running away wasn't going to improve the situation. The girl was a teenager, not an imbecile. I knew what she'd seen when she walked in. The next step was about damage control.

I looked up, raking a hand through my hair as I flashed the girl a winning smile, trying to put her at ease. "My date was sick. I came in to check on her."

The girl gave me a once over, taking in my disheveled clothes and kiss swollen lips. Then she did the same to Syd, stopping on her unbuttoned shirt, flushed face, smeared lipstick, and messy hair. She rolled her eyes. "Yeah, right," she said, snorting. "You know, they have stalls for that." Then she stepped into a stall of her own and locked the door.

I bit my lip and held back a laugh. Syd put her hand over her mouth to try to hold in her own giggle—which surprised me. I thought she'd be embarrassed and probably pissed. Apparently a little action was beneficial to her mood. Noted. We both quickly rearranged our clothes and hair before I took her hand, holding the door for her as we walked out of the bathroom together.

Neither of us had any interest in the movie. I was mostly interested in getting her in my truck, and then somewhere a little more private to continue improving her mood—and mine. We started toward my truck. "Thanks for making out with me in the light this time," Syd said, her tone teasing.

My lips curved up, remembering the kiss in the dark corridor of the haunted mine. Damn, that was a great kiss. If I hadn't been falling for her already, that kiss would have sealed the deal. "I thought about killing your date that night, but decided I'd much rather kiss you."

She lifted a brow. "It was an incredible kiss. You should have claimed it. Drew got credit as the ninja kisser for a while."

I snorted, completely annoyed. No one could kiss her like I could. I was offended she'd ever thought otherwise. "He wouldn't have been able to find the broad side of a barn in that dark hallway, let alone your mouth." I wrapped my arm around her waist and leaned in to whisper in her ear. "And Syd, if we hadn't been interrupted in the bathroom just now, I would have found a lot more than your lips."

If you enjoyed reading Tempting Sydney, please help others enjoy this book too by lending it, recommending it, or reviewing it on Amazon, Barnes and Noble, or Goodreads. If you do write a review, please send me a message through my website so I can thank you! www.angelacorbett.com

xoxo,
Ang

Adult
The Devil Drinks Coffee
Devilishly Short #1

Young Adult
Eternal Starling
Eternal Echoes

For special sneak peeks, giveaways, and super secret news, join Angela's newsletter!

Acknowledgments

Once again, there are so many people I couldn't have done this without!

My incredible production team! Ali Cross at Novel Ninjutsu; Rachel Morgan at Morgan Media; Ashley Argyle, Ph.D, at Inktip Editing; Laura Hidalgo at Bookfabulous Designs; Brad Olson Photography; and my super hot cover models, Sarah Singleton and Kevin Fulgham. Also, a massive thank you to my marketing/PR company, Bernard Books. And to Jean at Book Nerd Tours, I can't even thank you enough! You're always so supportive of me, and such a wonderful friend!

Jennifer Miller and Gypsy Rae Choszer, who heard my crazy idea and wanted to go nuts with me. I love having inappropriate discussions with you! And thanks to Gypsy, who provided very important jewelry-making info. Huge thanks to M. Clarke, LP Dover, Rebecca Ethington, and RaShelle Workman.

Dr. Ashley Argyle, my fantastic editor who pretended to be disappointed after first reading this book, and almost got a cookie thrown at her. Now I'm not allowed to have cookies at editing sessions. I absolutely couldn't do my job without her.

And of course, Dan, who makes me happy, and always

makes me laugh…especially when he's turning my books into his own version of Mystery Science 3000 Theater. Yes, Jax actually can make dinner with nothing but the heat coming off of his abs. :p

And my most important thank you goes to you, my readers! Without your support, I couldn't do what I do. Thank you for taking the time to leave reviews, and tell people about my books. Thank you for all of the kind words, notes, and posts on my social media pages. I treasure every single one of them! <3

About
Angela

Angela Corbett is a graduate of Westminster College where she double majored in communication and sociology. She has worked as a journalist, freelance writer, and director of communications and marketing. She loves classic cars, traveling, and listening to U2. She lives in Utah with her extremely supportive husband and their five-pound Pomeranian, Pippin, whose following of fangirls could rival Justin Bieber's.

You can find Angela online at
angelacorbett.com
@angcorbett